NOT A PLAYER

A.J. WYNTER

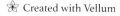 Created with Vellum

ALSO BY A.J. WYNTER

Hockey Royal Series

Puck King

Laketown Hockey Series

Not a Player

Hating the Rookie

The Coach Next Door

Wingmen are a Girl's Best Friend

The Captain's Secret Baby

The Defenseman's Second Chance

Falling for the Legend

Chance Rapids Series

Second Chances

One More Chance

Accidental Chances

A Secret Chance

Reckless Chances

Titan Billionaire Brothers

For Richer, For Poorer, Book 1

For Richer, For Poorer, Book 2

Her First Time Series

The Biker's Virgin

The Mountain Man's Virgin

The Rancher's Virgin

1

JESSIE

Laketown is known for two things: hockey and more hockey.

If anyone found out what I was doing to the precious ice surface at Laketown's McManus Place Arena I would be crucified. Triple toe loops, flying camel spins, and plenty of toe-picks, every single one of them gouging up their precious 'hockey players only' ice.

There is only one thing in the world that quiets the sound of the twisting metal of the car accident that killed my parents, and that's figure skating. Out here on the ice, I forget that my world has been turned upside down.

My ponytail flicked at my cheek as I skated backward around the faceoff circle. I've always done my warm-up to Queen. Freddie Mercury's voice had been with me over the years, from my first shaky single axel to my first solid triple, but this morning I strained to hear his voice coming out of my little speaker over the sound of my skates cutting into the ice.

Out of the corner of my eye, I saw a dark figure standing by the boards. I smiled and waved, and my dad's friend

Andy, the arena's custodian, waved back. I've known Andy for as long as I can remember, from back when I was a little kid and he had long hair and drove a rusty old van filled with guitars and amplifiers.

I picked up where I left off, and my breath started to come harder, puffs of steam escaping through my lips. Suddenly Freddie's voice blared through the arena's sound system and the full lighting system flickered and then blared brightly. Andy gave me a thumbs up from the system controls. Now that I could feel the music through my entire body, my chest felt like it was pounding with the bass. I stepped into my favorite jump, a triple toe-loop, and stuck the landing right in front of Andy.

When he clapped, my eyes stung with the worst kind of tears, the surprise kind. With a quick swipe of my sleeve, they were gone. "Thank you," I yelled over the music, but Andy had already turned and disappeared into the belly of the arena. Andy could lose his job for letting me skate here, and as intense gratitude washed over me, those sneaky surprise tears made another appearance.

I ran through my jumps and spins, finishing off with a flying camel spin and the only jump that still haunts me, my triple lutz. But, no matter how hard I flung myself into the air, it was under-rotated. I ran through the cues that my coach Veronica always shouted at me in her snooty British accent, but some days the lutz just eluded me – this morning was one of them.

Andy sounded the buzzer and I glanced at the time, 4:49 – early enough for him to get on the Zamboni and erase any signs that Jessie Moss had ever defiled the rink with her toe-picks.

2

KANE

IT'S A FACT. All hockey players are superstitious. I'm not weird. Mike, one of the defensemen, has to eat a sub before every game. Tanner, the captain, has to be the last person to leave the dressing room. Me, I have my gold coin.

Twisted in my sheets, I pulled my pillow over my head, trying to convince myself that losing my coin wasn't a big deal. But my heart wouldn't stop pounding in my chest and I sat up to take a sip of water. All night long, I'd been having the same dream: it's game seven, I'm the last player in the shoot-out, and my skates are so dull that I fall every time I charge for the puck. I keep getting up and falling, my team is screaming at me and the arena is deathly silent as the fans watch me flail about on the ice.

It was four-thirty in the morning, but it didn't matter. I kicked my feet free from the tangle of sheets and got dressed in my gray sweatpants and an Otters sweatshirt. There was no time for underwear, I had to find my coin. I grabbed the keys to my Land Cruiser and slipped my feet into my flip flops.

It has to be there, I whispered to myself as I drove down

the one-way gravel road, hoping that I didn't meet another car. There were only a few cottages on Mustang Point Road, but if you met someone, one of you had to reverse until the other car could squeeze by.

I emerged from the treed canopy, gunned the powerful engine of my vintage Land Cruiser, and headed into Lake-town, mentally retracing my steps from the night before. After practice, the team had gone to The Brewpub for dinner, then headed by boat to Tanner's place. I just hoped that the coin had fallen out somewhere between the arena and The Brewpub – and not in the lake. I popped open the console and pulled out the flashlight that I kept for emergencies. I planned to scour the parking lot of McManus Arena until it opened, and then convince the janitor to let me into The Otters' dressing room.

What the hell are the lights doing on? I muttered as I pulled into the parking lot and parked haphazardly by the front door. I jogged to the entrance and yanked on the door hopeful that is was open, but my heart sank when it rattled in my hands – locked. I shone my flashlight on the sidewalk, looking for any shiny objects. Then the custodian appeared, pushing a big broom across the lobby floor. "Hey," I shouted and pounded on the door.

"Hi, Fitzy." He opened the door and consulted his watch. "You're here early."

"Hey, Andy." I couldn't believe my good luck. "By any chance have you come across a coin with a pirate ship on it?" *Could it be this easy?*

"I haven't, but if I find it, I'll let you know."

He went to close the door, but I stopped him. "I think I forgot it in the change room. Do you mind if I go take a look?"

Andy had worked at the rink for years and knew all the

Otters' players by name. He had been a big player back in his day, but never made it past the Northern Professional League – and now he cleaned up after us. Whenever I saw him pushing the broom around after our games, I couldn't help but feel pity for his sad life.

He seemed torn, but then shrugged. "Go ahead." He pushed the door open wide and handed me the carabiner of keys from his belt. "The Otters' is the big blue one with your logo on it."

"Thanks, man." I grabbed the keys and headed through the lobby, scanning the floor for any sign of my lucky charm.

"Fitzy."

"Yeah," I turned.

"Don't go into the visitor's room."

Weird.

"Okay." I threw my arm up over my head waving acknowledgment and continued retracing the steps I would've taken the night before.

I checked the penalty box since last night I had spent two agonizing minutes in the sin bin. The Port Predators were the roughest, rowdiest team in the league. Their enforcer had set his sights on me in the first period and hadn't let up until I'd dropped my gloves with him in the third.

I shone the light under the home players' bench. Nothing.

Holy shit. The ice looked like hell. Gouges the size of tennis balls pockmarked across the ends, circled by deep grooves, but the telltale corkscrew circles gave the ice wrecker away – a fucking figure skater. In the hockey rink. The boards clanked as Andy stepped onto the ice with a bucket and shovel, manually filling the craters with ice shavings. The Otters' arena had been built by the team's owner

Jake McManus– a retired star from the professional league and was meant for hockey – and only hockey. Our ice was perfect because we didn't share it with anyone. My blood was boiling. I had to talk to someone about this, but first I had to find that damn coin.

The Otters' change room was the nicest one I've ever used, and it was all courtesy of Jake McManus. I headed to my cubby; the number 88 painted on the cement wall above where I sat to lace up my skates. I shone the light under the bench. Nothing.

I opened my locker and shook out everything that was hanging inside, my frustration mounting when the coin didn't drop to the floor. I searched every square inch of that room, but that coin was nowhere to be found.

I locked the change room and turned to continue my search, but my eyes were drawn to the visiting team's door. There was no way my coin was in there, but I wondered why Andy wanted me to stay out?

I looked at the keyring, feeling guilty at the very thought of going in after Andy trusted me with the keys. I heard the Zamboni circling the ice and started to walk away but couldn't help myself and nudged the door open with the toe of my flop and found it wasn't locked. I held my breath as I pushed it open, stepped inside, and peered around the concrete privacy wall.

Holy fuck. A gentleman would've turned around, but I was too stunned by her perfect back. I know that sounds weird, but the triangular shape of her torso showed that she worked out hard. My eyes trailed down her muscular body to the dimples on each side of her lower back, indents like that meant, yep, an amazing butt. Her round ass, the kind developed only from skating, filled out her yoga pants. As she pulled the hair elastic from her ponytail, wavy brown hair spilled down her back, almost to those perfect dimples. All the blood must have rushed from my brain to other parts of my body. That's the only way I can explain the loss of control of my hands. The keys dropped to the rubber floor into a loud, jangly pile. She whipped around, her forearm protectively pressing her breasts into two perfect mounds.

"What are you doing here," she screamed.

Brain, please start working. "I...I...I," I stammered. "Wrong room." I sounded like a fucking Neanderthal and stood there frozen.

She turned away from me and pulled her t-shirt over her head. "I'm sorry." I scooped the keys off the floor and started to back out. She turned to face me, my eyes were drawn first to her flashing green eyes, then to her nipples visible through the thin cotton of her shirt.

"Get out." Her voice was low and guttural, then a pink skate guard wind milled at me in slow motion. My brain wasn't functioning well enough to block it. "Ow, fuck," I muttered as the hard plastic hit me in the temple. I drew my hand to my forehead. No blood.

"Get out," she screamed again.

"Right, sorry." I turned and yanked the door open. The bottom of the door was the perfect height to peel my exposed toenail back. I inhaled sharply and bit my lip as pain shot through my body, but I'd be damned if I was going to scream out in front of the girl. I held my breath and hobbled as fast as I could into the hallway. "Dammit," I released my breath and glanced down to see the blood pooling on the side of my toenail. I ducked into the Otters' dressing room and opened the first aid kit, wrapping my toe in as much gauze as I could, allowing just enough room to slide it into my flip flop. I slipped out of the dressing room and limped towards the lobby, noticing that the pocked ice surface now gleamed perfectly, no sign of the scars from the girl's toe picks. "Thanks, Andy." I tossed the keys to him as I hobbled to the front door.

"Are you okay?" he asked.

"Fine," I grimaced.

"Hey, Fitz. About the ice--" he began.

I held up my hand to stop him. "As long as it looks as good as it does now, I won't say anything – but be careful. You know how the guys feel about toe-picks."

"Thanks, Fitzy." The relief on Andy's face was obvious. "They'll never be able to tell."

The Land Cruiser roared to life and I got the hell out of there as fast as I could, but every time I pushed on the gas pedal, my toe throbbed. I was definitely going to lose that toenail. I flicked on my high beams, my eyes scanning the road and the sidewalks as I continued on my journey to retrace my steps.

I didn't know that figure skater, or why Andy was letting her skate on our ice, but something inside me told me to let it go. I couldn't rat him out – he would lose his job. I just hoped that no one else discovered what could only be described as a betrayal, to the club.

By the time the sun had risen, I had looked everywhere – my coin was gone. I sighed. It had been a gift from my uncle, the black sheep of the Fitzgerald family. Uncle Joe didn't want to have anything to do with the family business, or the Fitzgerald family estate - Pine Hill. The cottage had been in the Fitzgerald family since the turn of the twentieth century, a staple on all of the Millionaire's of Laketown cottage cruises with its sweeping verandas and cobblestone pathways. Uncle Joe had chosen a simpler life and lived on a sailboat, dropping in and out of our lives over the years, until he didn't – we assume that his boat sank somewhere off the Amalfi coast, but no one has ever found him or his fifty-two-foot boat.

I don't remember the last time I cried, and today I fought the lump in my throat harder than I had in years, successfully willing the tears away. I turned onto Mustang Point Road and the Land Cruiser sputtered, its wheel shaking in my hands before the entire car shuddered and the damn thing ran out of gas. I groaned and dropped my head onto the carved wooden steering wheel. "I'll find it, Uncle Joe. I'll find it."

3

JESSIE

"WHERE DID YOU PUT THE KEYS?" Dylan's voice was loud from downstairs.

"They're in the bowl," I shouted. Getting yelled at by my brother wasn't my preferred way to wake up.

"No, they're not." There was irritation in Dylan's voice, and I heard him rummaging through the drawers in the table by the front door. "Come on, Jessie. I'm going to be late for work."

I threw back the covers, hopped out of bed, and found the keys in the side pocket of my skate bag. I ran to the top of the landing. "Here," I shouted.

Dylan held out his hands and I tossed the keys to him.

"Thanks," he shouted. "I'll see you later."

"Later," I grumbled. I yanked the curtains across my window, but the sun shone through the thin fabric. I pulled the covers over my head but sweat pricked my forehead. I pulled the sheet back, reminding myself that I needed to buy a fan, or else I wouldn't be able to sleep all summer. Even though I had grown up in this room, it felt foreign, like it belonged to another person. My skating trophies sat dusty on my bookshelf, a stuffed bear, its neck laden with medals sat beside them. Pictures of my childhood heroes, and skating icons, Evan Lysacek, and my all-time favorite – Kurt Browning, covered the walls. Until the accident brought me back to Laketown, it had been years since I'd slept in this room.

I gave up on getting a few more precious minutes of sleep and got out of bed. The fish and chips truck was open seven days a week and I was trying to pick up as many shifts as possible. After mom and dad died, Dylan and I had sat down and figured it out. If I worked six days a week all summer, combined with the insurance money from their death, I would be able to afford the tuition so that I could go back to the Figure Skating Academy. I pulled on a pair of jeans and a tank top that I didn't mind getting ruined from grease stains. The chip truck was a hot box and it wasn't even June yet.

For now, sneaking into the hockey rink in the middle of the night was going to be my only training. If I didn't get the lutz down before the end of the year, I could kiss my chance at the Olympic team goodbye. I hoped that the peeping tom jock that I saw this morning would keep his mouth shut.

He could ruin everything.

I rummaged through the basket in the front closet, trying to find a baseball cap to wear to work. Dylan was notorious for stealing my hats. "Damn you, Dylan," I hissed under my breath when I couldn't find my hat. I sighed and snatched his Otters hat from the basket and adjusted it to fit my head.

I heard some scratching on the door and let in Crosby, our tabby cat, home from his evening prowling. I held my breath and tried not to gag as I opened up a can of his disgusting food and mixed it in with some kitty kibble. He purred and rubbed up against my bare legs. "Lucky bugger." I reached down to pat him. He arched his back in appreciation and purred while he ate, preparing for his day of getting cat fur all over the sofa.

"Bye, Crosby." I slung my backpack over my shoulder and headed off to work. The chip truck was on the other side of town, beside the marina. Dylan and I took turns driving to work in the old Volvo station wagon. Carpooling wasn't an option as our shifts rarely coincided.

Laketown is known as cottage country, where rich stockbrokers and professional athletes come to play in the summer. The mansions that they call cottages, sit empty for eight months of the year, then Laketown's population quadruples in the summer months, as the wealthy descend in their private helicopters. I'm what they call a Laketownie – I was born and raised here and live in Laketown year-round. In the summer, a Townie's sole purpose is to serve the needs of the cottagers. Or at least that's what it feels like.

The sun beat down on my bare shoulders, and I knew the freckles that I hated were intensifying by the second. When I left three years ago, to live at the figure skating academy, I thought that my days as a Laketownie were over. That I'd escaped a life of serving rich people, but just when I thought I'd escaped, tragedy pulled me back in.

I tied on the apron and clicked on the deep fryers. The job sucked, but at least I got to spend time with my friend Paige. We were best friends in high school and had loosely stayed connected over social media while I was at the academy. Like me, Paige was a Laketownie.

The door to the trailer clattered open and Paige hopped inside. Her cheeks were rosy, her white-blonde hair perfectly stick straight even in the humidity. She looked like she stepped off the pages of a Swedish swimsuit catalog. "Sorry, I'm late," she said.

I glanced out the window and saw a sleek Mercedes pulling away.

"Fun night?"

"Super fun."

"You're glowing."

"My fake I.D. worked." She winked. Paige tucked her hair up under her hat and still managed to look good. "You should try to get your own. The bar was so good last night."

By good, Paige meant that a bunch of hot rich guys showed up and bought rounds of drinks for everyone at the bar. "Oh, yeah?"

"Yeah, you'll never guess who showed up."

I squashed a potato through the cutting machine and dropped the pieces into a bowl of brine.

"Who?"

"The owner of the Otters and the Thunder, what-shisname?"

"McManus. Dylan said that he's always there." I wasn't impressed. I dumped the pre-mixed batter into a huge bowl and tossed in the fresh pickerel that was delivered this morning.

"Yeah, I know. But he brought both of his teams." The Thunder was his NHL team, the Otters his Northern Professional League team. In Laketown, NHL players are bigger than movie stars, and I once saw Kevin Costner get pushed out of the way by a fan trying to reach a Thunder player.

"Ooooh." I roll my eyes. "Paige, you know that I don't like hockey players."

"Come on, Jessie. You've gotta admit that Jake McManus is one of the hottest guys you've ever seen."

She was right, but I'd be loath to admit it. "He's okay," I

shrugged. "Hey…" All this talk about dumb jocks reminded me of the doofus from the morning. "You'll never guess what happened to me after practice today."

"You landed the lutz?" Paige's voice was high with excitement.

"Not yet."

"Oh, you'll get it soon." She smiled and finished rolling napkins around plastic forks.

I hoped that she was right, but it seemed like the harder I worked, the more elusive the lutz became. "No, some hockey player totally peeping tommed me this morning."

"Ooh," she turned, her eyes wide with excitement. "Who?"

"I don't know," I shook my head. "I don't fangirl on the players, you know that."

"Well, what did he look like?"

I now had her full undivided attention and she set down the ketchup bottles she was carrying.

"I don't know."

"Come on, now. Was he tall?"

"Of course, he was tall." All the Otters players were behemoths who stood over 6'6 on their skates. "I don't really remember; I was trying to cover up my boobs." This was a lie. I could describe the man to a sketch artist in enough detail that a jury would have no doubt but to convict. "Light brown hair, blue eyes."

"Ice or Navy?"

"What?" I continued battering the slippery pieces of fish.

"His eyes, what kind of blue?"

I flicked some of the flour on my hands at her. "Blue. Just blue."

They were ice.

"He was wearing those stupid flip flops that all hockey

players wear and he had on sweatpants." *That left little to the imagination*, I could've added. "I guess he was cute... If I found hockey players hot, which I don't."

"I wonder who it was," Paige mused. The deep fryer beeped, interrupting our conversation, letting us know that it was ready to gurgle and sizzle all the fries we could feed it.

I laughed under my breath, remembering the stunned look on his face as my skate guard ricocheted off his skull. "Look for a guy with a black eye."

"You hit him?" Paige's eyes went wide.

"I wanted to, that pervert just stood there watching me change. But he may have accidentally walked into a flying skate guard."

"You should've invited him in to help you get dressed." Paige elbowed me, her fire-engine red lips wide in a conspiratorial smile. "When was the last time you got some action? There can't have been that many straight guys at the figure skating academy."

She was right, I hadn't been on a date in over a year. There were a few hot figure skaters that trained with me, but they were all spoken for – or gay. "I would never date a figure skater. Remember how that turned out last time?"

"Yeah, but Robbie was a dick."

Robbie had lost his triple axel; it was something that happened to skaters from time to time – and I still had mine. I couldn't handle the jealousy and had enough competition on the ice – I didn't need to compete off-ice with the guy I was dating.

"Maybe it's time to test drive a few hockey players."

"Ugh, they're worse," I shook my head. "Never in a million years. You couldn't pay me to go on a date with a hockey jock."

"Never say never," Paige smiled. She pulled the chain on the neon sign. We were open for business.

BY THE TIME I flicked off the sign, my tank top was soaked in sweat and my hair was stuck to my neck. "How are we going to make it through the summer in this hot box?" I stepped out the back of the truck, locked the door, and chugged back all the water in my aluminum bottle.

"I'm going to try to get a job at Valerock," Paige stated. The local bar was 'the' place to work for the summer. All the girls that worked there looked like models, and the tips they made were legendary. You had to be in the know to get a job at the Rock. Paige could make a real killing there, and it was selfish of me to try to stop her from leaving the chip wagon.

"Don't you dare." I shook the last drop of water from my bottle at her. "If you leave me in this truck alone, I will cut off that pretty hair of yours in your sleep."

"But just think, Jess. If I get in there, I could get you a job too."

I shrugged. "It's not really my scene." I couldn't imagine putting on the tiny black dresses and a full face of makeup every night. I glanced down at my B-cup chest, knowing that even if I did know the right people, I didn't have the Valerock 'goods.'

"Suit yourself." Paige wrapped her arm around me and pulled me in tightly. "And I'm coming to destroy every single pair of scissors that you own." She pulled the elastic out of her high ponytail and shook her long hair over her shoulders, there wasn't a ponytail kink in sight. "Want to go for a swim?"

I crinkled my nose as I glanced around the shoreline.

Despite the marina being home to hundred-thousand-dollar boats and a small shop that sold three-hundred dollar sweatshirts, it had a piddly rocky beach. Not exactly a relaxing swimming hole, and dodging wakeboard boats was not my idea of fun.

"I think I'll pass." I checked my watch. "Dylan should be done with his shift soon and I don't want to walk home in this heat.

"Do you think he'd give me a ride too?" Paige asked. Her skin was the kind of porcelain that tanned like a perfectly roasted marshmallow, but I noticed a slight pink flush in her cheeks.

"Come on, let's go find him." I set out towards the big corrugated metal building, and Paige followed me. As we reached the open garage bay, Dylan was leaning up against a Mastercraft, a beer in hand. The other mechanic, a guy named Ralph grinned as Paige and I approached.

"Ladies," Ralph tipped his oil-stained baseball hat at us.

"Dirtbags."

Ralph clutched his t-shirt, "Damn, girl. That's harsh." He set his beer on the side of the boat and pulled me in for a squeeze. "Sorry for your loss, kid," he whispered into my ear.

I pulled back and pursed my lips, trying to hold in the tears. The accident had happened almost three months ago, but I was still running into people who hadn't had the chance to say their condolences. "Thanks, Ralph," I murmured, the toes of my Converse all of sudden seeming a lot more interesting.

Dylan cleared his throat. "Speak for yourself, at least we don't smell like the food tent at the fall fair."

"Are you ready to go home?" I ignored his comment, eyeing his beer.

"Just have to finish this one." He held up the can.

"Can you give Paige a ride home too?"

"Sure." Dylan smiled past me at Paige. "You two want a drink?" Dylan's Cheshire cat smile was unnerving.

"Sure, I'll take one," Paige said and stepped up beside me.

Dylan fished a Coors Light out of the cooler, opened it, and handed it to Paige.

"Thanks." She took a big swig and smiled at my brother. I knew for a fact that Paige hated domestic beer.

"Jess?" he paused at the open lid to the cooler.

"I'll pass." I held up my hand. "One of us has to be sober enough to drive."

"Oh, lighten up," Paige said.

"Yeah, listen to your friend," Dylan grinned.

I couldn't believe that the two of them were ganging up on me, and somewhere along the line, my best friend and my brother were making eyes at each other.

"You know what? I think I'll just walk. Bye, Ralph." I walked away, waiting for Paige to catch up. But, instead of rushing to join me, she waved and took a sip of her beer, and then turned back to face the guys, all while twirling the end of her hair.

I hoped that my hat was enough to stop the late afternoon sun from burning my skin to a crisp. Unlike Paige, my skin went directly from white glue to lobster with no stops in between. Paige and I had been inseparable in high school, but I guess I couldn't expect that friendship to maintain its bond after being away at the Academy. Somehow during that time, Paige had gone boy crazy, and now my goofy ass brother was on her radar.

The cooling effects of the lake dissipated the closer I got to town. The cicadas hummed and the sweat had soaked through my baseball hat. The Volvo didn't have air conditioning, and I would've been stuck to its seats, but at least I would've been home by now. I cursed Dylan and wished that I had grabbed the keys and made him walk home.

A Mercedes cruised by, its tinted windows obscuring whatever famous or rich person sat in its air-conditioned sanctity, followed by three Range Rovers, and a Lamborghini.

The year-round community of Laketown was small – everyone knew everyone or at least knew of everyone – the whole first degree of separation thing. Before the accident, I was known as that figure skater, and Dylan was known as the fastest guy on the Otters. Now, we were those poor Moss kids. Not in the monetary sense, the pitiful sense – we were the orphans, the kids whose parents were killed by the drunk driver. I used to hate being known only for my skating skills but being known as the kid with the dead parents, was a million times worse.

The hair went up on the back of my neck as I felt electricity brewing in the air. The sky had grown black and ominous behind me, and then a low slow rumble of thunder shook the windows of the ice cream shop beside me.

I picked up the pace. Our house was only a few blocks away from Oak Avenue, the main street of Laketown, but the drops weren't having it. They started plopping down from the sky, exploding into steam as they met the hot pavement. I rounded the corner as the heavens exploded and was instantly soaked through to my underwear. I gripped the wet straps of my backpack, put my head down, and continued walking home. I didn't even bother avoiding the puddles, and as my shoes squished, I heard a car slow down behind me.

"Took you long enough," I shouted and turned, but it wasn't the Volvo. It was a red Jeep.

"Need a ride?"

The man inside looked to be in his thirties, but I couldn't be sure, the Otters hat he was wearing shielded most of his face.

"I'm alright." I blew a drop of rain off my top lip, then a flash of lightning lit up the sky.

"You should get in." The man stopped the car beside me. "It's only going to get worse."

A BMW swerved around the jeep and plowed through a giant puddle. A tidal wave rolled over my feet.

"Are you a serial killer?" I asked.

The look of shock on his face turned to a smile. "Close, I'm a hockey coach."

I jumped as another rumble of thunder growled through the air. I grabbed the door handle and hopped in. "That's worse," I smiled at him. "Sorry about getting your car all soaked."

"That's better than watching you get electrocuted."

The man's eyes crinkled when he smiled. He was too old to be a player. "Are you the new coach for the Otters?"

"New? I've been in Laketown for a year and a half."

Right, I had forgotten that life had gone on without me while I was away. "My brother plays on your team."

The man turned down the radio and glanced over at me. "Let me guess, Dylan?"

"That's him."

"You're the famous figure skater then, Jessica, right?"

"I guess so." I picked at the frayed threads from my jeans cutting across my knees. "And you're Coach Covington."

"You can call me Dean. It's nice to meet you Jessica, and I'm sorry about your parents."

"Thanks," I replied. My response was now on autopilot.

The windows of the Jeep were fogging up and he cracked the windows slightly. "What are you doing walking in this?"

"Well, Dylan was supposed to give me a ride home, but he was too busy drinking." I resisted the urge to squeeze the water out of my t-shirt, and instead, let it cling heavily to my body.

"Really?" The coach concentrated on the road, but I could see that his jaw had clenched. "He was supposed to be at practice this afternoon."

Oh, shit. Did I just get Dylan in trouble? "I mean, he was at work, just finishing up."

"Jessica. Is everything okay with your brother?"

I blinked at the coach. "I don't know how to answer that."

"Shit," he muttered. "I'm sorry. I just mean he's been missing a lot of practices lately."

"I don't know anything about that," I replied, keeping my response simple and safe. I had already said too much. Dylan didn't take the team seriously. He was a natural, the fastest on the team, and as long as the defensemen took care of him, his job was to skate fast and score goals, something he could do with his eyes shut.

"Is yours the brown house?" the coach asked. "I dropped Dylan off once before, but it was dark out."

"Yes, the one with the white trim." Coach Covington pulled into the driveway and I saw our little house with the eyes of a newcomer. My mom would've had heart failure if she saw how overgrown the gardens had become. The weeds were taller than any of the perennials that she'd worked so hard to curate over the years. Dylan and I took turns mowing the lawn, but with the heatwave, our once a week schedule wasn't cutting it – literally. The fuzzy-looking front yard was now a rainforest, battered and weighed down from the downpour.

"Thanks for the ride." I hopped out of the Jeep, giving the soaked leather seat a fruitless wipe with my hand before I shut the door. The coach rolled down the window. "You're welcome, Jessica. And get that brother of yours to call me if he wants to stay on the team."

"I'll do my best." I rested my hand on the door, "but you know what he's like."

"Headstrong." The coach smiled.

"I was going to say an ass. But I guess headstrong works too."

The coach laughed and I swore that he snorted a little bit. I stepped away from the SUV and waved as he backed out of the driveway, wondering why Dylan was missing so many practices.

4

KANE

Swimming always clears my head. I hung my towel on the hooks on the side of the boathouse and stood at the end of the dock. Lake Casper is the deepest of the five lakes in Laketown, and it's always the last one to warm up. I pulled up the thermometer from the water; it read fifty- nine degrees. It was almost balmy compared to the team's post-game ice baths.

I took a breath and launched into the clear water, hoping that the bandage on my toe was wrapped tightly enough to keep the nail in place. I let my body float just under the surface of the water for a minute. This was my meditation. I didn't need any mindfulness apps or any of that shit.

A boat droned by and a loon called in the distance. I hoisted myself on the dock and basked in one of the teak lounge chairs, totally zenned out until my phone chimed with a text message.

I saw that I had missed a call from The Otters' captain, Tanner, as well as three texts in a row. The last read, "Dude. Call me."

He picked up on the first ring.

"What's up?" I asked.

"You better have your A-Game on tonight."

I could hear the excitement in his voice and knew exactly what he meant. The scouts were going to be at the game. Coach never told us when they were there, he didn't want our nerves to interfere with the game.

'Which scouts are going to be there?'

'The Thunder and the Flames.'

'Holy shit,' I gulped.

'Yeah, holy shit.'

The New York Thunder was one of the original teams in the National League, and everyone who grew up in this part of the country dreamt about wearing the blue and white jersey. I pinned the phone between my ear and my shoulder to grab my towel. 'How did you find...'

I meant to ask how he found out that the scouts were going to be at the exhibition game, but the phone slipped and did exactly two slow-motion rotations before it disappeared through a crack in the dock boards, splashing into Lake Casper.

"For fucks' sake." I dropped to my knees to peer through the boards into the darkness beneath the dock, knowing full well that my phone was ruined. I hopped into the lake anyway, retrieved the phone, knowing that as I pushed the power button that nothing would happen. I sighed and walked toward the sandy beach and up the granite pathway to the cottage. I shoved the phone into a bowl of rice and pulled off my wet boardshorts, hanging them on the railing of the balcony – something my step-mom hated, saying it made the cottage look like a third world bazaar, but she only came to Laketown once a year – for the Island Club's annual gala.

I rubbed my chin, my playoff beard was gone, replaced with a five o'clock shadow. I couldn't believe that the scouts were coming to an exhibition game. I pulled on a pair of blue shorts and a white t-shirt, then gingerly stepped into my flip flops, and grabbed the keys to the Cruiser. Two seconds before I reached the car a fat drop of rain spattered on the windshield. I looked behind me to see that the blue sky had been overtaken by tall black thunderclouds. 'Shit,' I muttered and lunged for the door handle, but the downpour came on hard and fast as I jumped in the driver's seat, soaked to the bone.

If I didn't find that coin before the game tonight, I might as well kiss my dreams of being drafted goodbye.

5

JESSIE

"Jessie."

My eyes snapped open and I heard Dylan pushing around food in the fridge. I had dozed off while I was studying skating videos and my laptop was still perched on my thighs. I closed it, thankful that it hadn't fallen onto the floor.

"What time is it?" I asked and glanced out the window. It wasn't dark, so I couldn't have been asleep on the sofa for too long.

"Time to go to the rink." Dylan shoved a slice of cold pizza into his mouth, letting it hang while he twisted off the lid from a bottle of soda. "Can you drop me off?" he said as he swigged the Coke directly from the two-liter bottle.

"How are you not five hundred pounds?" Dylan was a garbage can – he ate whatever was in his path, and other than hockey practice, he didn't work out - yet he still had a six-pack.

Dylan shrugged. "Want a piece?" He shoved the box at me. I took it from his hands and put it back in the fridge. "You're looking skinny, you need to eat more than that rabbit food." He pointed to the blender cup on the counter crusted with the residue from my protein smoothie.

"I'm good." But he was right, ever since mom and dad died, I just didn't feel like eating.

"It's going to affect your skating, you know."

"My skating is fine." I didn't tell him that my hip was sore from continuously crashing with my lutz attempts. I shuffled into the kitchen, poured myself a glass of water, and chugged it back.

"Are you coming to the game?" he asked.

"I'm going to bed." I didn't go to Dylan's games for two reasons. One, the entire town was obsessed with his damn team, and the rah-rah Otters' cheers got on my nerves; and two, Dylan's groupies, aka the puck bunnies, were equally, if not more, annoying.

"It's one of the last exhibition games before summer camp."

"I'll pass. I'm exhausted."

"Ok, can you drop me off then?"

"Are you serious?" I gestured to my sweatpants. "I'm not going anywhere. I have to get up at three-thirty in the morning."

"Okay, but we're probably going to Valerock after. And I know that you don't like it when I drink and drive."

I could feel the blood rush to my face. Dylan never got behind the wheel when he was falling-down drunk, but for someone whose parents were killed by a drunk driver, the gall of my brother to even have one or two, but more likely four or five, and get behind the wheel made me want to scream.

"Don't. It's not hard." I grabbed my laptop and headed upstairs.

"Come on, you know how it is. We'll just go for a few. If I have too many, I'll get a cab home."

I gripped the handrail so hard my knuckles went white. I turned to face him as he lugged his giant hockey bag from the living room, where it now lived beside the television, in all its stinky glory. "I had to walk home in a thunderstorm today." I left out the part that his coach had driven me home.

Dylan smiled at me. "Right, that was a big one."

I stomped down the stairs and got in my brother's face. "I have to be at the arena at four in the morning. I. Need. The. Car." I held out my hand for the keys. "Call one of your jock buddies for a ride."

"It's too late." He shoved the keys in the pocket of his team hoody. "Jess, I'll only have one drink."

Dylan never had 'just one.'

"Ugh." I groaned at him. "Hold on. Let me change and then I'll drop you off." All I wanted to do was set my alarm and crawl into bed, but if Dylan got an impaired driving charge, he wouldn't be able to get to work, and I'd be driving his sorry ass around all summer. I marched up the stairs muttering under my breath. Dylan knew how to get to me.

I should just let him fuck up his life, I thought to myself as I changed into leggings and a light sweater. He was grieving, just like me, but in a vastly different way. But I couldn't lose another family member to drinking and driving. I twisted my hair into a loose top knot, my face bare from the steaming shower I had taken when I got home.

Dylan tossed his hockey bag into the back of the station wagon while I pumped the gas pedal a couple of times. The car was ancient and there was a technique to getting the old beast up and running. Thankfully, the engine roared to life when I turned the key.

I backed out of the driveway and started to head into town. Dylan grabbed my hand and stopped me from turning the wheel. "We've got to make one stop first," he smiled.

I gritted my teeth and leaned my head back on the headrest. "Where?"

"Paige's house."

Of course.

"She lives --"

"I know where she lives," I snapped. I shoved the car into gear and stomped on the pedal to go and pick up my supposed best friend. "Is this a date?"

"Nah." Dylan fiddled with the radio. Our car was so old it didn't even have a cd-player, and when he didn't find anything good on the radio, he popped in the cassette tape and his pre-game band, Motley Crue, blared out through the speakers. "I told her you were coming to the game too."

"Dyl! Come on. You know that I have to go to bed early."

He turned up the music even louder. "Relax. You need to have a little fun."

I gripped the steering wheel with one hand and turned down *Doctor Feelgood* with the other. "You need to grow up. Coach Covington told me that you've been missing practices."

This got his attention. He turned his body to face me. "When were you talking to him?"

"He saved me from getting struck by lightning today." I navigated the car through the narrow roads of Paige's trailer park, pulled into her driveway and honked.

"He shouldn't be talking to you about that stuff."

Paige flicked her hair as she jogged to get in the car. "You're right. He should be talking to **you** about why you are missing practice."

"Hi guys," Paige opened the car door and hopped in.

"Hi," we both said at the same time. I shot him a look and he shot one back, the conversation was over – for now.

"I can't believe you're actually coming to a game," Paige clicked into her seatbelt as I backed out of the driveway. I cut my eyes at my brother.

"I can only stay for the first period." Paige seemed too excited to let my words bring her down.

"I'll take it," Paige gushed. "I've been trying to get you to a game since ninth grade."

I glanced in the mirror and felt a pang of guilt as Paige smiled at me. Between my grueling practice schedule and my complete and utter disinterest in the game of hockey, I had pushed Paige away to the point where she didn't even ask me to go to the games anymore. "Dylan promised to score a goal tonight and then ride the stick," I said and raised my eyebrows at my brother.

"Oooh," Paige laughed from the back. "That'll go over well."

Dylan punched my arm. "I'll get destroyed on the ice if I do that." Dylan was a fast skater, but a fighter he was not. And showboating like that was a one-way ticket to a gloves-off beat-down.

The parking lot was bustling when we arrived, and I pulled into the first spot that I could find.

"What, you're going to make me walk from here?" Dylan put his hand over his eyes, pretending to strain to see the lobby doors.

"You're an athlete. You can walk." I shut off the car.

Dylan groaned, retrieved his bag, and strode off.

"Shouldn't he be at the game earlier than this?" Paige glanced at her oversized rose gold watch.

"Dylan thinks that being on time applies to everyone but

him," I sighed. I glanced around the parking lot full of fans carrying homemade signs and those annoying horns. I used to think that Dylan's ability alone was enough to keep him on the team, but after today's meeting with the coach, I wondered if skipping practice and showing up late were going to catch up with him.

We joined nearly everyone else in town and filed into the state-of-the-art facility. Laketown's ice rink was the best in the Northern Professional League and overbuilt for our little town – it came complete with jumbotrons and executive boxes for the National League players when they were in town.

I glanced at the seat number on my ticket – we were way up in the back, the blue seats. We settled into the nosebleeds and as I shoved the ticket into my purse, I noticed a familiar set of eyes. The creeper from the dressing room was staring up at me from the glossy ticket. "That's him." I shoved the ticket at Paige, "The guy from this morning".

Paige choked on her iced cappuccino. "Kane Fitzgerald?"

"This guy." I tapped my unmanicured nail on the photo.

"Yeah, that's Fitzy. Jessie, he's like the hottest guy on the team."

I glanced at the ticket, Fitzy's eyes were trained on something ahead of him, his body captured mid-stride, the puck on his stick, the number eighty-eight on his jersey which was half-tucked into his blue hockey pants. "He's not that hot in person." The clumsy tongue-tied guy from this morning couldn't have been farther from the action hero on the ticket. I shoved the ticket into my purse and settled into my seat. I was antsy, but I figured if there weren't any delays in the period, I could be home and in my bed in less than an hour.

"I heard that there are scouts here tonight," Paige

elbowed me, her eyes scanning the audience. "Do you think that they're checking out your brother?"

The Northern Professional Hockey League was just below the National League, and many of the New York Thunder superstars had started their careers as a Laketown Otter.

I rolled my eyes. My brother was a skillful player, but not National League material. "He doesn't want it badly enough," I shrugged.

"I heard that they're here for Fitzy and Tanner." Paige studied the executive boxes.

"Who's Tanner?"

The woman beside me raised her eyebrows and smirked. "Tanner is the captain."

"Are you sure you're from Laketown?" Paige smiled and thrust her drink at me. "Want some?" she asked.

I raised my hands in front of me. "No, thanks."

"Are you sure you don't want anything, popcorn, a beer?" Paige plucked a piece of popcorn from its paper bag.

"I'm good." I folded my arms across my chest as the lights went down and the sound system boomed out more Motley Crue. The Laketown Otters hockey team had all the theatrics: lasers, pyrotechnics, and even cheerleaders.

"Ladies and Gentlemen, please welcome to the ice, your hometown Oooooooooooootters." The announcer drew out the O in Otters and the audience all did the same, including Paige. The team burst onto the ice through a cloud of dry ice and the crowd roared. The girls behind us screamed and when number eighty-eight stepped onto the ice, they went even more batshit crazy. I shoved my fingers in my ears, but it was too late, the screams had already pierced through to my brain.

After the national anthem, the crowd settled into their

seats, the lights came up, and number twenty-seven, the captain, stepped to center ice and won the face-off. It had been years since I'd seen a game and I'd forgotten how enthusiastic the Otters' fan base could be. I scanned the lineup of players along the bench, spotting my brother lounging and laughing, his mouthguard jauntily stuck between his teeth. Beside him, looking much more serious, was number eighty-eight. His ice-blue eyes were trained on the action in front of him.

Dylan kicked his foot over the boards and sprang into action, his unorthodox upright skating style made him easy to pick out. He circled back into the defensive zone and number twenty-seven backhanded the puck to him. I couldn't help it, my heart jumped into my throat when my brother easily navigated past the blue line, deked out the Predator's defense and reared his stick back as if to take a huge slapshot - but instead brought his stick down and nudged the puck into the net behind the pads of the unsuspecting goalie.

Paige jumped to her feet, along with everyone else around me. I stood up and cheered. Dylan scanned the audience and when his gaze found us, I recognized his shit-eating grin.

"Oh no," I whispered. "Don't you dare. I. Was. Joking."

I cringed as my brother threw his glove up in the air and proceeded to 'shoot it' out of the air with his hockey stick. It only took a millisecond for one of the Predators to retaliate with a cross-check to his back. An audible gasp, followed by a collectively held breath by every person in the arena, quickly erupted into cheers as Dylan stood up shook his shoulders like a wet dog.

"Oh, thank God, he's okay," one of the girls said behind me. I turned to Paige and rolled my eyes. Dylan grinned and pointed at me in the audience and then dramatically flung his other glove onto the ice.

"Cocky son of a bitch," I whispered under my breath.

The referee blew his whistle as Dylan charged at the Predators player. They grabbed each other's jerseys and the momentum from Dylan's charge spun them around, but before any blows could be thrown, the referee and linesman pulled the two apart.

Dylan was ejected from the game for unsportsmanlike conduct and the Predators player got a five minute for fighting penalty, which would have to be taken in the second period. The teams filed out from their respective benches as Andy reversed the Zamboni onto the ice.

"He's kind of cute," Paige mused as she finished off her coffee slushy with a loud slurp, swirling the straw around to vacuum up the last drops her drink. "You know, for an older guy."

"Who?" I followed her gaze. "Andy?"

"Wait. That's the Andy that's been letting you in here in the mornings?" She pointed at him with her straw.

"Yes and stay away from him." I threatened.

"Ooh, is he bad news?" She bit the end of her straw and I saw the glint in her eye.

"No, he's just – he's a custodian." Andy was the nicest man I'd ever known.

"Is that what you think of me?" Paige put on a fake pout.

"You have a type, P. And thirty-eight-year-old Zamboni drivers are not it."

I waited for Paige to object, but her eyes grew wide as she stared at something over the top of my head. I jumped as hands clasped down on my shoulders.

"Relax, sis." Dylan shimmied past me and into the seat beside Paige.

"Nice goal." Paige bit the end of the plastic straw, flattening it between her teeth.

"Thanks," Dylan grinned.

"When did you turn into such a hothead?" I asked. The fight was extremely out of character for my brother.

"You said you'd only come to the game if I rode the stick. I went with the old 'shoot the glove'." He dug his hand into Paige's popcorn and crammed it into his mouth all while keeping a huge smile on his face. Everyone has their own way of dealing with grief, and I'm no psychiatrist, but Dylan's outburst on the ice, and cavalier attitude towards life in general, seemed to indicate that his was anger and denial.

"I was joking." I stared at the shiny sheet of ice as Andy finished his last lap. There was something about a fresh sheet that relaxed me - a clean slate – a fresh start. "You've been missing practices. The last thing you need is to get kicked out of the game."

"Want a beer?" He ignored me. The question was aimed at Paige, not me.

"Sure." Paige handed him her empty plastic cup.

"Jess?" He stood up and fixed his game tie.

"Shouldn't you be over with your team?" I glanced at the home bench as the Otters started their warm-up laps around the wet ice.

"Meh." He shrugged and started to walk backwards up the stairs. "So that's a no then?" he pointed at me. I shook my head as he walked away. I had been so preoccupied with my own life falling apart, I hadn't noticed that Dylan was making sure that his did too.

By the time Dylan got back precariously balancing four plastic cups of draft beer, the second period was well underway. "It was cheaper to buy two." He explained as Paige took the cups from his hands.

"Jess?" Paige held up the extra beer. "I won't be able to drink two before they get warm."

Dylan nudged Paige. "If she doesn't want it, I can help you with that."

"Actually, maybe I will take one," I grabbed one of the flimsy cups from Paige's hand and took a sip. I rarely drank and was surprised that the watery beer tasted good.

The Otters and Predators were tied one to one. I blocked out the giggling and flirting taking place beside me and started watching the game in earnest. The players were good, there was no doubt about it, but there were three that stood out – and they were all Otters. I found myself drawn to number eighty-eight, not because he was the guy from this morning, but because of his technique. The man knew how to harness the power of his edges but was leaving some speed on the table with his stride technique. But, for being such a behemoth of a man, I was impressed with his maneu-vering skills. Where Dylan was thin and lanky, eighty-eight was solid and powerful, yet managed to gracefully stick handle his weight in circles around the Predator's defensemen.

Fitzgerald passed the puck to Townsend, who arced around the back of the net, faked a backhand, and then passed the puck back to Fitzgerald who was ready and waiting to slap it into the top right corner of the net.

The goal light lit up and sirens screamed. Fitzgerald hugged Tanner and the rest of the team gathered around the duo.

"Wooo." Dylan was on his feet. "Yeah, Fitzy!" he screamed, raising his glass in the air.

There was no way he could've heard Dylan, but Fitzy's eyes scanned the audience and seemed to stop on him, then on me. Even from this distance, the intensity in his eyes was apparent. The Fitzgerald on the ice was a far cry from the bumbling jock from this morning.

I inhaled sharply and averted my gaze before he did, wondering if he could tell that I had been staring at him, and also wondering if he recognized me as the skate guard attacker. I finished the last sip of my beer and stood up. "I'm going home."

"Ah, come on, Jess. The game is just getting good." Dylan said.

"Is that because you're not on the ice right now?" I eyed the two empty cups under his seat and wondered how he had managed to get two fresh new drinks without me noticing.

"Touché," he laughed.

"Paige, can I drop you off at home?" It was an empty offer; I could tell by the way she was leaning into Dylan that she had found her spot for the rest of the evening.

"I think I'll stay," she shot a glance at Dylan and he gave me a smug shrug.

I slung my handbag over my shoulder and Paige and Dylan both drew their knees to the side to let me pass. The crowd erupted in cheers and I turned to see what I was missing. The Otters were short-handed, and number eighty-eight was on a breakaway, the red sweaters of the Predators flashed down the ice as they tried to catch the lone Otter. This time I wasn't impressed by Fitzy's blades, it was the intensity in his movements, the way his head remained perfectly still as his body worked its magic beneath him. He was in the zone, I could see it, I recognized it and my stomach constricted in excitement for him. The rest of the crowd was standing and screaming and I clutched my bag, my fingernails leaving crescent curves in the leather as number eighty-eight passed the blue line, wound up, but instead of faking, as he did with his first goal, he followed through with his stick and the puck launched, too fast for anyone's eyes to effectively follow its path, the only giveaway to its destination was the spasm of the net behind the goaltender. The screams and the bass of the announcer's voice reverberated in my chest. I knew that I had witnessed something magical and that one day, number eighty-eight was going to be a star.

"Bye," I shouted to Dylan and Paige.

They were both screaming and clapping, but Paige stopped to hug me. "Are you sure you don't want to stay?" Her eyes sparkled with excitement, and even though I saw the beginning of a mistake that was likely brewing between her and Dylan, I knew that she genuinely wanted me at the game too.

"I have practice in a few hours," I shouted.

She nodded. "Of course."

It had been my excuse for the past three months, and even though she said that she understood, I could see or hear the disappointment in her voice whenever I canceled. But she didn't understand what was at stake.

I reached the stairs and turned to look at the ice, Fitzy was back at the player's bench. Unlike Dylan, he didn't showboat or play to the crowd. His gaze was on the ice, but then I saw him break focus and look to the stands, to Dylan and Paige – and then to me.

There were thousands of people in the arena that night. There was no way he's looking at you, I told myself and my sneakers squeaked as I rushed up the sticky stairs. He's not looking at you, I repeated, but my stomach was gripped tightly in a knot and I was having a tough time catching my breath.

Why was I acting like a preteen girl at a Jonas Brother's

concert? I walked as quickly as I could out of the arena and into the warm night air, where my shoulders finally relaxed. I shook it off. I didn't like hockey players, and the guy that had walked into the dressing room this morning was the poster boy for exactly what I did NOT want in a man.

6

KANE

OUT OF ALL THE coaches I'd ever had, Dean Covington was my favorite. He somehow managed to inspire us without screaming and throwing stuff – but tonight, his eyes flashed, and his nostrils flared as he looked around the room.

"Who was out there tonight?" He raised his arms. "You boys might have won tonight, but that wasn't my team out there."

I paused with my fingers in my skate's laces. Since word had spread that the Thunder's scout was going to be in the audience, everyone had turned on their inner Wayne Gretzky. I was just as guilty, there were times when I should have passed the puck, but I waited, wanting to show off my skills.

"Fitzy, Leo was wide open on that last play – why didn't you follow our play?"

"I—I—" I didn't know what to say.

"I come in here, and you guys are celebrating a win, but I didn't see a win out there." He slapped the clipboard against his palm. "I saw a bunch of selfish assholes."

I shifted in my seat, my one foot on the floor, the other

still in my skate. The blood from my toenail had soaked through my compression socks.

"Townsend," Coach turned to face Tanner. "You're the captain of this team, and you and Fitzgerald were playing like there were only two of you on the ice."

Tanner opened his mouth to reply, but then hung his head.

"I know what happened out there tonight, and you boys need to forget who is in the stands. We have one more game against the Predators, and if I was their coach..." He shook his head. "I'd be rubbing my hands together because there are some serious holes in this team's armor."

I glanced sideways at Tanner, his hands were clasped, and his gaze was on the floor. The room was dead silent, no one in the room was going to challenge the coach, the only guy who was stupid enough to challenge him was out frolicking in the stands with those beautiful girls. Who was that figure skater, and why was she sitting with Dylan?

The silence lingered into extremely uncomfortable territory as Coach Covington stared us down. "Where's Moss?" he asked.

We all glanced from side to side. Dylan had been kicked out of the game in the first period, but instead of sitting with us, he had gone to drink beer in the stands. I scanned the room, his bag was sitting in front of his spot, but Dylan Moss was nowhere to be seen.

"Tanner Townsend, you are the captain of this team. Where is your player?"

Tanner exhaled loudly. "I don't know."

It was extremely unprofessional for Dylan to go and sit in the stands, but to not show up for the post-game, to stand united with his team, it was like he didn't care at all anymore.

"Well, Townsend. When that showboating motherfucker shows his face, you tell him that's strike two."

The room went silent. I looked from Tanner to Coach.

"You heard me. I won't tolerate behavior like that." He kicked the side of the plastic garbage can and it wobbled before toppling over onto the rubberized floor. "And don't you dare feel sorry for him." He pointed around the room. "Any one of you," he said. "That disgusting act out there could've cost you guys the game."

Coach was right. Dylan had put us all at risk to show off for some fucking puck bunnies. I put all emotion aside when I played, but now I felt rage. I clenched my hands into fists. What if we had lost tonight? That fucker could've ruined my chance at the National League.

"Get dressed." Coach paused at the door, turning to face us one more time, his face a little softer. "You guys won tonight, and I'm proud of you for that. Fitzy, beautiful slap shot, Townsend, great stickhandling out there."

All of our eyes were trained on the coach, he didn't play favorites, but he always selected a player to run the drills at the next practice. It was his version of 'star of the game.' He pointed to the shaggy-haired forward that we all called the Lion. The guy had a tan year-round and a mane of hair that all the bunnies said they'd kill for. "Leo will run drills at practice on Sunday."

Even with his tan, Leo's cheeks flushed pink. I understood where the coach was coming from, but it was usually myself, Tanner, Mike, or occasionally even Dylan, who ran drills. I concentrated on the laces of my skate; did I need to remind him that I had scored two goals? We would've lost if it wasn't for me.

The coach shoved the door open and disappeared into the bustling hallway. I pulled off my skate, and even though

I had already dumped out my hockey bag, I ran my hands around it one more time, praying that my fingertips would find my coin.

The mood in the dressing room was somber as we all showered and packed up our gear.

Tanner cleared his throat and stood. "Coach was right," he said.

"About what?" Mike Ryan, one of the defensemen muttered.

"Everything." Tanner's voice was stern. "Leo played his heart out today and deserves to be recognized." I looked at Tanner, waiting for him to acknowledge my goals, but he continued, "We didn't play as a team, and Dylan Moss is a selfish prick."

A couple of the guys laughed, and most of the team nodded their heads in agreement. "But we did win tonight. We ARE going to win this exhibition series." The mood in the room started to lift as players nodded and a couple clapped in agreement. Tanner stood in the center of the room, still in his hockey pants. "Leo's going to run the practice on Sunday but tonight we're going to celebrate this win – as a team." He clenched his fists at his side and then raised one into the air. "Got it?" he shouted.

"Got it," A couple of the guys replied.

"Got it?" Tanner growled loudly.

The team erupted in cheers, "GOT IT." Mike started with the guttural O at the beginning of the Otters' chant that rhymed with the song *Day-O*. I followed suit, soon the room was humming along with Tanner, "Oooooootters," he shouted and the rest of us mirrored it back. He shouted it again, this time louder and the rest of us stood up. "Oooooootters." Anyone standing on the other side of the door would've heard the chanting, and I sure hoped that Coach Covington was still there.

"Afterparty at Fitzy's place," Tanner smiled and glanced over at me. I shrugged and then nodded. Most of the guys lived at the Laketown Hockey Academy training camp dorms, but a few of us were cottagers and stayed at our own places, and a couple of townie kids still lived at home. My dad never came to the cottage, so my place just happened to be the fallback for all the parties. "Come on guys, let's go blow off some steam. You heard the coach…" he paused dramatically, "team-building."

The rest of the team cheered and clapped. Tanner was a natural-born leader and he was right; we could all blow off a bit of steam. I just hoped that the scout saw my goals and that this team building celebration was only the beginning of a series of celebrations for me. After I showered and got dressed, I picked up my hockey bag and it gaped open just after I had zipped it shut. I fingered the zipper pull and saw that it was broken. I sighed and carefully pulled the straps over the shoulder of my suit jacket. Tanner lingered by the door, while the rest of the team filed out of the dressing room. He waited for me so he could be the last one to leave. As my bag jostled against the frame of the door, the nylon strap slipped from my shoulder and all of my hockey equipment spilled to the floor in a heap.

"Really, Fitzy?" Tanner groaned.

"Zipper's busted," I said and dropped the now floppy bag to the ground to shove my equipment back into it. Leo didn't realize that I wasn't following behind him and the door dropped heavily against my ass, knocking me directly onto the pile of my equipment.

Tanner bent to help me up. I groaned as I rolled off the pile of sweaty hockey gear, my toe throbbing inside my brown dress shoes. "What's going on with you man?" he laughed as we stuffed the gear into my broken bag. I didn't dare tell Tanner that with one game left against the Predators, I had lost my lucky coin. Out of all the guys, he was probably the most superstitious of all. If he knew I lost my coin, it would play with his psyche, the way it was wreaking havoc with mine.

7

JESSIE

MY ALARM SOUNDED and I patted my nightstand in the dark, trying to find my phone. I squinted at the bright screen, ready to press snooze once, but the red button wasn't there. It took me a minute to realize that I wasn't looking at my alarm, it was a phone call. What the hell was Paige doing calling me in the middle of the night?

I accepted the call, resting the phone between my ear and my pillow. "Paige," I murmured.

"Jessie, I'm so sorry," she said as she slurred her words. Paige was drunk. "You've gotta come get me."

"Where are you?" I asked sitting up, bleary-eyed.

"I don't know. Jessie, you've got to come and get me. There was a fight and Dylan is ..."

As I swung my feet out of the bed, my heart started to race. Middle of the night phone calls were never good – the last one had been to tell me my parents were dead. "Where's Dylan?" I shoved my feet into my Birkenstocks, pulled a sweatshirt from my closet, zipping it up over the wifebeater tank top that I wore to bed, and tightened the string on my cotton pajama shorts.

"I don't know." A bubble had formed in her throat.

"What do you mean you don't know?" I grabbed the keys from the bowl by the door and rushed to the Volvo.

"He... there was a fight," she was full-on sobbing.

"You said that already, Paige. Where are you? I'm coming to get you."

I heard a fumbling and rustling and then a male voice came on the line. "The address?" The voice seemed to be talking to Paige before it redirected itself back to the phone conversation. "Hi."

"Hi." I shoved the key into the ignition and pumped the gas. "What's going on?"

"Your friend needs a ride. Do you know where Mustang Point Road is?"

I nodded as the car growled to life. I pushed the gas one more time and revved the engine - the other trick to keeping it running.

"Hello?"

I realized that I had nodded. "I know where it is." I glanced in the rear-view mirror and reversed the car out of the driveway.

"It's number ten-ten."

"Ten-Ten Mustang Point Rd. Got it," I slammed the car into gear and accelerated toward the lake. "Is everything okay? What's going on?"

I didn't recognize the voice, but it was low and somehow reassuring. "Everything is fine. Your friend has just had a little too much to drink."

I had already made it to the highway, the car shuddering as I got her up to sixty miles an hour. "What about Dylan?"

There was no response. "Shit," I muttered and dropped my phone into the coffee-stained cup holder. I had entered into the granite outcroppings that killed all cell signals for at least ten miles. "Ten Ten Mustang Point Road," I whispered to myself. The Volvo's headlights were old and yellowed, and I clicked them onto their high setting to read the road signs.

Ten-ten was the last cottage on the dead-end road, and easily one of the biggest. I turned into the driveway, past a gilded sign that read 'Pine Hill'. Dylan and I once joked that we should name our house, but the best we could come up with was Little Brown. There were several cars lined up around the circular driveway that led to a classic cedar shake sided cottage.

I hopped out of the car, tempted to leave it running to ensure that it started again, but the number of shadowy figures staggering around the driveway told me that it wasn't a good idea. It wouldn't be the first time that a town drunk woke up with a 'borrowed' car parked haphazardly in their driveway.

My text to Paige sat unanswered and I waited a minute by the car, watching the cigarettes and joints glowing orange in the dark as people came and went from the cottage. I glanced at my phone, still no response. I sighed and then headed to the door, suddenly very aware of my disheveled appearance. Everywhere I looked I saw eyelash extensions and even longer hair extensions – puck bunny city. What was the protocol for crashing a party at three a.m.? I raised my fist to knock on the door but changed my mind and let myself into the front foyer of Pine Hill. I was met with the stench of stale beer and blaring music. I followed the sound of the pounding bass, kicking discarded red cups out of the way and emerged into a great room, its crystal chandeliers glowing, reflecting in the twenty-foot-tall wall of windows that framed the darkness of the overcast night. A fully clothed couple writhed on one of the sofas and I averted my gaze, less out of privacy, and more out of disgust as the guy's hands clumsily fumbled down the back of the girl's pants, exposing her tanned ass cheeks.

There was no sign of Paige or Dylan. The kitchen was in worse shape than the great room and my feet stuck to the floor as I passed through. "Do you know Paige Thomas?" I asked a group of girls who were sitting on the counter, their lips stained the same vibrant pink as their wine coolers, two of them looked at me and shrugged.

"Check the lake. I think there are some people swimming?" the third girl suggested, a classic valley girl upswing making her statement sound like a question.

Great, I muttered under my breath and hurried out of the kitchen. The Paige I used to know wouldn't be that stupid, but this new boy crazy version might be dumb enough to jump in the lake while wasted out of her tree.

"Hey, Paige is over here." I turned toward the deep voice and was met with the ice blue eyes of number eighty-eight.

"Oh, it's you." He stepped back.

That's exactly what I was thinking. "Where is she?" I asked.

"Come with me," he waved his arm in a follow-me gesture.

I nodded and focused on his bare feet as he navigated through the maze of hallways to a bedroom. Paige was sitting on the edge of the bed, her face in her hands.

"Are you okay?" I rushed to her side.

She peered between her fingers. "Jessie?"

"I'll leave you two." The hockey player's bulky form turned in the doorway.

"Wait," I said.

He paused.

"What's going on here?" I asked.

The guy sighed and then stepped into the room. "Her boyfriend showed up here and started a fight."

"Her boyfriend?"

"Yeah, Dylan Moss. You know him. The guy you were sitting with at the game."

I stood in the space between Kane Fitzgerald and whimpering Paige. I hadn't imagined it. He had seen me at the game.

"He's not my boyfriend," Paige said a little louder than was necessary.

I was tired, and it was becoming very clear that there was nothing wrong with Paige, other than the fact that she was wasted. "Where is Dylan?" I asked.

Kane held the lever on the door as though it was a crutch, holding him upright. "I don't know." He shrugged.

Dylan was a clown, an entertainer, but he wasn't a fighter. One punch from a guy like Fitzy would level his lanky body to the ground. "Is he okay?" I tried to keep the tremble out of my voice.

Kane's eyes seemed to focus sharply on me, and he let go of the door. "Is Dylan *your* boyfriend?"

I turned to Paige, whose eyes were crossing as she attempted to direct a wand of lip gloss to her lips. "Paige, where is Dylan?" I repeated.

She huffed out a breath and set her hand on her thigh, the lip gloss wand dropping to the pine floor. "I don't know. He got in a fight and he..." her voice constricted, and the tears started streaming down her face, "he left me here." Her chest heaved in a sob.

I wasn't going to get any answers from either of these two. "Come on, Paige. I'll take you home." I held out my hand and heaved her off the nautical themed quilt. She stumbled toward me, stepping onto her lip gloss with her bare foot. She wavered and I caught her before she could hit the floor or break her ankle.

"Can you help me?" I groaned as I held all one hundred and twenty pounds of my friend on my shoulder.

"Right," Kane rushed to my side and scooped Paige into his arms like he was about to whisk her away on a romantic honeymoon. I stretched tall as her weight was released from my shoulder. The guy had picked her up like she weighed nothing at all.

I hurried into the hallway and Kane followed behind.

"No, this way," he said. The massive cottage was like a maze. We passed the kitchen where the trio of wine cooler girls was still camping and after passing through an extremely well-stocked pantry entered yet another hallway, one that led to a circular staircase.

"What is this?" I glanced into another bedroom as we made our way to the stairs.

"Servants' quarters," he said.

"Servants' quarters? How old is your cottage?"

"Why?" he turned to look at me, Paige's head lolled against his white t-shirt.

"Decommissioned servant's quarters? I mean, that's got to mean, maybe the twenties?" I guessed.

"I think it was built in the twenties, but we still have staff when my dad is here."

The room beside me was bigger than mine, furnished like the rest of the house, a blue and white quilt, made perfectly on a four-poster bed. He led me to a door, and we exited out the side of the cottage into a screened-in porch, complete with a swing. "I'm parked in the driveway," I said.

He pushed open the screen door and raised his eyebrows at me. "That's usually where people park."

My cheeks flushed hot. Was it condescension or was this asshole jock trying to be funny? His stupid flip flops slapped his feet as we made our way through the mess of cars. My hair blew in the wind and my chest prickled with goosebumps. I crossed my arms, trying to disguise the fact that I wasn't wearing a bra.

"The wind just shifted; did you feel that?" He stopped and pointed to one of the flags that snapped in the wind like an angry dog.

"I can walk," Paige murmured, her fingers looped around Kane's muscled neck.

"It's okay. I've got you." He replaced his hand on her back.

"Thanks, Fitzy," Paige murmured.

"Mine is the Volvo," I pointed out the rusty wagon at the end of the line of cars.

He nodded. "Nice ride."

"It's a car, asshole. Not all of us have mommy and daddy's Bentley at our fingertips."

"No." He gently lowered Paige until she was standing on her own two feet. The hinges of the passenger door groaned as he pulled it open and he helped Paige slip onto the worn leather seat. "That's not what I meant; this is a classic. I love these old wagons."

"Oh..."

"Is it a GL?" He gazed at the front grill of the car as he made his way to the driver's side.

"I don't know. It's a car, it has a steering wheel, and this is the key." I held up my keychain.

Kane held the door open as I pulled on the stained seat belt. My dad had been a mechanic, his hands permanently darkened with oil and grease, the dirty seatbelt a reminder that this had once been his car.

"I need to find Dylan. Do you have any idea where he went?"

"He disappeared with some townies. Why is it so important for you to find Moss? He's an inconsiderate piece of shit."

I yanked the door to shut it, but Fitzy's grip was stronger than my pull. He held it open, waiting for my response.

"That might be true, but he's my brother."

"Oh." Kane released the door and held up his hands as it slammed shut. I jammed the key into the ignition, stomped the gas pedal and turned the key.

Click.

Nothing.

"What's going on? Why won't the car start?" Paige fumbled with the volume button on the radio as I tried turning the key two more times. I felt Kane's presence at the window but didn't want to face him.

He rapped on the window with his knuckle and made the roll down the window motion with his fingertips. The car was old enough to have crank windows, making his miming accurate. I lowered the window.

"It's your battery."

"I know." I sucked in my breath. "Or the alternator."

He nodded. "Or your alternator."

I squeezed my eyes, trying to suck the tears back in before they fell. "What time is it?" I gripped the steering wheel with both hands.

"Uh," Kane glanced at his watch, "Holy shit, it's three-thirty."

I dropped my head to the steering wheel and turned the

key one more time. I knew it was fruitless, but I had to be at the arena in half an hour.

"Come on, let's go," Paige stared out the passenger window.

My vision flashed white with rage. "Paige, I'm trying," I said through clenched teeth. "I'm going to miss practice."

"Oh, no." She sat up straight. "Oh, Jessie. I'm sorry. It's all my fault."

It was all her fault, and Dylan's. I wanted to scream and tell her she was right. She and my selfish brother *had* ruined my night, but I was exhausted and after playing taxi driver to her drunk ass I was going to miss the only thing that mattered in my life – skating.

"Come on," Kane opened the door. "I'll take you."

"You?" While he seemed significantly more sober than when I had first arrived at Pine Hill, he looked like he was swaying on his feet. "You're drunk."

"Maybe a little." He extended his hand to help me out of the car. "You can take one of my cars."

I stared his hand, "It just needs a boost."

"If it's your alternator, you'll just be stranded at the next place. And, if you leave now, you might be able to make it to the arena for four."

"I couldn't."

He reached and grabbed my hand, pulling me away from the car. "Take one of my cars. Please. I will have yours towed to your garage first thing in the morning, or we can boost it."

"Oh no," Paige said. We both turned to see her fumbling to open the passenger door, one hand clamped over her mouth.

Both of us groaned as the contents of Paige's stomach splattered onto the paved driveway.

"Okay," I agreed. "But are you sure you want her in one of your cars?"

"Better now than thirty seconds ago." He laughed and tugged at my hand. I let him lead us into his five-car garage and hand me the keys to a Mercedes Sedan.

"Are you sure about this?" I took the keys.

"It's my stepmom's," he laughed. "It's also the crappiest car we've got."

I glanced at the rest of the cars gleaming in the fluorescent light

"Get going, or you're going to be late," he shooed me away with his hands. Paige had already gotten into the passenger seat. Kane pressed the button and the garage door opened behind me.

"Thank you." I slid into the buttery leather of the driver's seat, pressed the ignition button, and the powerful engine growled to life. Out of habit, I stomped my foot on the accelerator and the V8 engine roared.

"Easy there, tiger," Kane smiled then pushed the door shut.

I rolled down the window. "Thanks again, Fitzy."

"It's Kane," he said. He reached his hand in the window.

"I know." I shook it. "Your face is on the hockey tickets." For some reason, I felt like I needed to clarify exactly how I knew his name.

"Get going, Moss's sister. You're going to be late for practice."

He stepped away from the car. "It's Jessie," I smiled and put the car in reverse.

"Well then get going, Jessie Moss." He smiled back and patted the hood of the car like they do in the movies.

Without the rattle and shimmy of the Volvo to drown out all other sounds, the pounding of my heart hammering against my ribcage thudded loudly in my ears. I waved at Kane and noticed the tremble in my hand. The thudding in my ears intensified as he shot me a toothy grin and waved back. There was no denying it. Kane Fitzgerald was the first man to give me butterflies in years.

8

KANE

THE SHUTTERS CLATTERED AGGRESSIVELY against the cedar shakes outside my bedroom window. I sat up and rubbed my temple, trying to judge the severity of my hangover before I got out of bed. Check number one, the room didn't start to spin. Check number two, I didn't feel like I was going to barf. I chugged down the glass of water that drunk me left for morning me and stretched my arms over my head.

When I set down the glass on my nightstand, I noticed a set of keys on a pewter figure skater keychain. The events from the night before, while a little hazy, started to come back to me. The figure skater, she had been here. Dylan's sister. Last night I had jerked off to someone I could never have – my right winger's sister. I shook the image of Jessie's nipples from my brain and stumbled into the bathroom. I grabbed my swimsuit from its hook; a swim was the best hangover cure I knew.

"Hey guys, get out." I banged on the back of the sofa and a partially clothed couple groaned and entwined tighter into each other.

When I rounded the corner into the hallway I almost

ran right into Mike Ryan. "Whoa." Mike blinked and pressed the heel of his hand to his forehead. "Thanks for the party, Fitzy."

"You out of here?" I asked.

"Yeah, man. Back to the dorms. I've gotta go sleep this one off."

"You can stay here if you want, buddy." Mike pointed to the guest room and made a throat-slitting motion with his hand. I looked inside the room and saw a disheveled puck bunny, her mouth slightly agape, the pillow smeared with black eyeliner. "I'm gonna get out of here." He winked.

Mike was a total player, but I didn't feel bad for the bunny, it wasn't exactly a secret that he was a dog. "See you tomorrow," I said to him and then shut the door gently.

My to-do list grew longer as the hangover fuzziness subsided. I found my new phone amongst the tangled duvet on my bed and sent a quick message to Margie, the only cleaning lady I could trust not to rat me out to my dad, asking her to come and help with the mess.

Next on my list was to deal with that car. I pulled on an Otters hoodie and parked the Land Cruiser beside the rusty old Volvo. I hooked my car battery up to Jessie's with booster cables. "Shit," I swore as my knees bashed into the steering wheel, clearly set up for Jessie's height. I turned the key in the ignition and pulled the choke out slightly, just as Jessie had done the night before, pumped the gas pedal once, and then smiled as the car roared to life. It sputtered, but I gave it a shot of gas, and soon enough it was purring.

I waited a few minutes, then unhooked the cables, turned off the car, and held my breath before trying it again. The old rust bucket roared to life – it was just a dead battery.

I made my way to one of the bunkies, where my best

---

friend always crashed, "Tanner," I shouted, opening the door.

"Yeah." Tanner squinted at me.

"Get up, you've got to help me with something." I shut the door before Tanner had the chance to say no., I sat in one of the white Adirondack chairs and listened as the waves crashed against the shoreline.

"What's going on?" Tanner stepped out of the bunkie, ran his fingers through his disheveled hair, and pulled on a blue flat-brimmed Otters team hat.

"Coffee run."

"No way." Tanner turned to walk back into the bunkie.

"I'll let you drive," I taunted. Tanner loved my car almost more than I did. I smiled and tossed him the keys.

"You asshole," Tanner muttered and snagged them out of mid-air with authority. "Let's go." He grinned.

My phone rang as we sat in the drive-through of the local coffee shop. I glanced at the screen, wondering who could be calling so early in the morning, "It's Coach."

"I missed a call from him too," Tanner said. "I haven't called him back yet."

"I wonder what he wants..." My mind started to race with both good and bad scenarios.

"Maybe he wants to run some drills today or something," Tanner mused.

Both of us knew that was bullshit. The coach never had last-minute practices. The call was definitely about something else.

Neither of us said anything as Tanner inched the car up to the speaker box, the Rolling Stones' song on the radio the only thing that filled the air between us. We both knew that the scout from the New York Thunder had been at the game, but Tanner's silence told me that he was just as nervous about the call as I was.

"Are you going to answer?" Tanner pulled up to the window.

I pressed 'decline'. What if the coach had bad news for me and good news for Tanner? Or vice-versa. "I'll wait until after we order the coffee." The truth was that I didn't want to have that conversation in front of him.

We ordered a couple of trays of coffee and a box of donuts. We didn't know how many people had stayed at Pine Hill, so we got the family size just to be on the safe side. I opened the box and pulled out my favorite, a Boston Cream. I handed Tanner a chocolate glazed and neither of us acknowledged the fact that I wasn't rushing to call Coach Covington back right away.

"Do you think that he'll kick Mossy off the team?" Tanner peeled back the tab on his coffee lid and slurped a sip.

"Yeah, I do – if he keeps screwing up." I brushed some of the icing sugar off my sweatshirt. "If he gets another strike, Coach will make an example of him."

"It's too bad." Tanner signaled out of the parking lot and onto Oak Avenue.

I opened the glove box and pulled out my aviator sunglasses, giving them a quick polish before sliding them over my bloodshot eyes. Even though it was overcast, the brightness was proving too much for me. "Too bad? I think he should've been cut a month ago."

"He performs. We get the W with him."

"It just pisses me off," I took the first sip of my coffee and recoiled as it burned my lip. "The guy is so talented and doesn't give a fuck about going anywhere. I just don't get it."

"I've known him for years, Fitzy. That stuff with his parents really fucked him up."

"Shit, I'm an asshole." I knew that Dylan's parents died in that car accident, but I hated to admit that I'd forgotten about it. Dylan never talked about it, and hell, they hadn't even had a public funeral – so the team couldn't even pay their respects. "I guess that would mess you up pretty bad." My mom had died when I was little, but I didn't remember how I felt about it. Maybe I had blocked it out, or maybe I was just too young to process the fact that she was there one day and gone the next.

Tanner took another sip of his coffee and as he headed east on the highway, the sun broke from behind the clouds and we both slammed our visors down like shields. "I thought that Dylan was doing okay, but I think it's an act. He's losing it."

I couldn't believe how selfish I'd been. I was more worried about the game than one of my teammates. We were supposed to be brothers. "Hey, did you know that he has a sister?"

Tanner squinted through his sunglasses. "Yeah, but I've never met her. She's away at some figure skating school. Apparently, she's the next Tonya Harding."

I laughed. "I think you need to brush up on your figure skating knowledge, Captain." I laughed. It didn't make sense. If she was some hotshot away at skating school, why was she sneaking into our rink in the middle of the night? "The Academy in New York?"

"I think that's the one," Tanner replied. "Why do you ask?"

"She showed up at the party last night, looking for Dylan and that bunny he was with."

Tanner glanced at me. "Before or after the fight?"

"Late. Like three in the morning late." I hadn't seen the fight, only the aftermath. The coffee table had been knocked over and half the team was holding Josh, one of the newer defensemen, and the other half was holding onto Dylan. The two of them were trying to free themselves, flailing against the restraint of their teammates, eager to keep punching each other's lights out.

"Do you know where he went?" I asked.

"No. I think he left with a bunny."

"Did you see what happened?" I took a bite of my donut. "Why were they fighting?"

"You didn't see it?" Tanner asked. "Josh was chirping him about fucking up the game and then said something about Moss's mom."

"Oh." I sucked in some air between my teeth. "I don't know why, but I assumed that Mossy started it." I had been mad at Dylan since the game. "If Josh ever said something about my mom, I'd punch his lights out too." My anger at Dylan was fading. "I hope he's okay." I took another bite of my donut and the cream squeezed out the small hole and plopped onto my blue sweatshirt. "Oh, come on," I groaned and searched inside the glove box for a napkin.

"Maybe Coach wants to know what to do about Moss," Tanner suggested and signaled onto Mustang Point Road.

My eyes relaxed as the trees blocked out the aggressive sunlight. I took off my sunglasses and rubbed the bridge of my nose. "Maybe." I doubted it. "But, if Coach asks me what to do, I'm going to tell him to go easy on him."

"Is his sister hot?" Tanner smiled at me as he downshifted. "I've heard she's pretty cute."

"She's alright," I shrugged. Truthfully, just the memory of the dimples on her lower back made my cock pulse. I hardly knew the girl, but already I knew that I didn't want any of the Otters to get their hands on her. "Too bad she's off-limits for everyone," I added.

Tanner nodded. He had two sisters and had threatened the entire team with death if any of us touched them. "No sisters," he said as if reminding me.

I picked up my coffee cup and blew through the small opening, slowly testing another sip. It was still too hot to drink.

"Oh shit!" Tanner yanked the wheel and jammed on the brakes. In my reflex to grab something, I squeezed the cup and the lid popped off. Coffee sloshed all over my lap.

I sucked in air as the searing pain from my thighs reached my brain. The car skidded to a stop in the middle of the road and I saw the flick of a white-tailed deer as it disappeared into the sea of pine trees. "Sorry, dude," he said.

I had to get the hot fabric away from all that was important to me and pulled down my pants. My thighs were red with the heat and I gently dabbed at them with the rest of the napkins. The box had slid from my lap and I kicked at the sprinkled donuts with my feet. I breathed a sigh of relief. My junk had escaped the hot lava, but my boxer briefs were soaked.

"Are you alright?" Tanner's knuckles were white as they gripped the steering wheel. Both of us were breathing heavily while the hit of adrenaline faded from our systems.

"I think so. Nothing important got burned." I pulled the box from the floor and set it down on my lap. I wasn't shy, but it felt weird to be driving around with one of my teammates in my boxers.

"Nice undies." Tanner pushed in the clutch and eased the Cruiser to a much slower speed.

I glanced down. They were one of my favorite pairs – bright yellow with pizza wedges.

"Thanks." I knew he wasn't serious, but I loved my novelty boxer briefs.

"You're having quite the streak of bad luck."

I wanted to agree with him. But to a superstitious guy like Tanner, admitting that I was in a bad-luck slump was akin to saying we'd never win another game again. "It's just a bit of coffee." I brushed off the comment, but he was right, the bad luck sure was piling up.

Tanner parked the car and hopped out. "Do you want me to get you another pair of shorts?" he asked.

"It's okay, man." I grabbed my coffee-soaked sweatpants and gingerly eased out of the car. I didn't think the burn was too severe, but it still stung. "I'll just go jump in the lake."

"That's your cure for everything," Tanner laughed.

He was right. "Are you coming with me?"

He tossed me the keys, walked past the main building, and threw his hand up in the air – I was dismissed. "Where are you going?" I yelled.

He turned, "Back to bed."

I locked up the Land Cruiser, took stock of the three unknown vehicles in the driveway, and headed inside. I had to call the coach to see what he wanted, but as my finger hovered over Covington's number my stomach wrenched with angry butterflies. I'd call him after my swim.

I tried to stay positive as I made my way to the shoreline, but if my recent spate of bad luck had anything to say, I knew that the news wasn't going to be good.

9

JESSIE

SLEEP ELUDED ME. I glanced out the curtains, looking for any sign of Dylan, and was momentarily caught off guard by the gunmetal gray Mercedes in the driveway.

The steam billowed out of the shower as I stepped inside. This morning's practice had been brutal. Not only had I eaten it every time I attempted my triple lutz, but I also fell on my easiest jump – my toe loop, and I can perform that damn jump in my sleep.

I wrapped the towel around my chest and padded to my bedroom, glancing into Dylan's dark green disaster of a room, hoping that the unmade lump of twisted sheets now contained my brother, but there was no sign of him.

The wind hadn't let up all night, and even though the sun had just come up, it was still almost pitch black in my room. I toweled off my hair and then piled it into a messy bun on top of my head. Luckily, both Paige and I had the late shift today, and as much as I knew that I should try to get some sleep, I wasn't going to be able to rest until I knew what had happened to Dylan.

I dialed Paige's number but wasn't surprised when it

rang again and again until her voicemail picked up. I cursed myself for not getting Kane Fitzgerald's phone number, but the car was a reminder that I was going to have to go back to Pine Hill anyway.

This wasn't the first time Dylan had disappeared in a drunken stupor, and I knew that he was going to show up after sleeping it off at one of his loser friend's houses. But I couldn't stop worrying. *Damn you, Dylan*. I got dressed in a pair of leggings and a t-shirt. I caught a glimpse of myself in the hallway mirror and backtracked to the bathroom where I quickly layered some cover up on over the dark circles under my eyes. The girl that looked back at me looked tired. I shook my head, wondering why I cared what Kane Fitzgerald thought about me. I would never be a puck bunny – nor did I want to be. Nevertheless, I swiped a thin mascara layer on my lashes and applied some tinted lip gloss.

I started the Mercedes, but before I could put the car into reverse my breath caught in my throat as the black and white appeared in the rear-view mirror. I felt my life go into slow motion; police cars this early in the morning were never a good thing.

I held onto the steering wheel, unable to move. The car's engine purred and Celine Dion sang her heart out on the radio, but both of those things were white noise to me. My eyes were glued on the mirror and when a police officer opened the rear door and my brother stepped out of the car in one piece, I managed to open the door and collapse into a heap beside the running car.

"Jess, are you okay?" Dylan's black Vans slapped the cracked pavement as the police car pulled away.

"I'm fine," I muttered and tried to shrug his hand off of me.

"Sweet car." Dylan stared past me while maintaining his grip. His nonchalant attitude sent a fire into my belly. The strength that I had lost came rushing back and I pushed him away like The Hulk.

"What the fuck, Dylan? Where were you?" I stepped away from him. My hands were shaking, and I was trying my best not to slap that inconsiderate bastard across the face.

"Whoa, easy, Jess."

"*Easy Jess*? I was worried about you!" Anger had cycled through, and now relief that my brother was okay washed over me. I sank back onto the driveway, this time, my body overtaken with wracking sobs.

"Shit," Dylan whispered. "Come on." he reached his hand to try to pull me up.

"Leave. Me. Alone," I managed to croak out between sobs.

"No, I'm not going to leave you out here like this."

"What do you care?" I looked at him. The sun had just peeked out from the dense cloud cover and he was ringed in its light. Instead of trying to haul me up off the ground again, he crossed his feet and sat down with me. He reached his arm around my back and rubbed my shoulder.

"You don't have to worry about me. That's not your job," he whispered.

My spine sagged as the anger left my body and I let my big brother hold me. "I can't help it. You haven't been your-self since..."

"I know," he squeezed my shoulder again.

I wiped away the tears and sat up a little taller, my butt was starting to feel the cold as it seeped from the pavement. "Promise me something."

I felt him stiffen. "I know what you're going to ask, and I won't. I won't drink and drive, I promise."

I couldn't help but smile at him. We had drifted apart in the three years I had been away at the Academy, but deep down, we knew each other, and no matter how much time or distance spanned between us, we had that. "Thanks, Dylan." I stood and brushed the dirt off the back of my leggings.

"Where were you going?" Dylan stood up beside me.

"I was going to find you – and return this car," I gestured to the Mercedes.

"Whose car is that? Where's the vulva?"

I rolled my eyes and he grinned and winked at me. We each had our nicknames for the car, his, The Vulva, was much cruder than mine: Penny, on account of all of her rust spots.

I slid into the driver's seat and rolled down the window. "None of your business."

"Hold on a minute," Dylan held onto the bottom of the open window frame.

"Ugh, you smell like a brewery." I waved my hand in front of my face, avoiding the question.

"Jess," he sighed. "I thought our policy was honesty. Here, I'll go first. Last night I got into a fight and ended up spending the night in the drunk tank. More or less. Now, your turn."

I let my hand slip from the gear shifter. "Paige called me in the middle of the night."

Dylan's gaze fell to the ground.

"Crying," I added.

"Shit," he muttered. "I forgot about…"

"Her?" I folded my arms across my chest.

"Is she okay?" He wouldn't meet my gaze.

"She's fine. She was drunk and irrational. I dropped her off at her house last night. She's probably sleeping it off, or has her head stuffed in a toilet right now."

"I should probably call..."

"No," I interrupted. "You should probably stop whatever is going on between you two. It's not going to end well, and she's my friend."

He looked up, "You were at Fitzy's?"

"Yep. Penny wouldn't start, so he lent me this." I tapped my hand on the steering wheel. "He said something about towing the car to the mechanic's today."

"Shit." Dylan shook his head. He ran around the car and hopped in the passenger seat. "I'm coming with you. We will boost the car and take it to the marina; Gary's shop is way too expensive."

I hadn't thought past the logistics of picking up the car. "Fine."

"Does he know you're coming?" Dylan craned his head to look through the back window of the car as I reversed out of the driveway – an annoying habit of his.

"I don't have his number, I left in a hurry to get to the arena."

"Oh, Jess. I'm sorry. Did you make your practice?"

"Barely," I pursed my lips, put the car in gear, and our heads jerked and hit the headrests as I stomped on the gas. "Whoops, this gas pedal is a little more responsive than Penny's." I glanced at the dashboard and saw that we were already going seventy miles per hour. "Are you sure it's a good idea for you to show up there today?"

"It was a misunderstanding, as long as that bastard Josh is gone, it will be fine."

"Are you sure?" I kept him in my peripheral vision as I navigated the car through town.

He waved it off. "I've been on the team longer; it's all good."

"Maybe give Fitzy a heads up." I tapped Dylan's phone.

"Fine." He reluctantly scrolled through his contact list. "Shit, we're in the dead zone," he held his phone up searching for a signal after the third dropped call. "It will be fine," he said as if trying to convince himself, but I heard the hesitation in his voice.

10

KANE

THE SMELL of bacon sizzling wafted from the open kitchen window as I headed to the main cottage from the lake.

"I thought you were going back to bed," I yelled from the balcony as I draped my wet towel over the railing.

Tanner was dressed in a pair of workout shorts, prodding a pan of bacon with a fork. "I couldn't sleep. I guess the coffee woke me up."

"Yeah, me too, but in a different way." The cold lake water had worked its magic on my legs, the redness barely visible underneath my board shorts.

"You alright?"

"Yeah, but I sure could use a coffee," I grumbled and plucked a piece of bacon from the plate beside the stove and Tanner pretended to jab at my hand with the fork. "I put on a pot. There are still a few people sleeping." He pointed to the wing that housed the guest rooms.

A blue recycling bag sat in the middle of the great room, stuffed with red plastic cups. "Thanks for starting the cleanup."

"No problem, buddy. I sure hope your parents aren't going to pull a surprise appearance today."

When I was a kid, my mom used to spend the entire summer at the cottage and my dad came and went as business meetings permitted. Now that I have a stepmom, my dad rarely comes to Pine Hill at all. My stepmom can't handle the mosquitos and never really took to the family estate. "They aren't coming up until the gala."

I shook open another recycling bag and picked up where Tanner had left off. "I called Margie, the cleaning lady -- the one that I can trust – she's coming by tomorrow."

"Oh, thank God. This place is a wreck." Tanner looked visibly relieved.

"I know." I stacked fifteen cups into each other and dropped them into the bag. "We should probably start making people bring their own cups. This isn't exactly good for the environment."

Tanner shrugged. "How do you want your eggs?"

"Poached."

"I can only do scrambled." Tanner pulled the carton of eggs from the fridge. "I don't even know why I asked," he laughed.

"I'll take 'em scrambled then." I went back to collecting empty cups and beer bottles.

"That smells good."

We both turned to see a disheveled woman emerge from one of the bedrooms.

"I hope you like scrambled," Tanner held up the spatula.

"Mmmm." The girl stretched her arms above her head. "Have you seen Mike?" she asked.

I glanced at Tanner. He hadn't seen Mike pull his escape earlier this morning, but he wasn't stupid.

Tanner stirred the eggs in the pan with the spatula. "He

said that he had something important to do for the coach this morning." Tanner gave her his million-megawatt smile, covering for his teammate.

She blushed and smiled back. "Oh, okay."

The toaster popped and Tanner slathered the pieces with butter. "Here." He handed the still-unnamed girl a plate topped with his surprisingly good-looking breakfast.

She picked up the piece of toast like it was laced with arsenic and dropped it onto the next plate. "Carbs," she said.

Tanner handed her a fork and rolled his eyes at me. "Fitzy, you're up."

I set down the bag and washed my hands in the kitchen sink, the stale beer smell had almost ruined my appetite. The banging sound from the wrought iron door knocker interrupted our conversation.

"You expecting someone?" Tanner paused with a plate in his hand.

"Maybe Margie's here early." I shook the water off my hands and jogged through the great room to the rear entryway and pulled the door wide open.

"Hi."

It was Jessie. Her eyes looked tired, but her cheeks glowed pink as she handed me the keys to the car.

"Hi." I hung the keys on the hooks by the door. "We're just making breakfast; do you want some?"

"Sure. Smells great." Dylan stepped out from behind the stone pillar and stood beside his sister. I don't know how I missed it, the resemblance between them was uncanny, with their high cheekbones and tall lanky frames, they were practically twins.

"Oh, hey." I couldn't believe that he would show up after the scene he caused. He also had dark circles under his eyes, but his were bruises.

Jessie put her hand on her brother's chest, stopping him. "Where's our car?"

I leaned against the doorframe. "It's in the garage. I left it on a charge. You should probably take it to Gary to make sure there isn't something else wrong with it."

"We have a family friend who fixes our car," Jessie explained.

I saw her gaze travel up and down my entire shirtless body and it wasn't my imagination, she flushed from her jawline down the center of her chest. I only glanced at her tits but had to turn away quickly when my cock stirred in my boardshorts. "Let me grab a shirt, come on in."

"We'll wait out here," Jessie said.

"Suit yourself," I said. Her cheeks were still red, and she appeared to be studying the trees between the main cottage and the bunkie.

As I LED the two of them to the garage, I asked as casually as I could, "Did you get a call from Coach today?" I still hadn't gotten the guts up to call Covington.

"I did, but I missed it," Dylan said. "I was a little busy. Did he call you too?"

"Yeah." I opened up the garage.

Dylan whistled as the fluorescent lights lit up the car collection. "I think he's going to give me shit about last night."

"You think?"

Dylan laughed under his breath. "I'm probably going to get kicked off the team."

I wanted to tell Dylan about the two strikes comment

that Coach had made after the game, but figured it wasn't my place.

"Do you care?" I couldn't help but ask.

"Not really," Dylan shrugged. "I wonder why he called you though."

"I don't know. I'll call him back later," keeping my voice even, trying to sound nonchalant.

I wanted to hate him, but I couldn't. I didn't know why Coach Covington had called, but I had to call him back. Dylan wasn't a bad guy; he was just going through a tough time. If Coach asked, I was going to tell him to go easy on the poor guy. I kept glancing at Jessie. She looked exhausted, and she had an air of sadness to her. I felt for the two of them, but it looked like Jessie had her hands full with her brother. If helping him, meant helping her, something deep in my heart told me that I needed to do it.

Not going to make it today.

I stared at the text from Paige - sent twenty minutes after her shift was supposed to start. The line at the chip truck snaked around the side of the truck down to the shoreline and I cursed Paige every time I dropped a basket of fries into the grease.

The good part about being run off your feet is that the day goes by fast – the bad part is – well, angry customers. I had packed my lunch but hadn't had a chance to eat any of it. As I locked up the truck for the day, I pried open the lid of my Tupperware and crunched on a piece of celery, thankful for the hydration.

I ran up to the marina, waved at Ralph, and beelined it for the bathroom.

"Hey Jessie," Ralph shouted and waved me over. He had removed a propeller and was examining its curved edges.

"Whoa, did someone run over Secret Island again?" Secret Island was actually a pile of rocks that, for most of the season sat just below the waterline and claimed its fair share of propellers over the summer.

"I think that this one was a log." He turned the heavy piece of metal in his hand. "Dylan told me about your car."

"Yeah." I didn't know what else there was to say.

"I will replace the battery for you and check over the car. You will just need to find the money for the battery and any parts you might need."

Relief washed over me. "Thanks, Ralph."

He turned to unscrew a bolt. "Anything for you guys." He was back to work but kept talking, "I know things are tight right now, kid. Don't worry, I'm sure that insurance money isn't too far from coming through."

"That's what everyone keeps telling us." I waved and left.

Boat engines whined in the distance as I walked away from the marina. Even though I'd had a rough day, I found a renewed spring in my step. Ralph was going to fix our car for free, and as soon as the insurance money came through, I'd be able to go back to the Skating Academy.

Dylan and I were not going to get rich from my mom's life insurance policy, but it would give us some breathing room – and pay the Academy's tuition. I didn't know what Dylan planned to do with his half, but he was right, I wasn't the mom – I would have to trust that he wasn't going to blow it all.

I KICKED off my Birkenstocks and tossed my grease-stained baseball cap on the folding chair on the porch. I made a beeline for the basement. If I didn't strip and throw my clothes directly into the washing machine, the whole house would reek of deep-fried fish for days. Crosby wound around my feet and then scurried out the door behind me.

Dylan was sitting at the kitchen table in silence.

Something was wrong.

"Everything okay?"

Dylan had a piece of paper in his hand and when he realized I was there he hid it behind his back.

"What's that?" I lunged to grab it from him.

He stopped and held the paper high above my head. At six foot five, there was no way I'd be able to jump and grab it.

"Nothing," he said.

"Doesn't look like nothing." I put my hands on my hips.

Dylan exhaled heavily, then relented and handed the paper to me. He took a seat at the table, turning the empty envelope in his hands while I read the letter.

"No. They can't do this."

Dylan leaned back against the chair. His eyes were ringed in dark circles, the lids were red like he had been crying. "I talked to Frank. They can and they are."

I glanced at the piece of paper, hoping that I had misread it. The Insurance Company's logo, a yellow sun peeking out from behind a line drawing of clouds mocked me. "Are you sure?" I whispered.

"It's bullshit." Dylan rested his forehead in his hands.

I sat and flattened the letter out on the table. Apparently, mom's policy was null and void.

"We have to talk to someone about this." My voice quivered.

"Who?" Dylan looked at me. "Frank is the best lawyer in town, and we can't afford a second opinion."

"There has to be something we can do."

"I don't think there is, Jess." He stood, his thighs ramming against the wooden table hard enough that the salt and pepper shakers wobbled. He started pacing.

"We will figure this out." I heard myself say the words, but I didn't believe them.

"I appreciate your optimism, Jess. But we just got royally fucked."

The room started to tilt, and I gripped the edge of the table and took a breath. My vision narrowed and the dated wooden cabinets of the kitchen came in and out of focus. I remembered thinking that I was lucky I was sitting down, and then everything went black.

The darkness fizzled away, and I squeezed my eyes together tightly as the kitchen came back into focus. It took me a minute to figure out where I was, the perspective from the floor was confusing.

"Oh, thank God. I was just about to call 911." I felt Dylan's deep voice through my back and realized that my brother was behind me, holding me upright.

"Are you okay?" he asked.

I shook my head slowly. "I don't know what happened."

"You fell out of the chair and almost clocked your forehead on the table."

I pushed against the floor in an effort to stand.

"Why don't you just give yourself a minute." Dylan held me down.

"I'm fine," I swatted at him and stood. My legs shook but did their job. He bounced up behind me and grabbed a banana from the hanging holder beside the fridge.

"When was the last time that you ate?" he asked.

I honestly couldn't remember. "Lunch at the truck," I lied.

He peeled the banana, handed it to me, and then poured me a glass of water, adding in one of his electrolyte tablets. I took a sip and a bite, and the room became a little clearer. Dylan pulled out a chair. "Sit. Let's figure this out."

❄

I CAN'T REMEMBER WANTING to be anything but a figure skater. And it had been so close, one more podium finish and I would've made it to Nationals. Now, I looked at the piece of paper that Dylan and I had been scribbling on for the past three hours and there was no way I could afford to go back to the Academy. I held my phone in my hand. The number had been on the screen for almost an hour, but I couldn't bring myself to push send.

Now Dylan was on the sofa, the light from the TV flickering on his face while he slept.

I jabbed the 'send' button on my phone and swallowed the lump down in my throat as far it would go.

"Jessica."

"Hi, Veronica." I tried to put on a chipper tone.

"What's wrong?"

I paused. "I'm not coming back."

This time it was her turn to pause. "What do you mean you're not coming back. I thought we agreed that you were going to come back as soon as your parents' estate was settled. We have so much work to do – especially on your short program."

Veronica was high strung, and her sentences sped along like she was in warp speed.

I sighed. "The insurance money. We're not getting it."

"What, what do you—"

"Veronica, I don't want to get into it right now." I was glad I wasn't in front of her so she couldn't see my lip tremble. "I can't come back. I can't afford the Academy, or..."

"Me." This she said quietly. Veronica Hunter was one of the most sought-after coaches in the country. She had sent at least one skater to every World Championship or Olympics for the past fifteen years.

"Right." My voice wavered. I wanted to get off the phone before the waterworks started. Veronica was tough as nails but as harsh as she could be, had never made me cry.

"My dear. You need to fight for that money. You are a warrior, a survivor. I know that you will come up with something."

I wanted to believe her, but short of winning the lottery, or selling my body, I was done. "Promise me you won't give up." She didn't give me time to think of an excuse. "Jessica Moss. You will figure this out."

"I'll figure it out," I said without conviction. My voice cracked on the last word. "Bye," I said without waiting for her response and hung up the phone. She said exactly what I expected her to say.

"Was that Veronica?" Dylan asked from the living room.

"I thought you were sleeping."

"Just resting my eyes." He clasped his hands on his chest and kept his eyes shut. "What did she say?"

"Nothing much. Just told me to figure it out."

Dylan sat and slunk into the back of the sofa. "She didn't offer her protégé any help? No scholarships? Nothing?"

"It doesn't work like that." Part of me had hoped that Veronica might come through with some kind of a plan, even though I knew it wasn't likely.

"Fuck." Dylan shook his head. "I'll find the money, Jess. You just keep sneaking into the arena at night. And maybe you can join the Laketown Figure Skating Club. I think we can swing that."

The Laketown Figure skating club was where I cut my teeth. It was run from the original arena in town, an old school rink where little kids took lessons – the coaches there had probably never even seen someone do a triple jump – let alone coach someone who was doing them.

"Pfft." I shook my head and headed up the stairs to bed.

"Don't scoff. Right now, it's your only option," Dylan shouted.

"I'm going to bed."

I barrel-rolled onto my bed, cocooning myself like a burrito. I didn't have tears; I didn't have anger. I didn't have anything.

It was pitch black when Dylan knocked on the door.

"What?" I grumbled.

"It's your phone. It's Veronica."

I struggled to pull my arms out of my swaddle and sat up. Dylan cracked the door open. "Here." He handed me the phone. My hands shook as I took it from him.

"Veronica?"

"My dear. Have you figured it out yet?"

Did she think I was a fricking miracle worker? "Still working on it," I mumbled. I raised my shoulders and eyebrows at my brother, who was standing in the doorway straining to hear the other end of the conversation.

"You can stop working on it. I will tell you what you're going to do."

The air sucked out of my lungs and I bolted upright. "What is it? I'll do anything."

12

KANE

Margie's car was in the driveway, along with a red jeep. "Shit," I muttered to myself as I parked the car in the garage.

"Hello," I shouted as the screen door slammed behind me. I could hear clanking in the kitchen and the sound of the dishwasher running.

Margie stepped out of the kitchen and shook her head at me with a smirk on her face. A tea towel was balled up in her fist. "Quite the party the other night, Mr. Fitzgerald?"

"You aren't going to tell my parents, are you?" I couldn't believe that I was twenty-two and still worried about this stuff.

"Your secret is safe with me. You're giving me an extra day of work." She winked at me. "Or two." She bent down to pick up a bottle cap off the floor. "Your coach is down at the dock."

I looked around the great room. "Did he come in?" What I was really asking was, did he see the mess?

"I poured him a coffee and sent him to the boathouse to wait for you. I told him that he was going to have to stay out of my way, or else." She slapped the tea towel on her hand and laughed.

"Thanks again, Margie," I said. I walked through the cottage and leaned over the railing of the main house. The royal blue of Coach Covington's Otters hat was visible over the back of one of the Adirondack chairs.

The lake had calmed down significantly, and the sun sparkled on the ripples as the water lapped at the shore. The dock jostled as I stepped on it and Coach turned. "Hi, Coach." I waved and threw an extra hustle into my step.

"Have a seat, son." Coach gestured to the empty white chair beside him.

I obeyed and perched on the edge of the wooden seat. "I was about to call you." It had taken me almost a full day to get up the nerve to call him back and he beat me to it with this surprise visit.

Even though Coach's eyes were shaded behind his aviator sunglasses, I could see his eyes crinkle as he smiled at me. "I have good news for you."

"You do?" I was always a glass half full kind of guy, but for some reason, I had been dreading calling him. I cursed myself for not calling earlier. I could've saved myself hours of agony. "There's something I want to talk to you about too."

Coach sighed. "Ok."

"I think you should go easy on Dylan."

"Really?" Coach took off his sunglasses. "After the stunt he pulled?"

"He's going through a lot, Coach. I think that hockey is the only thing that's stopping him from spiraling out of control."

Coach squinted and then slid his glasses back on. "I'm not going to kick him off the team – yet. But he has to have some consequences, and I'm going to suspend him from the rest of the exhibition games. After that, we'll see."

"That seems fair." It was more than fair and a hell of a lot better than kicking him off.

Coach took a sip of his coffee. "Listen, Fitzgerald. You're one of the strongest players out there."

"I feel like there's a but coming," I flattened my lips and crossed my arms.

"Not exactly." He held up a hand as if to stop me, "And let me finish, please."

I gulped and took a seat in the chair. "Yes, sir."

"I heard that someone let it slip that there was a scout at the last game."

I rubbed the back of my neck, "I might have heard something like that."

Coach's gaze followed a boat as it made its way between the islands that sat in front of Pine Hill. "I might have heard that there was a party here after the game, too."

"I guess we both heard things that we weren't supposed to hear." I was pushing Coach, but I was on the edge of my seat, literally. "What's the news Coach?"

"The scout was interested in two players."

My heart thudded against my chest. "Oh, yeah?" I slid fully into the chair, trying my best to look nonchalant.

This time it was coach's turn to sit up. "I wanted you to hear it from me first."

"Okaaaaay."

"Shit," Coach took off his sunglasses. "This is harder than I thought it was going to be."

"Coach, I thought that you said this was good news." My heart was pumping so hard the whooshing in my ears was drowning out the sounds of the waves hitting the dock boards beneath us.

"The scout thinks you have potential. Serious potential."

"That's good, right?" I couldn't help it. I gripped the armrests of the chair and stood up. "That means he's interested."

"It does," Coach smiled. "But not for next season."

"Oh."

Coach stood up and gripped my arm. "All I'm saying is you could go all the way; we just have some work to do. Are you prepared to work hard?"

"Of course, Coach." I nodded. "It has been my dream to play in the National League since I was four years old."

"And you're prepared to cut back on the partying?" He nodded towards the cottage.

"Yep. I'm getting a little tired of cleaning up after everyone anyway." I smiled, my lips wavering. "Did he say what I have to work on?" My mind went to the hours I had spent on our backyard rink, shooting pucks until my hands went numb.

"It's your skating."

I reared back like Covington had reached out and slapped me. "My skating?" I repeated.

"I was surprised too, but I watched the game tapes and I can see it. You're leaving a lot of maneuverability on the table. I think he's right, it's the missing piece. Tighten that up and you will be an all-around solid player."

"My skating?" I was still thrown. My slap shot, maybe, but my skating, that was fucking crazy. "I guess I'll work on that. Do some drills or something..."?

"I've got one better for you. Have you ever heard of the Skating Academy?"

I shook my head, but then it dawned on me, "Just the one in New York."

"Yes, it's based in the city."

I looked at Pine Hill. Playing for Laketown was perfect. I got to live at my cottage and everyone in the town worshipped the ground the players walked on – it was the closest I'd ever been to being a celebrity. "I don't know, Coach, that's a long way to go for some edge lessons, and the city isn't really where I want to spend my summer." Already I could smell the rotting garbage and feel the heat radiating from the pavement.

"I thought you would say that." The coach finished his coffee and shook the last drops into the lake. "I know the owner of the Academy, she's an old friend of mine, and it turns out one of her top skaters lives right here in Laketown."

"Is he here to coach the summer camps?"

"I don't know the details. All I know is that this coach lives here and is willing to take you on, one on one. Private lessons."

I took a deep breath, "Beats leaving Laketown."

"Now, these sessions, they aren't cheap, but I spoke with your mom this morning."

"Step-mom," I corrected.

"Right, sorry. Step-mom. And your dad agreed to pay for the sessions."

"Wait, this is all said and done before any of you even consulted with me?"

Coach clapped me on the shoulder. "We all know how badly you want to make it to the National League, Kane. You'd jump in hot lava if I told you to."

He was right. "When do we start?"

"Tomorrow. Five."

"Five. Got it."

"You know there are two five o'clocks in the day, right Fitzy?" Coach rarely called me by my nickname, and it caught me by surprise. I saw the sides of his lips turn up into a smile.

"Five in the morning?" I gasped.

"It's the only open ice time and the only time this skating coach can make it. Is it going to be a problem?" Coach took off his sunglasses and stared me down.

"Not a problem, sir. I'll be there tomorrow at five." In the fucking morning. I wasn't a morning person, but if it meant going all the way to the pros, I would do it. Also, I'd be lying if I said I wasn't excited at the prospect of crossing paths with a certain figure skater.

"Good." Coach handed me the empty coffee mug and started to walk away.

"Coach," I shouted.

"Yeah," He turned.

"The two. The guys the scout was interested in. Who are they?"

Coach pursed his lips. "You're going to find out anyway, but it's Townsend and Moss."

I stopped in my tracks, the mug hanging loosely from my fingertips. Tanner, that made sense, but Dylan?

"I told him Moss's season with the team is over, so don't worry about any competition from him. I already talked to Tanner."

Jealousy or envy, I didn't really know which was which, but one of them burned inside of me. I couldn't believe that the scout was interested in Dylan - especially after his performance. And Tanner, he was my best friend, but it still stung that he was going to be one step ahead of me.

My hands shook as I watched coach leave. I breathed out hard through my nose and paced back and forth on the dock. I had played better than both Tanner and Dylan. What the fuck was going on? I worked harder than those two put together. Now, I had to go to some kind of remedial skating school? I pictured orange pylons scattered around the ice and some fat man with a thick accent screaming at me to bend my knees. I whipped around on my heel and chucked the coffee mug as hard as I could, watching the blue pottery sail through the air before it splashed into the lake and disappeared from sight.

Was this some kind of sick joke?

13

JESSIE

MY THIGHS BURNED as they pumped up and down, propelling me forward on the rusty mountain bike I had ridden all through high school. It's a good warm-up, I told myself, trying to turn my miserable, misty commute into something positive.

The last thing I wanted to do after skating practice, was to stay on the ice and teach some hockey jock about edge control, but when Veronica told me how much they were going to pay me, there was no way I could say no. With the chip truck and the power skating sessions, I should be able to save enough money for one more semester at the Academy. Enough to polish up my long program and get ready for the American finals.

The bike rack still had dew on it as I shoved the bike into one of the slots. I didn't bother with a bike lock, the brakes didn't really work, so if someone wanted to steal my bike – karma in the form of no brakes would get them back.

Andy was waiting to let me in. "Hi, Andy."

"Hi, kiddo." He locked up behind me.

"Someone is coming at five for power skating," I said as I hurried past him.

"I got the memo," Andy yelled.

I laced up my skates and tried to smooth out the frizzies in my hair courtesy of the misty bike ride. The fresh sheet of ice gleamed in wait for me. I hopped on the surface, hoping to leave my problems in the dressing room. I warmed up quickly and then did three back to back run-throughs of my long program – Veronica had chosen the music from *Swan Lake* and I was thrilled, but I couldn't get the lutz. The first time I popped it – a single, the second time it was under-rotated, and I stepped out of it – the third, I just totally caught my edge and bailed – hard. By the end of the session, the ice had been mopped clean by my ass.

"Dammit," I shouted as I slid backward into the boards one last time.

"Toepick!" I heard someone yell – someone who wasn't Andy.

"Fuck off," I said under my breath. I would've screamed it but I didn't have the energy. I paused on my hands and knees, catching my breath, and then made my way to the exit. The door opened as I skidded to stop. "Thanks, Andy," I said without looking as I grabbed my skate guards from the ledge.

"You're welcome?" The voice wasn't Andy's.

I turned to see Kane Fitzgerald holding the door. "I thought you were Andy," I said, running my fingers down the blades and shaking off the snow on the rubber mats.

"I see the toe-pick is tripping you up. Literally."

I rolled my eyes at him. Ever since the movie *The Cutting Edge*, hockey players have found it funny to scream out 'toe-pick' every time they witnessed a fall. "And I'm surprised that you know how to use the word literally."

"I just guessed." He grinned. "Are you alright? That last one looked like it hurt."

I marched to the visitor's dressing room and paused with my hand on the heavy door. He followed behind me. "Are you coming in here again?" I turned, blocking the doorway.

"No, I'm going in there." he gestured over his shoulder to the Otters' dressing room with his thumb.

"What are you doing here so early? Do you secretly live here?"

"Sometimes I feel like I do." Kane backed away from me.

The bulge in his sweatpants was like a solar eclipse. I didn't want to look at it directly, but secretly I wanted to stare at it. Did the man walk around with a semi in his boxers, or was his cock just that big? "Me too." I leaned against the door, training my eyes on the space above his eyebrows. I tried looking at his eyes but felt the color rushing to my cheeks. Was there no place sacred on this man – somewhere that wouldn't set my heart beating just a little bit faster? "But really, what are you doing here?"

"Fuck," he muttered. "I'm here to take skating lessons."

I had just swigged a mouthful of water and I squeezed my lips together to try to stop the spray, but it was too late, and water shot out of my mouth like the show at the Bellagio.

Kane jumped back as splatters from my fountainhead impression landed on his flip flops.

"Skating lessons? You? No." I wiped my mouth with the sleeve of my warm-up jacket.

He looked at me sideways, a hint of a smile on his face. "You think it's ridiculous too?"

"I've seen you play. You're alright." This was an under-statement; he was one of the best.

His eyes sparkled as he nodded and leaned against the

Otters' door. His arms windmilled as the door opened behind him - he obviously thought he was leaning on something solid, but his arm span was wide enough for his fingertips to catch the doorframe.

"That's very *The Matrix* of you," I laughed. He seemed suspended at an unbelievably low angle, his body in a reverse tabletop position. There was no way he was going to be able to stand up. I strode across the hallway in my skates and offered him my hand. He accepted and I leaned back and hauled him to a standing position.

My hand was clammy and sweaty, and I pulled it from his grip as quickly as I could. I nonchalantly put my hands on my hips, hoping that the fabric from my leggings would absorb some of the dampness.

"Thanks." He checked his watch and glanced behind me. "Have you seen anyone else here, besides Andy?"

"Nope," I backed away, gripping my skate guards in my left hand.

"I wonder where he is then?"

"Who?"

"This hotshot coach." Kane's lips flattened. He was clearly not happy.

"What makes you think your coach is a man?" I crossed my arms across my chest.

Kane screwed his face and snorted air out through his nose. "You're kidding right?" I tilted my head and waited and then he continued his rant. "There's no woman in the world who could teach me anything about skating." His eyes widened. He must have figure out how sexist he had just sounded. "Hey, no offense," he added.

"Plenty taken."

"Whoa, sorry." Kane shot me a smile and held his hands up stickup style.

I turned and strode to the ice surface, watching as Andy completed his last lap in the Zamboni.

"Wait, where are you going?" Kane shouted.

"I have a five o'clock lesson." I stepped onto the ice and shouted. "I have to teach a dumb jock how to skate."

14

KANE

"Whoa, whoa, whoa." I jogged and caught up with Jessie. She was tall in her skates and her eyes just about met mine directly. "You're the power skating coach?"

"I am." She held onto the boards and shuffled her skates back and forth in place on the ice. "And you're the player who needs to work on his edge control." She sounded amused and looked me up and down.

"There's nothing wrong with my edge control."

"That's not what I heard." She started scrolling through the music on her phone and I winced as the opening notes to *Fat Bottom Girl* rang out through the arena's sound system.

"Well, Mr. Fitzgerald, how about you go put your skates on and show me that great edge control of yours." She pushed against the boards and glided backward.

"I will on one condition," I shouted.

"What's that?" she started skating along on one foot, pumping her free foot in the air for momentum.

"We're changing the music." I pointed to the speakers suspended above center ice.

She pointed to the time clock, which read seven minutes after five. "No. Now go get your skates on."

How could they do this to me? This was the ultimate humiliation. I'm Kane Fitzgerald. Number eight-eight – the best player on the damn team – and I'm getting lessons from a figure skater?

In the dressing room, I sat in front of my number and shook my head. I was tempted to keep walking, get into my car, and tell Covington to go fuck himself, but I wanted to succeed too badly. 'Suck it up,' I whispered under my breath and shoved my feet into my skates.

At the far end of the ice, Jessie was gliding like a balle-rina, seemingly in her graceful little world – one that I was about to invade. Feedback cracked through the speakers as I plugged my phone in and angry guitar filled the cold arena air.

Jessie skated towards me, stopping and spraying snow all over my skates. "No." Was all she said and unplugged my phone.

"Come on, you can't expect me to—"

"You can't warm up to this, it's the wrong BPM."

"BPM? Beats per—"

"Minute," she interrupted and turned up her terrible music even louder. "Now, start by doing crossovers around the faceoff circle, slowly, one cross per beat."

"This is fucking stupid," I whispered under my breath.

"Excuse me?"

"I didn't think you could hear that with your crappy music playing." I leaned against the boards. "And I'm not doing a figure skating drill."

"It's not a figure skating drill. It's a skating drill." She emphasized the word 'skating.'

"Well, then let me do it to my type of music. I'm not skating..." I mimicked her voice, "to this garbage. Before I could unplug her phone, she snatched mine out of my hand, turned and skated away before I even knew what had happened.

"You want to change the music, hotshot?" she shouted. "Fine, but you've got to catch me first." She held my phone hostage above her head. She was already at the blue line, her ponytail swinging as she skated away from me. I pushed off from the boards and within three aggressive strides was up to speed. There was no way she was going to outskate me. She rounded the edge of the rink, gracefully crossing her feet over faster than I had ever seen anyone do without doing jump strides. I arced a shortcut across the ice, but just as I reached my hand out to tag her, she did some kind of crazy jump turn. Once she was backward, she lowered her center of gravity and practically doubled her speed. Her strides were wide and powerful, and I could feel my heart racing, my breaths coming harder and faster as she ever so slightly widened the gap between us.

"Don't you dare..." I shouted, my breath a little more ragged than I expected. As a player, I specialized in short bursts - this extended sprint was pushing me out of my cardio comfort zone -"... drop my phone."

She shoved my phone into the pocket on her leggings and skated around the center circle. I followed, cutting the circle a little smaller each time we went around, and I don't know if she was slowing down, or my shortcut was paying off, but I finally got close enough so that I could touch her. I reached and lunged at her with my hand, "There," I shouted. But instead of feeling solid shoulder bone, I felt something soft and curved. It took both of us a second to realize that I had just totally copped a feel of her boob. I pulled my hand back like her chest was a hot ember, something burning I had to shake off. "I'm..." I gasped, "Sorry."

She was staring at her chest where my hand had just been.

"I didn't mean it, I swear."

"I know." She turned and skated away. I put my hands on my knees, my breaths leaving my body faster than they should have. I stared down at the laces on my skates, knowing that the flush in my cheeks wasn't just from the extreme cardio.

"I'm going to go." I skated hard and fast to the door and was off the ice before she even turned around.

"Wait," she shouted, but I was already halfway to the dressing rooms. I was equal parts fuming, and equal parts turned on. I ripped the skates off my feet. How was I supposed to make it to the National League if I couldn't even keep up with a girl?

15

JESSIE

"Hi, Sis," Dylan shouted from the kitchen and I nearly jumped out of my Birks. I kicked them onto the pile of shoes by the door and followed the sound of clanging pots to the kitchen.

"Smells amazing." The bacon was sizzling in the pan on the stove and Dylan was spreading what looked to be a tablespoon of butter onto some rye toast.

"How do you want your eggs?" Dylan held up the spatula and wiggled it at me.

"Thank Dyl, but I already had breakfast."

"What, one of those gross smoothies?" He wrinkled his nose and cracked two eggs directly into the bacon grease.

"Maybe you should try one," I said. "Your heart might thank you." But my mouth was starting to water and it took all of my willpower not to pluck a piece of crispy bacon from the folded paper towel on the counter.

Dylan patted the front of his mechanic's shirt. "I'll stick with real food. Here." He nudged the plate of bacon at me.

"No, thanks," I pushed it away.

"Ah, come on, Jess. There's nothing to you," he said.

"Yeah, and I'm trying to keep it that way. You don't have to wear a competition dress in a few months."

Dylan broke a piece in half and shoved it into his mouth and handed me the smaller piece. He was relentless. I popped it into my mouth and my eyes practically rolled into my head as the salty crunchiness landed on my tongue. The taste brought me back in time and I could practically see my dad standing at the stove, in his mechanic's uniform, not unlike Dylan's, making his bacon, lettuce, and tomato sandwich before heading off to work.

"How was your lesson?" Dylan assembled his heart attack platter and sat at the kitchen table. I poured myself a cup of coffee and joined him.

"I didn't think he was even going to get on the ice."

"Why? Fitzy always does what he's told."

"I don't think he's ever been told to do something by a..." I paused. I wasn't sure which was the bigger problem for him, "woman, or a figure skater."

Dylan took a swig of his coffee. "Figure skater. There are lots of women who teach power skating."

I nodded, thankful that Kane wasn't both a chauvinist and an asshole. "Wait, Jess. Did you wear your figure skates?" Dylan's eyes were wide.

"Of course, I wore my figure skates. I don't have hockey skates." Dylan popped the last bite of his sandwich into his mouth and stood up before he was finished chewing. "Come with me."

"What? Where?" I followed Dylan down the creaky old stairs into the unfinished basement. He pulled the string and the bare lightbulb lit up the dingy space. Dylan started rooting through a plastic bin. "What are you looking for?" I peered over his shoulder.

"These."

He stood up and presented me with a pair of his old hockey skates.

"What am I supposed to do with these?" I brushed the dust off the boots of the skates, the laces yellowed from time.

"I'd start with getting them sharpened. Andy can get them all cleaned up for you."

"Are you nuts? I can't wear these."

"Why?" Dylan shut off the light and we both bounded out of the basement, pushing each other out of the way to get up the stairs first. As kids, we were terrified of the low ceilings and cobwebs of the basement and had always raced up the stairs.

"Dylan, these skates are over ten years old. And, are you forgetting? I wear skates with picks on the front."

Dylan put his plate in the sink and poured himself a to-go mug of coffee. "I wore them when I was eleven, they should fit those tiny feet of yours perfectly. Fitzy might take you a bit more seriously if you start speaking his language." He pointed to the skates. "I've got to go." Dylan shoved his sock feet into his work boots but didn't lace them up.

"You're going in early," I glanced at the microwave, it was only six-thirty.

"Ralph and I are going to work on the Volvo and he's picking me up." Dylan pulled back the curtain. "And he's here, bye!" he shouted and somehow managed to run with his laces flying.

While riding my bike was great cross-training, I was certainly going to be happy to have the car back for my early morning practices. I chugged back the last of the coffee and sent Paige a text asking her for a ride to work, and then turned on the shower as hot as I could get it.

New bruises were forming on top of the old bruises and

I winced as the loofah passed over the hip that took the brunt of my falls. I'd never lost a jump for this long before. It seemed that the harder I tried to get the lutz back, the further it got away from me.

It wasn't my job to make Kane stay on the ice, I reasoned, as I lathered up my hair with shampoo. If anything, he should put on some figure skates and learn how to harness the power of his edges with finesse, not brute strength. But, as I wiped the steam off the mirror, I realized that if Kane Fitzgerald didn't get on the ice, I didn't get paid – and I needed that money more than anything.

I eased myself onto the edge of my bed and picked up the picture of my mom and dad that sat on my nightstand. It was their wedding day and my mom had worn my grandma's cheesy eighties wedding dress, complete with puffy sleeves. I tiptoed to their room, opened my mom's closet and wrapped my arms around her blouses. I knew it wasn't healthy, but somehow, I felt like I was hugging her. I stepped back and ripped the clothes off the hangers and screamed as I slammed them onto the floor. We didn't have the money for a therapist, but I knew about the stages of grief, so when I felt anger growing inside of me, I welcomed it.

My phone chimed and I saw a message from Paige. It was short and to the point and didn't help my volatile mood. I typed and retyped several angry messages to my so-called friend but ended up deleting them. Paige had quit the chip truck and was going to work at Valerock.

I took a deep breath and then resigned myself to the fact that I was going to spend my summer frying fish and then trying to find a job for the winter – probably at the tinfoil factory.

16

KANE

MOST OF THE guys on the Otters love the actual game of hockey but hate the practices. I'm not one of them. I live for the drills, the camaraderie, and if I'm being honest, feeling I'm the best out there on the ice – giving it my all. But today, I was dreading it.

The dressing room was buzzing. Leo and Mike were laughing a little too hard at something on Leo's phone, and the rest of the guys were clowning around. We had one more exhibition game and I couldn't believe they weren't taking the last practice seriously. The dressing room door opened, and Coach Covington stepped inside, drawing on his clipboard while he walked. Tanner elbowed me and I looked up from my skates just as the room went silent. Jake McManus, the team's owner had just walked into the room.

"Boys," Coach Covington smiled. "The last game showed me that we need to get back to the basics. Teamwork. There are twenty players on this team, not just Fitzy and Tanner. You win games as a team, not as a player." He paused and surveyed the room. Everyone was sitting at attention. Jake McManus was a star, and most of the guys had never even met him. "Jake is here to help you today. Jake." Coach stepped aside and let McManus speak.

"Hi, guys," Jake smiled. "Coach asked me to come and skate some drills with you."

I couldn't believe it. I was about to stand shoulder to shoulder with one of my heroes. He looked at Coach's clipboard. "Which one of you is Leo?"

Leo practically shot out of his skates. Jake continued, "Leo and I are going to run this practice together. Come on and show me what you've got." Jake clapped his hands together. The room erupted in a cheer and we all got up from the benches. Leo looked like he was going to shit his pants. He wasn't ready for something like this. It should've been me running the practice with McManus, not him.

The team filed out behind Jake like a bunch of puppy dogs – me included.

"Fitzy, can I have a word with you?" Coach caught me before I was able to leave.

"Sure, Coach."

Tanner lingered behind me.

"Tanner, get going." Coach pointed at the door with his clipboard.

Tanner paused; his mouth open like he was about to protest. He shot me a glance and I knew exactly what he was thinking. Both of us were equally superstitious, and I still hadn't told him that I lost my coin. The last thing the team needed was more bad luck.

"One sec, Coach." I took a step into the hallway, technically I was out of the room, allowing Tanner to leave, superstition intact. He smiled as he passed and then I stepped back into the room. "What's up?"

"How was your training this morning?"

Coach's face didn't give anything away. I couldn't tell

whether he was asking, or if he knew that it had been a disaster.

I rubbed the back of my neck. "It was good."

"Good?" He raised his eyebrows at me.

"Yeah, I think it went okay."

Coach put one foot up onto the bench and leaned his elbow on his knee. "You did what she said and got some good pointers?"

I didn't want to lie. "Coach, it got off to..." I wanted to say a rough start, but truthfully, the whole thing was a disaster. "I mean, I guess..." I was faltering.

"You refused to get on the ice and then pulled a hissy fit and left early?"

A hissy fit? I guess it wasn't too far off. "Coach. She was wearing figure skates."

"I don't care if she was wearing mukluks." He glanced down to the paper on his clipboard. "She has some really good insight into your stride. Son, check your ego, show up early, and do exactly what this girl tells you to do."

I narrowed my lips, holding in a groan. "Roger that, Coach." I shoved my hand into my glove. "Can I go now?" I gestured to the door.

"You're going to sit on the sidelines for this one, Fitzy."

"Coach, are you serious? That's Jake McManus out there." I pointed in the direction of the ice where I could hear pucks ricocheting off the boards like gunfire.

"I know exactly who is out there, and until you get your head out of your ass and start doing what you're told, you're not going to see any more ice time." He smacked the clipboard on his knee and then strode out of the dressing room.

"Fuck," I slapped the blade of my stick on the floor.

The door opened and Coach peeked his head in, "I heard that. You coming?"

"Yes, Coach." I breathed out slowly and followed that asshole to the box, where I sat and watched the Entire. Fucking. Practice.

Hissy fit? I stewed while I watched Tanner practice slap shots with my idol. Stride issues? My hands were shaking by the time practice was over, and only part of that was from sitting in the cold. Anger coursed through my veins.

After all I did for her? This is how she paid me back? Ratting me out to my coach? I should've never lent her my car. Hell, I should've never even let a Laketownie like her into my cottage.

The sky was pink as we exited the arena. The days were getting so long, that soon it would be sunset well after nine at night.

"Want to hit up the Brew Pub?" Tanner asked as he got into the passenger seat.

"Hell, yeah," I put the car in gear and revved up the engine. "I need a fucking drink. That Covington is such a prick."

"He's trying to bring out your potential."

I rolled my eyes and jammed the car into reverse. "You try and take pointers from a figure skater."

"Well, is she a good skater?"

The rest of the team followed behind us. "I guess. But, she's still a figure skater." I flicked on the headlights and we pulled out of the arena parking lot.

"I hear you, buddy. I wouldn't want to take instruction from a figure skater either, but if it gets you back into Coach's good graces, you might want to do it."

I sighed. "I know."

"Hey, is everything alright with you?" Tanner turned down the radio. The host had been yammering on about record high temperatures and water levels.

"What do you mean?"

"You just don't seem like yourself."

I glanced at Tanner as I drove. "I've got to tell you something, but you have to promise not to freak out."

"Ooookay."

"You're one of the only guys who will get it, and this has to stay between us." I shifted gears and slowed as we approached the busy parking lot of the Brew Pub. I didn't give Tanner a chance to guess, "I lost my coin."

"Your lucky coin?"

"What other coin would I be talking about?"

"Easy," Tanner held up his hands.

"Sorry dude. It's just, ever since I lost that damn coin, everything has been going wrong. I mean everything."

"Don't you think you're being a bit dramatic?" Tanner clicked out of his seatbelt and turned to face me.

"From the guy who wouldn't leave the dressing room until I stepped outside?"

"Touché," Tanner chuckled. "Fitzy, I get it. Have you looked for it?"

"Come on," I opened the door and got out of the car. "Of course, I looked for it."

The headlights from the caravan of hockey players' cars poured into the small lot, filling up every last parking spot. "Don't you dare tell the guys," I whispered.

"I won't, but Fitzy. You're going to have to find it – or find something to replace it."

"I know, I know..." But both of us knew that it didn't work that way. I couldn't just 'pick' something new to be my lucky thing. My missing uncle gave me that coin and as much as I wanted to believe that I could just get a new lucky token, deep down, I was afraid that things were only going to get worse until that chunk of gold was back in my pocket.

17

KANE

I SAT ALONE at the bar, the second beer dousing my anger.

A pretty brunette sidled up to the bar beside me. "Want to buy me a drink?"

"Not really," I grumbled. Okay, maybe the beer wasn't helping my mood. The smile dropped off her face and I instantly felt bad. "What are you having?" I raised my finger to get the bartender's attention. As quickly as it had disappeared, her smile came back. "Vodka soda." Her voice was high pitched, and she did that annoying baby talk thing that girls seem to think that we like.

She rested her forearms on the edge of the bar and arched her back, presenting her quite, nice looking breasts to me. She had all the trappings of a puck bunny, the same chunky necklace that they all wore, the fake eyelashes that made them look dopey, and wavy long hair that probably wasn't all hers. It made me wonder. Had I been at this too long? Were all the women starting to look the same?

She tapped her manicured nails on the bar while she waited for her drink. "How was practice?"

Yep. Puck Bunny.

"How did you know I had practice?"

"You're Kane Fitzgerald, right?" Her voice went up an octave at the end of her sentence. She twirled the end of her hair and batted her eyelashes at me as she sipped her drink.

The girl in front of me could've been any of the women I'd met in the last year. Except for Jessie. She didn't baby talk. Hell, the girl didn't even wear makeup. If I was a betting man, I'd wager ten thousand dollars that the Barbie doll in front of me wouldn't set foot outside of her house without spending two hours doing her makeup first.

I shook my head to try to get the image of Jessie's freckles out of my mind, and the feel of her breast from my palm, while the girl in front of me yammered on about some music festival.

It would be easy. I could take this bunny back to my cottage and, no, I wouldn't even have to take her back to my cottage. I could probably get a quick B.J. in the parking lot and never have to speak to her again.

Glancing around the bar I saw that most of the team had either disappeared or were currently entertaining some iteration of the girl in front of me. Hell, I was considering it. I was horny - she was there.

"I'll be right back," she whispered, letting her fingertips trail along my forearm. As she slid back from the barstool her handbag swung, knocking my entire pint of beer onto my lap. "Shit." I slid back, but most of the beer had already either soaked my shirt or pooled on my lap.

"Oh, no." She grabbed a napkin and dabbed at my shirt and then gave me a wink and dabbed at the zipper of my jeans.

"It's okay," I sighed and took the napkin from her hands.

"I'll get some more paper towels." She disappeared into the crowd.

I slapped a hundred down on the bar and waved to Nate, the bartender. Before the woman, Kari, Katrina, Katie... fuck, I couldn't remember, came back to the bar I was out of there.

The night was cool, and my skin prickled with goose-bumps. I hopped into my car and fumbled to get the keys into the ignition. I wasn't drunk, but I smelled like a brewery. Three drinks in one hour might put me over the limit, I couldn't risk it. I reclined the seat and closed my eyes. I would have to wait it out with a quick nap. A DUI could ruin my career.

I WOKE up shivering and I reached into the back seat, hoping that there was a sweater within arm's reach. I swigged a mouthful of water and rubbed my eyes as I checked the time on my phone.

"Shit," My fingertips found a hoodie in the back seat and I shrugged it on over my t-shirt. It was four forty-five. I found a stick of gum and checked my reflection in the back of the visor. My eyes were bloodshot. I took a whiff inside my shirt and recoiled, I smelled like a Budweiser brewery. No cop in the county would believe that I had just slept off a few drinks.

I locked the car and my brisk walk turned into a jog, with my damp jeans chafing my thighs as I ran. As much as I hated the power skating practices more than I hated the Predators, I had to suck it up, be a man, and just get the damn things over with. My flip flops slapped the pavement and the oxygen pumped through my body as I ran through town and turned onto Oak Street.

The door to the arena was open and the loud scream

from the skate sharpener echoed through the lobby. "Hey, Andy," I shouted even though I knew he wouldn't be able to hear me.

I took a few minutes in the change room to splash some water on my face and smooth down my hair. I put on my warm-up pants and laced up my skates, thankful that I had somehow woken up just in time to get to the rink, and that I wasn't going to have to skate in my beer-soaked jeans.

"Hey," I said as I approached the ice.

"Hey." She kept her gaze on the Zamboni as it passed by.

I leaned beside her. "What are we working on today, boss?"

She turned to face me and visibly recoiled. "Are you drunk?"

"No."

"You stink." She scrunched her nose and looked away. "I'm not going to work with someone who's been drinking."

"You can't do that."

"Do what?" She put her hands on her hips, her eyes narrowed at me.

"Make that call. You've been hired by my coach. Your paycheck is coming from my parents. I could show up here tripping on acid and you'd still have to do what you're told."

"Do. What. I'm. Told?"

Shit. Maybe I was a little drunk.

"That's not what I meant."

"I'm out of here." She turned and walked away, her gait clunky, courtesy of her figure skates.

"What's your fucking problem?" My cheeks felt like they were on fire and I saw my entire career swirling down the drain, the plug pulled courtesy of this holier than thou bitch.

She paused at the door to her dressing room. "My problem?" She looked over her shoulder. "My problem?" Her voice grew louder. "I'm trying to do a job. I'm trying to *help* you and you've been nothing but an inconsiderate..." she turned around, "unprofessional...", she took a step toward me, "spoiled rotten..." Now she was shouting and had to take a breath in between each insult. "Meathead." She was close enough to slap me. I had nowhere to go and I braced myself for a stinging cheek. "Drunk...Jock...Asshole." She jabbed my pec with her surprisingly strong pointer finger as she continued to sling insults at me.

My nostrils flared. She wasn't wrong, I was all of those things. But I was also a lot of good things too.

"You didn't care that I was a spoiled rotten meathead asshole when I gave you my car." I raised my eyebrows at her and instead of backing away, I took a step closer. Any player knew that the closer you were, the harder it was for someone to get a good punch in. "Did I get the insult right?"

"Is everything okay here?" Andy stood in the hallway behind Jessie.

Jessie blinked. "Fine," she said through gritted teeth.

Andy glanced from Jessie to me and I stepped back. "I'm done with your skates." He handed Jessie pair of well-worn Bauers.

"Thanks," she took them from him. "See you tomorrow, Kane. Don't bother showing up if you're under the influence again."

Then she stepped around Andy and disappeared into her dressing room. "Dammit," I hissed.

"Fitzy, if you're wasted, I'm going to have to ask you to leave." Andy crossed his arms.

I sighed. "Andy. I had a couple of drinks last night, and one spilled all over me. I didn't want to risk a DUI, so I slept in my car."

Andy shook his head. "That explains it." He looked toward the dressing room. "She's a little..." he paused as if debating on whether to finish his sentence "sensitive to drinking."

"But I'm not drunk."

Andy smiled while simultaneously shaking his head. "You smell wasted, Fitz." He opened the rinkside door for me. I grabbed my stick and stepped onto the ice. "You should explain that to her, and maybe apologize."

"Apologize?" Had he been in a different room? "Maybe she's the one who should apologize for overreacting." I bit my tongue, wanting to add being a drama queen and pulling some kind of power trip to ruin my life.

"Trust me, she's not like that." Andy smiled. "Figure out a way to get that girl on your side. Or get on her side. You two can probably help each other out more than you think."

"Doubt that." I was already trying to think about how I'd explain this morning's disaster to Coach.

I looked at the fresh sheet of ice and turned to ask Andy a question, but he'd already walked away. Instead of skating around the ice, I walked away from it and did something I knew I'd regret.

18

JESSIE

THE KNOCK on the door was soft.

"Just a second." I had one foot in a skate. I hobbled over to the door and pulled it open, expecting Andy, but finding Kane. One elbow rested on the doorframe above his head, his other hand poised to knock again.

"I thought you were Andy." I stood on my left foot, the one on the ground, and Kane towered over me, but his head was bowed.

"I'm not drunk," he said. He pulled out his sweatshirt, wafting it – "Someone spilled a drink on me at the Brew Pub last night."

"And you put it back on?" I crossed my arms across my body and let the heavy door rest on my shoulder.

"Is that better than sleeping in it?" His lips turned up slightly and I noticed that his whole face changed when he smiled. It lit up.

I tapped my lips with my finger as if thinking. "Not really. Why did you sleep in it?"

He rubbed the back of his neck. "I had a couple of drinks last night."

I knew it.

"It's not what you think. I didn't want to drive, I didn't want to go to Valerock with the team, I just thought I'd have a catnap in my car and when I woke up, it was, well, quarter to five and I ran here."

"You ran here?"

"Yeah." The smile neck rub combo came out again. "If I get a DUI, it'll ruin my life. I'm pretty careful about that. I'm sorry for showing up late. I promise I meant to come and listen to you, to hear what you have to say. I'm ready to take this seriously."

My heart started pounding harder than it should have. He was talking about our training sessions, but it sounded like words that every girl wanted to hear. Promise. Serious. Listen.

I was ready to accept his apology, but when my eyes met his, I was rendered unable to form complete sentences.

"Jessie?"

"Yeah," I shook my head and blinked hard.

"Can we skate now?"

I thought about it for a second. "You're not drunk, and you ran here in flip flops. I think that deserves a little ice time."

He stepped away from the door and gave a slight bow.

"Let me put my skates on."

"See you out there." He smiled and when the door clanked shut, I realized that I had been holding my breath. I rested my back against the closed door, allowing myself, and my heart, a minute to calm down. Don't you dare fall for him, I whispered to myself, knowing that it was too late.

I TEETERED to the ice surface; the hockey skates felt loose on my ankles and rocked me in an unfamiliar way as I walked. Kane was skating slow smooth laps and I gripped the boards as I stepped onto the ice.

"Whoa." He scraped to a stop beside me. "You're wearing them."

"Only seems fair." I shrugged.

"Have you ever skated in hockey skates before?" he raised his eyebrows at me.

"Nope."

"This should be interesting."

I pointed. "Meet me in the middle."

"It's called center ice."

"Okay, meet me at the center ice then." The sound system crackled as I plugged in my phone. I glanced over to Kane who was waiting patiently, his chin leaning on his hockey stick.

I thumbed through my playlist, passing by my usual warm-up songs, but I didn't have any Metallica or any other hard stuff.

"Put your stick down," I instructed. He skated over to me and leaned his stick against the boards.

The opening notes of *Bad Moon Rising* filled the arena and he cocked his head at me. "CCR?"

The guy knew his classic rock. "I hope it's satisfactory, I'm fresh out of Jock Jams 1996."

He almost snort laughed. "Too bad. It's a great album."

"I know, it's every hockey player's anthem." Having a hockey player brother meant I knew every track on every Jock Jams compilation from front to back.

"Alright, let's start at center ice." I took a stride, forgetting that the blades on my feet didn't have picks and my arms flailed in a wild circle. I almost recovered with a succession of quick steps backward, but those didn't save me either. The lights of the stadium blurred, and my movements seemed to go into slow motion as the betraying skates flew into in the air, impossibly high in front of my face. This fall was going to hurt.

Instead of my tailbone hitting the ice, two tree trunk-sized arms thrust underneath my arms and my back slammed into Kane. I could feel his chest shaking as laughter rocked his body.

"You're going to teach me how to skate?" His voice was deep and reverberated in my back.

"Put me down and I'll show you." I was stiff as a board in his arms, my feet just inches above the ice.

He lowered me but didn't fully release me. His breath was warm on my earlobe, and it sent goosebumps down my neck that fanned across my chest. I shivered and Kane rubbed my arms. "Thanks," I murmured, but it wasn't the temperature that had sent that chill through my body.

"Kane," I turned, this time cognizant of the blades beneath me. "You're losing your power by easing up on your edge too early. That's it. It's going to be an easy fix if you can focus on it."

"You care to show me, coach?"

Even his smirk was cute, and I looked away, hoping to hide my burning cheeks. I took one stride and it felt good, the next stride, even better. I picked up speed and ran out of ice. I pictured the way Fitzy had darted around the Predators' player in the last game, his stick wagging like a dog's tail leading him down the ice. I shook the figure skater out of my body, balled my hands into fists, and almost ran as I rounded the corner. I headed towards Fitzy, pumping my arms like a speed skater, and then put all of my weight into an aggressive hockey stop, spraying snow up to his shins.

"Nice work." He sounded genuine.

"Finish the stride, Fitzy. That's all you've got to do." I cocked my hip and crossed my arms. And once again, forgot that there was no 'back' to my blades. This time Fitzy wasn't there to catch me, and my butt slammed to the ice. "Ow." I winced and squinted my eyes. When I opened them, Fitzy was in front of me, holding out his hand. "It might take me a minute to get used to them."

"I think I see what you mean," he smiled and pulled me up from the ice like I was a feather. He didn't let go of my hands and I didn't move to pull mine from his.

"Show me," I whispered. I didn't let go. Instead, I squeezed tighter and turned backward, and like I had done when I had taught little kids, held Kane's hands, completely unnecessarily, as he quickly adopted the technique I recommended. I let go and Kane took off. I shouted cues at him every once in a while, but the guy had it. I grabbed his stick and tossed it to him. "Let me see how you perform with your stick."

He grinned as he snatched it from the air.

"I mean…" I stammered but couldn't finish my sentence.

"Was that a Freudian slip?" Kane laughed.

"Just go, let's see your stroking…" My face flushed with heat. "I mean, oh my God."

"Stroking?" This time he was full-on belly laughing.

"That's what it's called." Now I was laughing too, shaking on my feet as I wiped the tears from the corners of my eyes.

"I think I could charge you with harassment right now." Kane swiped away his tears of laughter.

By the time Andy sounded the buzzer, both Kane and I had our feet under ourselves. "You're a great skater," I said as we headed off the ice surface.

"You're not so bad yourself." He reached over the boards

and he opened the door for me, gesturing with his hand, "Ladies' first." We walked down the corridor to the dressing rooms in silence. On the ice, the joking and laughing came easily. Off the ice, awkwardness set back in.

"I guess I'll see you tomorrow then?" I paused with my hand on the door to the dressing room."

"Do you want to get breakfast?" Kane asked. Then added quickly, "I mean, we could discuss everything we talked about on the ice, I think it would be really helpful, for, you know, coaching purposes."

There it was again, the smile that bordered on a sexy smirk and I couldn't say no. "Sure. I could go for a coffee right about now and I'm not the one who slept in their car."

19

KANE

"Pink sky in the morning..." I mused as we left the arena.

"Sailors take warning." Jessie finished the old saying. "They're not calling for rain." She looked up at the sky. "But those old sayings aren't usually wrong."

Jessie pulled an old crappy bike from the rack at the front door. "Can I put this in the back of your car?" she asked.

I scanned the parking lot, panicking when I didn't see my beloved car, and then remembered my early morning sprint. Shit. "I walked from the Brew Pub."

"That's right." Jessie grabbed yanked the bike from the rack. "It's not too far from here."

I took the pink bike from her hands and threw my leg over the seat. "Hop on," I patted the handlebars.

"You've got to be joking," she scoffed.

"I'm starving. Get on." I patted the bike again.

"Kane Fitzgerald, if I get hurt before Regionals..."

"Regionals? For what?"

She looked at me like I had two heads. "Figure skating. I need to make it past regionals if I want a shot at the National team. And I have to get on Team USA to skate in the Olympics."

"You're that good?" Sometimes I should think before I open my mouth.

"I used to be," she said as she took a deep breath.

"Hey, if there's anything I've learned, it's that you don't talk like that. Mindset is everything, Jessie. I'm going to make the NHL. I tell myself that every day." As long as I find my coin, I thought to myself.

"It's easy for you."

"Easy?" I walked the bike along beside her as we headed toward the main street of town.

"I shouldn't say that," she looked up and sniffed. "I know that you work hard."

"I do work hard. And I'm trying my best not to be offended right now." It wasn't the first time someone assumed that I was successful because my dad was rich. "You of all people should know how hard we have to work if we want to go pro. I was up every day before school, shooting pucks in the back yard."

"I'm sorry, Kane. I just... I've had a rough go this last little while." Her voice cracked.

"I know." Was it callous of me not to say sorry about your parents? I wanted to, but I didn't know if it would make her too sad. "It must be hard." It was lame, but it was the best I could come up with.

"It is." She resumed walking. "But things are going to work out."

From the tone of her voice, I could tell that she didn't believe her own words.

"Get on," I ordered and pointed to the handlebars. "I promise, I won't hurt you." The girl had more on her shoulders than anyone her age should have to deal with. It wasn't my job to protect Jessie, but I knew that I could.

She looked at me sideways, but then stopped. "Okay." She stepped over the front wheel and sidled her Lululemoned ass onto the handlebars. "Where do I hold on?" She looked back at me and my chest involuntarily constricted. Her eyes were the greenest I'd ever seen, not an emerald, more like the green of a freshly unfurled leaf.

"Here," I placed her hands on either side of her butt. "Now, hold on," I shouted and pushed hard on the pedal. She extended her feet in front of her and squealed. "Fitzy..." The ends of her hair flicked at my face as we picked up speed. I pumped steadily and evenly, and eventually, her grip loosened on the bars and she relaxed her feet down.

"This is actually kind of fun," she said without looking back.

"Easy for you to say. There's a giant hill coming up." My breaths were already starting to labor up the incline.

"Get those quads moving," she laughed. A genuine laugh, the kind that I rarely heard. There was nothing fake about Jessie and I wanted to hear that giggle again. I stood and pumped the pedals hard, my heart pounding against my chest, Jessie's laughter fueling my legs.

We reached the Brew Pub and she hopped off the bike, rubbing her butt. My gaze followed her hand and my balls tensed. Shit. I averted my gaze, opened up the Land Cruiser, and put her bike inside.

"You've earned your breakfast." She reached for the passenger door, but I jumped past her and opened it. I was raised to be a gentleman.

"Thanks." She looked amused.

I glanced at her as we drove down Oak Avenue. The first

rays of the sun beamed low across the lake as we crossed the suspension bridge, the tires humming on the metal grates.

My heart sank when I pulled into the parking lot of The Crepe House and realized that it was closed.

"Oh no," she sighed.

"Shit," I whispered. "I don't think any of the other breakfast spots are open for the season yet."

"It's a ghost town until after Memorial Day," she said.

I liked the peace and quiet of Laketown in the off-season, but today, I wished for some of the hustle and bustle when the warmer weather brought hordes of cottagers and weekend warriors alike.

Something magical had happened on the ice and I didn't want to break the spell. "I'll make you breakfast." I put the car in reverse before she could object.

20

JESSIE

"I'm really not that hungry." I squirmed uncomfortably on the teak barstool at Kane's giant kitchen island.

Kane rubbed his belly over his t-shirt. "After the workout you put me through, I'm starving." He cracked a seventh egg into the bowl and whisked in some milk. The smell of bacon and the sound of the whisk against the stainless-steel bowl transported me back in time, and my stomach clenched with nostalgia.

"Seriously Kane, you don't have to make me breakfast. I should get going."

He paused mid-whisk. "I thought that you had the day off today."

I shouldn't have told him; it would've been the perfect excuse to get the hell out of his cottage.

"I usually just have a smoothie after practice, that's all. You know, something quick and easy. I don't want you to go to all of this trouble for me."

Kane poured his scramble mixture into the hot pan and spoke a little louder over the sizzle, "For you?" He tapped the whisk on the bowl. "This is for me. What are you having?" His smile was infectious, and I fought to keep the sides of my lips turned down. "Just kidding." He grabbed a wooden spatula from a pottery container on the counter and pushed the eggs around the pan. "But I can make you a smoothie if you'd prefer."

A giant grumble from my stomach interrupted the conversation and Kane raised his eyebrows at me.

"Eggs are fine. Thanks." I held my hand on my stomach as if it had the power to stop the growling. "Is there anything I can do?"

"Grab some napkins." He pointed to a drawer.

Napkins? I lived with Dylan, and the idea of a young hockey jock using napkins seemed absurd. The drawer was filled with neatly folded linen napkins with little Adirondack chairs hand-embroidered on the corners.

Once Kane had our breakfast plated, he handed me a polished silver knife and fork. "What no silver spoon?" I regretted it as soon as I said it. Sure, Kane had grown up a spoiled rich kid, but aside from being a dick about my coaching, he had been nothing but kind to me. "Sorry, bad joke." I backpedaled.

"Come on." He jerked his head toward the balcony and opened the screen door with his foot. "After you."

"Wow." The view of Lake Casper was breathtaking. "This is beautiful," I paused, staring at what had to be a multi-million-dollar view.

"Wait until you see it from the boathouse."

We ate our breakfast, complete with linen napkins, at a teak table on the roof of Kane's boathouse. The breeze tickled my neck as I watched Kane unfold the napkin onto his lap. I followed suit, feeling ridiculous. Some nights Dylan and I ate off paper plates, and ninety percent of the time he was hunched over the coffee table, fork in hand, shoveling food into his face like a farmhand.

"These eggs are delicious." I took a bite, cutting a piece of bacon in half and resisting the urge to pick it up in my fingers, forked it into my mouth. I moaned as a combination of sweet and salty hit my tongue and then clapped my hand over my mouth.

"It's the maple syrup," Kane's eyes sparkled as he finished his breakfast. "I'll let you in on a little hint, it's my secret ingredient in almost everything."

"Okay, Buddy."

"Buddy?" he leaned back in his chair.

"The elf from the movie Elf." I smiled and pushed my plate to the middle of the table.

"I love that movie." He grinned like he had just scored the winning goal in overtime.

"Of course you do."

Kane wiped his mouth with his napkin and set it on the table. "What's your problem, Jessie?"

"My problem?"

"Yes. I like Will Farrell movies. They're funny. You know what, I also like Citizen Kane. And, the silver spoon thing? From earlier?"

My seat suddenly felt hot. "I should go." My hands were planted on the table as I prepared to bolt.

"No, Jessie, sit." Kane's steely eyes were locked on mine and I eased back down onto the chair. A boat droned by in the background. "What's your problem with me?"

My cheeks burned against the cool breeze that came off the water. "I don't have a problem with you, Kane." I did have a problem with him, the kind of problem that involved my heart beating like I had just finished my long program whenever he smiled at me. The kind of problem that made me imagine what his hand would feel like wrapped around my waist, rather than his hockey stick. "You wouldn't understand."

"Try me." He rested his elbows on the table and leaned in.

"You and I, Kane… we come from different worlds."

"So?" His brow knitted.

"Laketown, this place. I can't believe I'm back here," I sighed. "Listen, Kane. You're a cottager. I'm a Laketownie. Oil and water."

"That's bullshit." He shook his head almost impercep-tibly and rolled his eyes.

"Is it? How many locals do you know?"

"Lots." Kane smiled. "Dylan, Jack…," his voice trailed off.

"The guys from your team." I counted two on my fingers. I pointed to his cottage. "I've never been in one of these old cottages, I've never been to the Casper Lake Yacht Club, or gone to a hundred-dollar Pilates class at the Casper Zen Center. I have to work. Townies clean the Zen Center; we don't meditate there. We don't spend our summer boating around in hundred-thousand-dollar wakeboard boats. I didn't spend my nights going to exclusive boathouse parties." I pointed at Kane and then back to me. "In the natural world, you and I would never be sitting across the table from each other."

"Oh, come on," Kane scoffed.

"It's true."

"Do you ever think that you're not friends with cottagers because of your salty attitude?" He smiled and tossed his napkin at me.

The napkin landed on my hand and I batted it away. "I'm serious, Kane. I get it. You can't help that you were born with a silver spoon in your mouth. I don't have a problem with you, per se, but all this?" I pointed to his cottage. "We are different."

"I've never judged you. Not once." Kane's voice was quiet. "I don't care where you grew up or what your last name is, Jess. I think what you're doing, all this judging – it's not coming from a good place."

The tears came. I never plan on crying, no one does, but these tears caught me off guard. It wasn't one lone drop either; my shoulders shook from the ferocity of a full-on gasping sob. "Oh, no. Jessie, I'm sorry." Kane shot up from his chair and wrapped his arms around my shoulders. I pushed him away and wiped at the ugly sheen on my face.

"Jess, I—"

I held up my hand. My elbows slipped to my knees and I hung my head while I processed what had just happened. The weight of Kane's warm hand on my shoulder brought me back to reality. I cleared my throat and stood up. "A cottager killed my parents. He was drunk, coming back from some party at the yacht club..."

"Oh..." Kane's voice was soft, and his hand slipped from my shoulder.

"He was never charged, He got off on some technicality." I stood and shrugged Kane's hand from my shoulder. "I guess it's that, that's my problem." I brushed at invisible crumbs on the thighs of my yoga pants. "I should go."

"Jessie, wait." Kane's fingers wrapped around my forearm. I turned to face him. "Come with me." His hand slipped to grasp my hand. I resisted, but he tugged, and I followed.

"Where?" I asked. He led me inside his boathouse. The sound of water lapping against rocks echoed louder inside the building as five boats rocked, moored in their slips.

Kane let go of my hand and pulled at the lines securing a wakeboard boat.

"What are you doing?" I asked.

"You've never spent the day lounging on my - what did you call it? -hundred-thousand-dollar wakeboard boat? That's practically a crime." He grabbed my hand. "Get in." I glanced at the door to the boathouse as if looking for an escape. "Come on," he urged. "It's your day off." I sighed and then kicked off my Birkenstocks and stepped into the boat, the leather of the seat squeaking at I sat down. Kane hopped in behind me and started the boat, its engine purred as he navigated into the main body of the lake. The air was chilly, but the sun was warm enough to keep me from shivering.

"Hold on." Kane smiled, turned his baseball hat backward, and then pushed the throttle down. The wake flattened as we sped down Lake Casper at forty miles an hour. Kane pointed out all of the islands and rattled off their names. Every time we passed another boater he smiled and raised his hand in a wave – and the other boater did the same.

I released my ponytail from my fist and gawked at the cottages as we sped by. Most of them were like Kane's, built at the turn of the century with sweeping screened-in porches and shuttered windows, but some new builds dotted the shoreline, the angled modern structures glinted like broken glass amongst the sea of evergreen trees.

"Are you cold?" Kane pulled back the throttle.

I realized I was hugging myself tightly and rubbing my arms. "Just when we're going fast," I admitted.

Kane pulled his t-shirt off and tossed it to me. "Here."

His left, very round, very defined bicep twitched as he navigated the boat towards the shoreline. How did he have a golden tan this early in the season? I draped his shirt over my chest and the smell of sandalwood and Irish Spring soap sent warmth through to my core. I had to remember that he was a jock, a shirtless, backward hat-wearing, jock. As my eyes traveled over his body, he became more than that, though. He was big, strong, and muscled. *Stop it, Jessie.* I tell myself. He's still a hockey player, exactly the type of guy I had avoided my whole life.

A shiver ran through me. The kind of shiver that had nothing to do with the cold.

A rock wall loomed beside us and Kane shut off the boat's engine. "You're up first."

"What?"

Kane winked and pointed to a rope hanging from a pine tree.

"Are you joking? The water has got to be fifty degrees!"

"Sixty-two today," Kane grinned and laced his fingertips behind his head.

I pointed to the rope. "Let me get this straight. You want me to swing on the rope of certain death, into water that could literally still have ice chunks in it?"

"That's a bit dramatic, and not the correct use of literally." Like a giant cat, Kane hopped onto the edge of the boat and then leaped into the air in an impressive swan dive, slipping beneath the surface with barely a splash.

I waited, but he seemed to be under for too long. I rushed to the edge of the boat and shielded my eyes with my hand, looking for air bubbles or any sign of him. "Kane?" My eyes scanned the surface of the water. "Kane?" This time my voice pitched higher. Shit. There was no sign of him. Do I call for help? My mind raced with worst-case scenarios.

Did he hit his head? Did the shock of the water stop his heart?

Save him.

I didn't think twice before jumping in – feet first. The temperature took my breath away and I fought for the surface, "Gah!" I screamed when I emerged. My breathing was rapid and shallow, but the need to save him surpassed my own body's need to get out of the freezing water. I took a deep breath but before I dove, I felt something brush by my feet. "Eeeek," I screamed. Kane emerged in front of me – and the bastard was laughing.

"I knew I could get you in here." His wet hair was plastered on his face and rivulets of water ran alongside his piercing eyes.

"You asshole!" I flailed my arms and kicked my legs to get away from him, not caring if I connected with his junk – secretly hoping I would. "I thought that you drowned." I swam as fast as I could to the platform at the stern of the boat. He followed and before I could haul my half-frozen body out of the lake, I felt the heat from his body behind me. He placed his hands on the platform on either side of me. He was so close I could feel the warmth of his breath on my earlobe. "Give it a second," he whispered. "Your body will get used to it."

"I don't want my body to get used to it," I seethed through clenched teeth.

He slipped his hand around my waist. "Relax, breathe into my arm." I was stiff as a board. "Let go. I'll hold you."

My teeth chattered and I could see my fingertips turning blue as they gripped the platform. "Trust me," Kane whispered.

I never trusted anyone, but Kane's forearm tightened around my waist and I melted into him and for the first time in a long time, I let myself be held. My hands slipped from the platform and onto his muscled forearm. "Now take a deep breath in," he instructed. I nodded and followed his instructions; and while the water didn't miraculously get warm, it became bearable. The teeth chattering slowed and when it completely stopped, I turned my face towards Kane, resting my forehead against his scruffy jawline. The only sound that I could hear was that of our breaths, our chests rising and falling in sync.

"Cryotherapy." Kane squeezed me a little tighter. "It's really good for you."

That's when I felt it.

It.

Any question about whether or not Kane Fitzgerald was into me disappeared as I felt his very large, very hard erection between my thighs. I shivered.

"Are you ready to get out?" he asked.

Instead of responding, I spun to face him, holding onto his shoulders. Now our warm breath met in the inch between our faces. I knew that I shouldn't, we shouldn't – but he bridged the gap between our lips, and my breath hitched as his lips met mine. Kane kissed me gently at first, and I responded, our lips nipping and exploring each other, but he quickly grew ravenous. I wrapped one leg around his waist, arching into him, and I could feel his desire surge impossibly harder against me. I rocked my hips gently against his cock, gasping into his mouth and gripping his shoulders tighter as he kissed me harder.

Then, just as quickly as it started, it stopped. Kane pushed away from me, launched himself onto the swim platform like a gymnast, and then turned and pulled me from the water by my hands. I hopped into the boat. Kane was half a step behind me and pulled my sopping shirt off over my head from behind before I knew what was happening. His lips were warm and hungry as he nipped at the space between my shoulder blades. I turned to kiss him again, but he stopped me. "You need to get warm first. I didn't expect you to jump into the lake in your clothes."

My soaking wet yoga pants had gained a few inches in length. I felt the release from my bra band and then Kane's massive hands as they slipped under the shoulder straps, sliding it off my arms. I turned to face him, brushing his abs with my desire-pricked nipples.

"Oh. My. God." His voice was guttural. He cupped one of my breasts in his hand while the other squeezed my ass. He pulled me tightly to him then dropped to his knees and one by one, kissed my pink nipples while his hands kneaded and rocked my ass toward him.

"Kane," I moaned. My skin was cold, but I was on fire inside. My fingertips lingered in his thick hair while he kissed up my sternum. I arched my neck and closed my eyes, my fingers fisted in his hair as his lips made their way up my neck.

He stood and cupped my cheeks. "You're the most beautiful person I've ever met, Jessie, I hope that you see it one day." Then he kissed me gently and my knees shuddered. I held onto his forearms like they were crutches because there was no way I was going to be able to stand after that kiss.

I didn't want to be the one to break away and so I let my lips linger on his. When Kane pulled away, I brought my fingertips to my lips and tried to hold in my smile. "Lift your arms," he whispered and grabbed his t-shirt from the Captain's seat. I threaded my arms into the giant sleeves and the shirt fell to my mid-thighs. Kane bunched the hem of the shirt in his hands and slipped his fingers into the waistband of my pants.

I grabbed onto his wrists. I wanted to feel the warmth of his hands on my ass, and it took all of my self-control to push pause on the sexiest moment of my life. My body was trembling, but even though I wanted it more than I've ever wanted anything in my life, we couldn't go any further.

"I know," he nuzzled into my neck as if reading my mind. "I just want to get you out of your wet clothes."

He was a hockey player, emphasis on player, but at that moment, I saw something different in him, and I released his wrists. As he promised, he slid the wet fabric over my ass and then allowed gravity to take over. The yoga pants fell to the floor with a splashy thud and I stepped out of them. "Turn around," I said and swirled my index finger in the air.

He smiled, put his hand over his eyes, and turned away from me.

My wet panties rolled as I slid them down my thighs. I looked over my shoulder at Kane as I squeezed them out over the side of the boat. He remained still; his hand clamped over his eyes. I ensured that the t-shirt was in place before whispering, "Okay."

He squinted as he lowered his hand and then started rummaging under all of the seat cushions. "There's got to be some towels in here somewhere." He found a blue and white striped towel and tossed it at me. "Here." I caught it and I used it to squeeze the water out my hair. Kane wrapped another towel around his sculpted abs, tucking the end in under the V that darted out of sight below the towel. I smiled, as my eyes followed the V as far as I could. That chiseled lower abdomen muscle was what Paige liked to call the sex muscle, and Kane's was the most defined I'd ever seen. He shimmied out of his shorts under the towel and his bathing suit joined my panties on the floor.

The knowledge that there were only a couple layers of cotton separating our desire made me want to rip the damn towel off, and I wondered if he was thinking the same thing.

The breeze fluttered the hem of the t-shirt before making its way between my legs. The sensation of the wind on my bare sex didn't help the situation. I was more turned on than I'd ever been in my life and I'd be lying if I said I didn't want Kane to rip the shirt off and bend me over the back of his boat.

"I'm going to dry off a bit," he said while he reclined on the swim platform. "Join me." He patted the space beside him.

I eased down beside Kane and he pulled me closer so I could rest my head on his shoulder. The sun beat down, drying, and warming our bodies. "Kane," I whispered. "This is a bad idea, isn't it?"

"Yep."

My heart sank when he agreed with me.

"We shouldn't do this again, right?" Please disagree. Please disagree.

"Probably not."

A distant boat's rolling waves lapped against the hull of Kane's boat, slowly rocking it back and forth. Neither of us said a word. I closed my eyes and inhaled his scent, trying to commit it to memory, and wondering if this was the last time I'd ever be this close to him.

I don't remember the moment when I fell asleep, but I do remember the moment I was abruptly woken up.

"Oh, shit," Kane shouted. The vibration in his chest traveled through my entire body and my eyes snapped open. "It will be okay, Jessie." Kane shot to his feet and I blinked, trying to figure out what the hell was going on.

21

KANE

PUFFY marshmallow clouds bumbled their way across the sky, and I played with Jessie's hair as she slept on my chest. This girl was different. This girl jumped into the lake in her clothes to save me. Her breaths were slow and rhythmic and even though my arm had fallen asleep at least half an hour earlier, I couldn't bring myself to disturb her.

I was content letting the boat drift while holding Jessie in my arms. She was wrong, there really wasn't a good reason why we shouldn't be together. Screw the hockey bro-code. Dylan was probably going to get kicked off the team anyway. Jessie Moss and I belonged together, and I would prove it to her.

I let my eyes fall shut for what I thought was just a moment, but when I opened them again, the puffy clouds had been replaced with angry, dark, 'I'm going to rain the fuck all over you,' clouds.

I told her everything was going to be okay and then glanced around. Lake Casper was about thirty miles across at its widest point and somehow, we had drifted into the middle. I scanned the distant shoreline for any defining markers, anything that would tell me which direction I needed to head – and fast. Glancing at the sky didn't help - the sun was long gone, and a flash of heat lighting flickered high in the atmosphere.

"Come on, Jessie, get under here." I pulled up the bimini top, snapped it into place, and started the engine. The lighthouse at the north end of the lake flashed in my peripheral vision. *Thank God*, I thought to myself, and turned the boat southbound, gunning the engine. The rain line chased us down the lake, inching closer and closer by the second. The wakeboard boat wasn't meant for high speed runs across choppy water and it was a rough ride, but once we were in the channel, the waves subsided but the rain didn't stop her chase and finally caught us. The first few drops plopped heavily onto the windshield of the boat before the monsoon unleashed its fury directly on top of us. Sheets of rain danced on the lake and rain battered the windshield like wet ball bearings.

Jessie turned to me; her green eyes vibrant in all of the gray. "This is awesome," she grinned.

"So are you," I said under my breath.

Back in the shelter of the boathouse, Jessie hopped out of the boat and quickly tied the lines. "Nice knot," I pointed to her expertly tied daisy chain.

"My dad was a marine mechanic," she smiled. "I used to help him at work and sometimes I pumped gas at the marina."

"You've never pumped gas for me." I gathered up our wet clothes and squeezed the water from them into the open water of the boathouse slip.

"How do you know that?"

My t-shirt clung tightly to her small body in all the right places. As she stepped out of the boat, I was a gentleman and averted my gaze just before I got a glimpse of anything higher than her well-developed figure skater thighs. Of course, I wanted to fuck her on my boat. It was a fantasy of mine that I'd never fulfilled, but my brain was glad that we didn't – my cock on the other hand was furious and I shifted uncomfortably as it throbbed in frustration.

"Let's wait here until the rain lets up," I suggested, knowing that my towel was not doing a particularly good job hiding my raging boner.

"What for? We're already soaked." She pulled at the t-shirt and it clung to her and snapped back against her body causing my cock to twitch a little harder.

"Come on then." I grabbed her hand and she squealed as we ran up the pathway to the main cottage. Our bare feet slapped on the flagstone pathway and she had no problem keeping up with me. My towel, on the other hand, gave way to the intense soaking and dropped to the ground. "Shit."

I turned to grab it, but we were already three steps ahead. My stiff cock rejoiced in its freedom, standing tall in his own personal rain dance. Jessie clapped her hand over her mouth and turned away. The fat raindrops continued hitting the path and water ran down both of our faces.

Jessie let go of my hand and backtracked to the dripping wet towel. With her eyes squeezed shut she tossed it to me, hard, and it slapped into my chest with a wet thud that almost knocked me over.

Jessie's hands returned to cover her eyes. She looked fucking adorable, the sopping shirt nearly reached her knees now, and her hair was plastered down her face. I knew she was going to tell me that we couldn't be together, but if she left my cottage today and I didn't get to kiss those lips again, I knew I'd regret it for the rest of my life. I dropped the towel and our clothes on the pathway with a sloppy thud and took her cheeks in my hands. She peeked between her fingers, her green eyes locking with mine. "Kane," she moaned as she grabbed onto my wrists.

I didn't let her finish.

Hungry. That's how I felt, and I think she did too. I kissed her as though I would never kiss another woman again – and she kissed me like she was starving. It didn't seem possible, but the rain started to fall harder with buckets from the sky dumped on us. Her face was wet and slick in my palms, but the warmth of her lips a haven in the storm. At this point, my cock was rock fucking hard. She squeezed her hands into my lower back and when she pulled my body to hers, my dick fucking throbbed for her.

Wanting a woman is one thing. Needing her is another – and I needed Jessie. She squealed as I scooped her up in my arms and carried her the rest of the way to the main cottage.

Her face was buried in my neck and she didn't move it even when we were in the safety and warmth of the cottage. Leaving puddles behind me, I took Jessie to my bedroom. With her feet safely planted on the rustic floorboards, Jessie's modesty returned, and she averted her gaze from my buck-naked body. I helped her into my terrycloth robe, cinching the belt tightly around her small waist.

"I'll be right back," I whispered into her ear and headed to the linen closet to find some more towels. But, before I left the bedroom, I glanced back and caught her following my every move.

"Hurry," she smiled, her dimples denting her freckled cheeks.

I glanced around the linen closet for any of Pine Hill's monogrammed guest robes. This will have to do, I thought to myself as I pulled on the only robe I could find – a pink fluffy one and armed myself with a stack of towels.

She was standing exactly where I left her.

"Where are your matching kitten heel slippers?"

I handed her a towel. "Kitten heels?"

"Right, I forgot I'm dealing with a dude." Her smile lit up her entire face. "They're the little tiny heels that all the housewives wore in the fifties."

"Kitten heel this." I grabbed her hips and yanked her hard against me, my mouth covering hers. I slipped my hand inside the front of the robe and Jessie moaned into my mouth as my palm cupped her breast.

"Kane," she whispered.

"Jessie." my voice was raspier than I expected.

She tucked her chin, pulling her lips away from mine. I knew what she was going to say, so I beat her to it. "We shouldn't do this?" I stated. "Why, Jessie? Give me one good reason." She was killing me. My erection throbbed against the fluffy pink fabric, threatening to make an appearance through the opening.

"I really like you," she whispered.

"I really like you too." I cupped her face and rubbed her cheek with my thumb.

"But..." she held onto my wrist and her gaze fell to our bare feet.

"Kane?"

Her gaze snapped to mine, her eyes wide.

"Kane?" My father's voice echoed through the cottage.

"Who's that?" she whispered.

"It's okay. It's just my dad."

"Your dad?" she hissed. She let go of my hand and pulled the robe tighter against her body.

"Wait here." I kissed her on the cheek.

"What is all this water doing on the floor? KANE?" I shut the door quietly behind me, leaving Jessie, and her explanation hidden away in my room.

22

JESSIE

TWO DIFFERENT WORLDS. He would never understand. My dad was a mechanic who fixed his dad's boats. I fried pickerel all summer to make ends meet. He tinkered with one of his seven cars and belonged to the country club. Pine Hill oozed old money. My house, it oozed, well, no money.

I sat down on Kane's bed, perfectly made by the housekeeper, and looked around his room. Other than the fact that it was ten times bigger than mine, Kane's room wasn't so different. Trophies lined the walls of both of our rooms. I picked up the beveled glass award that sat on Kane's nightstand and ran my fingers across the engraved 'Player of the Year' stamp.

The Laketown Otters photo was prominently displayed on his dresser and Kane's face popped amongst the players, his eyes and million-dollar grin standing out in the sea of blue and white. Kane was going to be a star.

If I didn't make it to the Olympics, I would just be another Laketown townie. If I were lucky, maybe I could get a job waitressing at Valerock, and when my looks started to fade, I would probably get a job as a secretary somewhere.

I set the award down. Kane didn't want a townie. But an Olympic figure skater, that would be enough to bridge the class gap between us. My bruised hip throbbed as if to prove the point that my Olympic dream was slipping through my fingertips.

I leaned to press my face into his pillow, inhaling his scent. My body ached for his, but I knew I couldn't do something casual and that's all this would ever be.

"Gimme a second." I heard Kane's voice from the other side of the door and shot from his bed, smoothing out any sign that I had just been nuzzling his pillow.

"Hey." He stepped inside the room and closed the door. "Um..." he rubbed the back of his neck. "My dad and stepmom are here."

"I kind of figured that out." My chest tightened as I realized that my clothes were somewhere between the main cottage and the boathouse. "I thought that they didn't come here?" My mind raced, wondering could I jump out the window? How was I going to get past Kane's parents wearing nothing but a bathrobe?

"They don't. My stepmom hates it here, but the water main broke at their main house."

I sat down on his bed. "How am I going to get out of here?"

"Get out of here?" Kane disappeared into his walk-in closet. "Jessie, we're not in high school anymore. Come and meet them. You'll like my dad, my stepmom..." he hesitated, "well, you'll see..."

"Meet your parents?" My heart leaped directly into my throat. "In this?" I smoothed my hands over his gigantic soft robe.

Kane emerged from his closet and handed me a pair of

sweatpants, a Laketown Otters t-shirt, and a hoodie. I held up the giant sweatshirt in front of me, "Seriously?"

"Would you rather go out in the robe?"

I glanced at the window again, it was looking like a better option.

"Come on, Jessie. I want to introduce you to my dad. He's been asking me about the power skating lessons and I told him that you were the best thing to happen to my career in years."

"You did?"

"Of course. Although I may have left out the fact that..." There it was again, the neck rub, Kane's 'tell.' He was nervous.

"That what?"

"He assumed you were a man and I didn't correct him." Kane shrugged.

It wasn't the first time this had happened to me and sometimes I liked the fact that Jessie or Jesse confused people. I put my hands on my hips. "Why, are you embarrassed?"

"I was," Kane admitted. "But that was before I found out that you really know your stuff."

"How are we going to explain this?" I pulled the sweatpants up under the robe. Even though he had seen enough of my body to piece together what I looked like naked, I still asked him to turn around while I got dressed in his Otters' stalker starter pack.

"The truth," Kane smiled and grabbed my hand. "Come on, they're waiting."

I padded behind Kane. How was he going to introduce me? How was he going to explain why my hair was soaking wet and why I was wearing his clothes? Kane opened the door to the screened-in porch and I took a deep breath as I stepped out in front of Mr. and Mrs. Fitzgerald looking like a sewer rat.

"Dad, this is Jessie Moss."

I did a quick double-take between Kane and his father. Mr. Fitzgerald could've passed as Kane's older brother. "Pleased to meet you, Jessie," Mr. Fitzgerald stood and shook my hand. His eyes were the exact same shade of blue as Kane's, but his had crinkles at the side.

"Nice to meet you, Mr. Fitzgerald."

"Please, it's Kent." His smile was just as warm and bright as Kane's. "This is my wife, Tiffany."

"Pleasure." Tiffany stood and shook my hand, but unlike Kent's, her handshake was cold and limp like pickerel before it was fried. "If you'll excuse me for a moment." Tiffany clomped by us in her high heel wedges and stepped into the cottage, but her cloud of Chanel Mademoiselle lingered long after she disappeared.

"Please, have a seat, Jessie," Kent Fitzgerald gestured to one of the white wicker chairs. "I'm having Margie make up some coffee."

The instant comfort I felt around Mr. Fitzgerald unnerved me. Was it because he could've been Kane's older brother? "I'd love some coffee," I smiled and held my hands together in my lap amongst the sea of sweat pant fabric.

"Looks like you two could use some." He raised his eyebrows and the wicker creaked as he relaxed back into the floral cushions. "Rough morning?"

I glanced at Kane and shot him my best 'what the hell' look, but Kane didn't see it. What did he mean by 'rough morning?' Did his dad think we had spent the whole morning in bed?

An oblivious Kane started digging us into a hole. "She

sure cracked the whip this morning, dad." Kane laughed. "I'm beat."

I shot him another shut up look, wishing I could facepalm, and he furrowed his brow at me.

"Is that so?" Kane's dad looked puzzled.

"Her stroking technique is a little unorthodox, I'll give you that." Kane leaned back and grinned at me.

I was mortified.

"Son, why don't you change out of your stepmom's robe, and when you return with coffee for your guest, please bring your manners."

My eyes met Kane's and that's when he realized that everything he had just said had been misinterpreted as a sexual innuendo.

"Dad, she's my skating coach. Get your mind out of the gutter." He brushed it off and disappeared into the cottage.

I ran my fingers along the arm of the wicker chair and spoke without looking up. "I'm Jessie Moss. Kane's power skating coach. And this…" I held out the sweatshirt. "We got caught in the rain in the boat this morning. My clothes are soaked." I didn't mention that they were in a pile on the floor of the wakeboard boat.

I heard the chuckle and let myself look at Mr. Fitzgerald. He rubbed the back of his neck just like Kane. "I guess now it's my turn to be embarrassed." He crossed his legs and cleared his throat. "How is he doing then? With the… stroking."

Even though we had shifted into skating talk, both of our cheeks were the same shade of red.

I giggled nervously. "He's doing great." It was true. "All he needed was a couple of tweaks and I've already noticed a huge improvement in his maneuverability."

"He works hard that kid." Kent smiled and I could hear the pride in his voice.

"It's only a matter of time before he's drafted." Even as I said it, I felt a sense of sadness. Ten years from now some reporter might ask him about his path to superstardom and I would be nothing but a blip on the radar.

"If that's what he wants," Kent said.

I was shocked. I thought that part of Kane's drive was to please his father, who had played professional hockey himself.

"If that's what who wants?" Tiffany was back and had changed into white jeans and a floral tank top. She sat on the wicker love seat next to Kent and draped her manicured hand over his leg, her wrist limp, as though her dime-sized diamond was weighing down her hand.

"Kane," Mr. Fitzgerald clarified. "If he wants to play professional hockey, or not – it's up to him."

"Please," Tiffany groaned and then let out a terrible fake-sounding laugh. "That's all that boy can do."

It was slight, but I saw the way Kent shifted away from his wife. "Tiffany." His voice was low.

"Don't Tiffany me," she grinned at me and lightly slapped Kent's knee. "What's he going to do? Go to business school?" That laugh again.

"If he wants to, yes." Kent crossed his arms across his chest. "Where's Kane with those coffees?"

As if on cue, the screen door creaked and Kane gingerly stepped through, holding a serving tray of four coffees as well as a crystal cream and sugar set. He placed the tray on the coffee table. "Jessie, what do you take in your coffee?"

"Just black," I replied. He handed me a bone china mug.

"Dad, Tiffany, yours are ready to go." He pointed to the steaming cups.

"You should let Margie do this." Tiffany's eye roll was slight, but I still caught it. I took a sip of my coffee and shivered as she trained her gaze on me. "That's a cute outfit sweetie. Is that what the kids are wearing these days?"

I could've sat and talked to Mr. Fitzgerald all afternoon, but with the addition of Tiffany to the mix, all I wanted to do was get the hell out of there. She had an edge to her, and I couldn't figure out why. Did she and Kent fight during the drive out to the cottage? They seemed to be walking on eggshells around each other.

"They got caught in the rain." Mr. Fitzgerald answered for me. "Kane, Jessie was just telling me about your sessions. It sounds like they're paying off."

"She's a good teacher." Kane squeezed my thigh. I gave him a quick side-eye, wondering if it was subconscious.

The coffee was some of the best I'd ever drunk, and part of me wanted to savor it, but instead, I gulped it back.

Tiffany sipped with her pinky finger extended and set her lipstick-stained mug on the tray. "Where's your cottage, Jessie?"

I held the empty mug in both of my hands. "I live in town."

Tiffany's lips quivered and then the smile disappeared from her face. "Oh," she said. "I see." She stood, slapping Kent's knee out of her way. "I'm going to the club for the gala meeting. Tell Margie to make me a salad for dinner." She leaned down and kissed Kent on the cheek.

"Would you like a refill?" Kane asked, taking the empty mug from my hand.

"I should get going too." I stood up.

"Jessie." It was Kent who stopped me. "Please stay for as long as you'd like. I'm going to go play a round of golf this afternoon. You two will have the place to yourselves." Mr.

Fitzgerald stood and shook my hand. "Thank you for helping out with the skating. I'm so happy that Kane has someone looking out for him.

Kent and Tiffany left, and Kane held both of my hands in his. "Sorry about that."

"About what?" I pulled my hands from his. "Your father is lovely."

"He's alright," Kane smiled. "He's just made some bad decisions in his life."

I couldn't help myself. "Does one of them start with a T and rhyme with Biffany?"

Kane snorted and I thought coffee was going to come out his nose. "She's the worst. She hates me."

A breeze fluttered the napkins on the coffee table and sent a chill down my spine. I sat and pulled my knees up inside the roomy sweatshirt. "I can see that," I said. "Why?" Before he could reply I added, "Is it because you look better in her housecoat than she does?"

This time Kane did spit out his coffee. "I made that thing look good." He wiped his mouth with one of the mono-grammed napkins.

I smiled and nodded. "Like it was made for you."

"If I had to guess, I'd say it's because my dad made her sign a prenup, and I'll get everything – not her." Suddenly, I felt like the most selfish person on the planet. We had talked all morning about my family and my problems, and I just assumed that he didn't have any.

"Kane," I whispered. "Where is your mom?"

Kane glanced behind him, probably checking to see if his dad and Tiffany were gone. "She died when I was five."

"I'm sorry." Those were the words I'd been hearing over the last two months, and I knew that they weren't enough, but I didn't know what else to say.

"It was a long time ago." He finished his coffee. "Jessie, I need to tell you something."

I reached out to hold his free hand. "I need to tell you something too."

"You go first," we both said at the same time.

THE STORM HAD PASSED, but every time the breeze picked up, raindrops fell from the canopy of maple trees that ironically surrounded Pine Hill. Fresh cups of Americano sat steaming on the table in front of us. We had shifted to the love seat and Kane sat facing me, his apprehension apparent. He handed me a fluffy throw blanket.

"You've been trying to tell me something all day, Jess. I don't think that I want to hear it."

I sighed and pulled my feet out from beneath my legs and draped them across his thighs. "Kane, I was going to tell you that we can't keep fooling around."

"I know." He didn't look at me. "I mean, I know that's what you were going to say, but I don't agree." He squeezed the blanket over the top of my feet. "I mean, technically I can't date any of the guys' sisters."

I blinked. "That's your reason?"

"Yeah," he half shrugged. "I thought that's what you were going to say too."

Not. At. All. How could he be so clueless? "Kane, I..." I couldn't say the words. Maybe he was different. Maybe this whole townie-cottager class divide was in my head. When I looked at Kane, I didn't see a rich guy who was going to lose interest in me as soon as the novelty wore off, I just saw... Kane.

Could this be the moment that I looked back on years

from now and pinpointed where it all went wrong? I didn't care. My mind was made up. I was willing to risk it all for this hockey player. "I was going to tell you," I emphasized 'was,' "but life is short. I like you Kane, but I think whatever we do, we should keep it between us.

Translation: maybe it won't hurt as much when you break my heart if I pretend this is casual.

"Jess, are you serious?"

"As your slapshot." I looked at him sideways and smiled. "Whatever this is," I pointed at him and back at me, "we should keep it on the down-low. You know, because of Dylan."

That wasn't the reason at all, but I knew it would make sense to Kane. Also, Dylan would probably murder him, so there was that too.

He pulled me onto his lap and I wrapped my arms around his neck and for the first time, I kissed my secret maybe-boyfriend slash hockey player, Kane Fitzgerald – and it felt like I had just won a gold medal.

But better.

23

KANE

I'VE NEVER BEEN what I would call a 'morning person,' but the last week that changed. When my alarm clock went off at 4:30 in the morning, I'd already woken up, and I knew it was because my body was ready to see Jessie. I woke up aching for her.

Jessie had been riding me in my dreams. The imagery was so vivid I swore I could still feel where her figure skater thighs had been clamped around my thighs like a vice, my toes curling as I pushed up as high into her as I could. I woke up with a raging hard-on but didn't have time to rub one out, so I hopped in the shower and high tailed it to the arena.

She was waiting for me on the ice. "Metallica again?" She joined me at the boards, stopping with a spray of snow.

"It's my day to pick the music." I like Metallica. Not only am I superstitious, but I'm a creature of habit. I listen to *Master of Puppets* before every game, it gets me nice and pumped up. "You subjected me to Elton John twice this week."

She slipped her fingertip into the waistband of my warmup pants. "You liked it."

I did, but I wasn't going to tell her that. She tugged and I involuntarily glided toward her.

"Professional on the ice," I whispered in her ear and she snapped the elastic as she pulled her fingers out of my pants.

"Whose dumb idea was that?" Her hands were on her hips and her face lit up with her wide grin. She had at least five separate ways of smiling at me, and each of them lit up her face in a unique way. Her joking grin brought a certain sparkle to her eyes that made me want to rip her damn Lululemon pants down to her skates and fuck her hard against the boards.

She put me through another grueling training session, and today I was sweating so much that the front of my hair was plastered to my forehead. We met at the boards and she unplugged her phone from the sound system. "Coach Covington called me last night," she said as she slipped her phone into the pocket of her warmup jacket.

"He did?" I took a huge swig from my water bottle and passed it to Jessie who took a small sip.

"Mmmhmm," she nodded and handed the bottle back to me. "He wants to know if you've 'gotten it.'" She used air quotes. I knew that our training sessions couldn't go on forever, but they were the only time we could legitimately get together without anyone asking questions.

"And what did you tell him?" I leaned on the boards and balled my fingers into a fist to stop them from reaching out to her hips. She rocked her Bauer's now, and even though she was sexy in her figure skates, Jessie Moss in hockey skates was the stuff of *Maxim* magazine dreams.

"I told him that you were co-operating, but that you still have some work to do."

"I do?"

"Sue me. I lied." Her eyes glinted. My heart rate had just started to come down, but that joker smile revved it back up again.

"You little devil." I didn't care if the coach thought I needed more work, I wanted to keep coming to the rink every day, just to see Jessie in those skates.

Jessie skated off the ice and I followed her to the door of the visitor's dressing room. She turned and leaned against the heavy metal door and I knew exactly what she wanted. She arched her back and pressed her hips against mine and I wrapped my hand around the back of her neck and kissed her hard. She pushed against the door, opening it with her ass, and pulled me into her dressing room. The Otters have a strict policy of no women in the dressing room, and I didn't dare break that rule. It was another superstition, like sailors and having women onboard their ships back in the day. It didn't matter, I'd just started joining Jessie in the Visitor's room.

She stumbled backward and I held her arms, so she didn't fall. The momentum pulled us to the far wall where I pressed up against her, knowing that she wanted me to press my cock between her legs. She hadn't told me as much, but she moaned into my mouth every time it came close to her warmth. She threaded her fingers behind my neck, and we pressed our hips hard against each other. We had been taking it slowly, well, slowly for me that is – and had somehow managed to keep our clothes on this past week. But today, she scratched my lower back with her nails and pulled my shirt over my head.

I knelt and held each of her ass cheeks in my hands and

kissed at the front of her yoga pants. She fingered my hair and I glanced up in time to see her breath hitch as the warmth of mine met her body between her legs.

"Sit down, Jessie." I pushed on her belly and she took a seat on the slatted wood bench.

She played with my hair while I worked to loosen the laces of her skates and then pulled them off. She stood on the floor and wrapped her arms around me.

"Hey, short stuff." I bent to kiss her.

There was a different glint in her eye today, one that I didn't recognize. She stepped onto the bench, unzipped her warmup jacket, and revealed a bra with a pink bow that matched the color of the nipples that peeked out from behind the lacy pattern. She held onto my shoulders and wrapped her legs around me monkey-style and I held her tightly with one arm.

As she inhaled, her chest pressed against mine, but even with the warmth of our skin to skin contact, we both had goosebumps. I kissed the spot on her neck where it met her powerful shoulders and let my lips linger, inhaling in as much of Jessie Moss' scent as I could, vanilla with a little bit of icing sugar. I smiled to myself and lightly bit her shoulder.

She inhaled sharply and squeezed the side of my body tightly between her thighs. "Kane." Her words were breathy.

"Being here, with you, it just..." she kissed my lips and then continued, "feels right."

"I know, Jess. This has been the best week of my life." I ran my hand up the bumpy ridge of her spine, and she arched her back, grinding herself against me. I had been riding a strange line. I wanted to fuck her, but I also didn't want to fuck her. And that's how I knew that I was falling in love with her.

"Make love to me, Kane," she whispered, her breath hot on my ear. She let her lips linger and then took my lobe into her lips, and I almost came in my pants right then and there. We had been playing the long game, our touches slow, always pulling back before we went too far – but today, she didn't have to ask me twice. "Let me get out of these skates." I set her down on the bench and bent down to unlace them.

"No," she said. "Leave them on," and hooked her thumbs into the waistband of her skating tights and started to pull them down. A man possessed, I shoved my fingers into the back of Jessie's pants and yanked everything, her pants, tights, and lacy undies down to her ankles. If she'd been standing on the floor, the skates would've made what happened next impossible. She bent at the waist and held onto the coat hooks. I fumbled with the string on my pants, my cock ready for its breakaway, strained at the soft fabric. I pulled them down just enough to free my raging hard-on.

Jessie kicked at her duffel bag that sat on the bench, "In the zippered part at the end, there's a condom."

The lacy underwear and bra – the condom in the skating bag – Jessie knew what she wanted this morning and her take control attitude turned me on even more.

"Are you sure, Jess?" I rolled the condom on and held her by the hips. "Don't you want this to happen somewhere special?"

She looked over her shoulder, a smile on her face. "This place is special to us, isn't it?" She emphasized the word 'us' and it sounded so right. Us. Jessie and Kane; Fitzy and Jess.

"Take me, Kane."

She never ceased to amaze me. "You're the woman of my dreams," I growled. She bent over further, and I dug my fingers into her hipbones, pausing at the opening to her warmth. Maybe *she* didn't want it slow and tender, but I started to wonder if I did. She looked over her shoulder, her eyes flashed, and she arched her back a little more. "Fuck me, Fitzy." And with those words coming out of those sweet lips, any second-guessing on my part flew right out the door of that dressing room.

24

JESSIE

"Hello. Is there anybody in there?" A woman's voice yelled over the sound of the gurgling grease. Sometimes, it was so loud that I didn't hear people approach the chip truck. I took a deep breath and put on my imaginary patience hat.

"I'll be right there," I pulled the basket out of the oil and shook some salt on the fries.

No one could bring me down today, I felt like I was gliding around the world, high on a drug named Kane. Our mornings now consisted of skating hard and fucking harder. At the rink, we were animals but at home, our touches were softer. I winced as I turned, Kane hadn't been gentle this morning. The bruising and tenderness between my legs a welcome reminder of our morning session.

"Glad to see you're alive."

Paige leaned in the window, her voice sounded angry, but she had a smile on her face.

"Paige." I smiled. I was genuinely glad to see her. "I could say the same thing about you. Ever since you got the Vale-rock job, you've been MIA."

"Let's catch up," she grinned.

The morning dew had evaporated, and the picnic tables all sat empty. "I'll be right out." I unlaced my apron and tossed it onto the counter. As we hugged, I tried to mentally calculate how long it had been since we'd seen each other.

We sat on the bench seat of a picnic table and I opened the umbrella to protect us from the strength of the morning sun.

"You look good, Jess."

"So, do you, P."

"How's the skating going?"

It was the conversation of two friends that had let things slide; the small talk of once close friends now reduced to weather and generalizations – and I hated it. "I've been landing my lutz about fifty percent of the time."

"That's amazing, Jess." Paige's eyes sparkled and I knew that she was genuinely happy for me.

It was as though sleeping with Kane had changed me, shifted me somehow, maybe even relaxed me enough to let my muscle memory take over and give me back my hardest jump.

"It's getting there. It's still not one hundred percent." I didn't want to think about it. "How's the serving gig?"

"It's good." She played with the tips of her blond hair. "I mean, some people are real assholes, but the tips make up for it." Her gaze flitted behind me to the chip wagon, "I definitely don't miss this shithole."

"It works for me," I shrugged. I hated the chip truck too. Smelling like fried fish and sweating my ass off for minimum wage sucked, but the schedule worked with my skating.

"I could try to get you in at Valerock. I think my manager

wants to sleep with me." Her cheeks flushed scarlet and I knew that she had already slept with him.

"Those hours wouldn't work for me," I sighed. "The money certainly would though. Did I tell you that the insurance company has been giving us the run around?"

"No, Jess," she exclaimed. "What the hell?"

"It sucks." I took a sip of water. "I've had to take on a coaching job, it pays really well, but I'm still not sure if it's going to be enough to go back to the academy."

Paige rested her manicured hand on my freckled arm. "There's got to be something someone can do."

"I'll figure it out." I didn't want to dwell on the insurance or the academy. "Guess who I'm coaching?"

My words didn't seem to reach Paige, she was somewhere else. "That explains it."

I had been ready to drop a bomb on Paige. She was going to lose her mind when she found out that I had been spending every day with one of the Laketown Otters. "That explains what?"

"Why Dylan is working that second job."

"What?" I screwed up my forehead. "Dylan doesn't have a second job."

Paige looked at me like I had two heads. "Where have you been, Jessie? Your brother has been working nights at the marina. He never goes out anymore, all he does is work. We've hung out a couple of times and he's been too tired to do anyth—" her voice trailed off and I guessed what Dylan was too tired to do. I shook my head to get that imagery from my brain.

Dylan and I had opposite schedules, but how could I have missed this? Kane had been spending almost every night at my place since his dad moved back to the cottage. "I just assumed he was out partying." I couldn't believe that I had been so oblivious, that I hadn't noticed my own brother, who lived under the same roof, had taken on a night shift job. My closest friend had a new job and was probably banging her boss, and I didn't know about that either. My life had been filled with skating, but now that it was wrapped up in both Kane and skating, I had squeezed out the rest of the world.

"This is news to me." I traced my finger over the carved hearts in the surface of the table. I was hiding my relationship with Kane from Dylan and he was busy hiding his second job from me. But, was he hiding it, or was I just a terrible sister?

"Maybe he just needs some extra cash," Paige said.

I hoped that she was right and that my brother wasn't working himself to the bone for, I hated to think it, me.

The sun sparkled on the water and I squinted as a shiny antique boat cut through the ripples and approached the dock. The gas attendants ran, scrambling to grab the mooring lines. My heart clenched. My dad had always admired those antique wooden boats, but there was no way we could have ever afforded one. They were usually only kept by the 'old money' families on the lake, like the Fitzgerald's, and I held my hand over my eyes to see if it was the boat from Pine Hill.

"Maybe," I mused as I watched the man step out of the boat, reverting my gaze to Paige when I realized it wasn't Kent Fitzgerald.

"We need to spend some time together, Jess, I really miss you." Paige pulled at the cardboard sleeve on her coffee cup.

"I miss you too, Paige." Until that moment, I hadn't realized how much I missed having someone to talk to, someone who wasn't sharing my single bed.

"Oooh." Paige sat up straight and slapped at my arm. "I

just thought of something. I know how you can make some extra money."

"I don't know if I like the sound of this," I grinned. "I'm not ready for a *Pretty Woman* storyline just yet."

"Nooo." Paige rolled her eyes and smiled at me. "The gala. Valerock is catering the annual fundraiser for minor hockey at The Island Club."

The Island Club Gala is 'THE' event of the spring in Laketown. I had never been, but the newspapers always rolled out a full-page spread of the celebrity-studded event. "I could get you a job, just for the night, serving cocktails. It pays a-mazing and all you have to do is walk around with platters."

"I don't know if that's really my scene…"

"Who cares?" Paige said. "You need money to get back to the academy, right?"

I nodded reluctantly.

"And if you do a decent job, there are plenty of private parties you could work over the summer. Suck up your pride, Jess. All you've got to do is put on a dress, smile, and rake in the cash. My boss mentioned that we are under-staffed for the Gala, so I know I could get you in."

I needed the money and I hated it, but I sighed, "Okay."

"Okay?" Paige repeated and then smiled. "Omigod. I'm so excited, Jess." She grabbed my arms and shook me, then pulled me in for an almost rib breaking hug.

A rumble caught both of our attention and what looked like a supermodel strutted along the main dock. Her boho dress flapped out behind her and she held onto her over-sized sun hat with her free hand while clutching a leather overnight bag in her other. A man trailed behind her drag-ging two giant Louis Vuitton suitcases.

The man in the boat kissed her on both cheeks and then helped her into the boat.

"Ugh," Paige groaned under her breath.

"Do you know her?" The boat pulled away from the dock and cruised away slowly.

"That's Bronwyn Yates." She said it as if I should know. When I didn't respond, she continued, "Yates Petroleum..."

"Oh." The Yates Estate made Pine Hill look like a rundown squatter's cottage.

"She must be in town for the Gala," Paige said. "I've heard that she's a real bitch."

"Whoa. Jealousy doesn't look good on you Paige."

Paige cocked her head at me. "I'm not jealous, everyone who works at Valerock says that she's a total beehive and tips less than ten percent."

"Yikes."

We both watched the boat disappear past the island.

"Hey, does anybody work here?" A voice called out followed by a knock on the metallic siding of the chip truck.

"I've gotta go." I jumped up from the picnic table.

"I'll text you the info." Paige stood and we hugged once again. "I can't wait to work with you, Jess. If that's the only way we can hang out, I'll take it."

A pang of guilt clenched in my gut. "Let's hang out soon." It was weak and non-committal, but I meant it.

"Sure, Jess."

"No, I mean it." I grabbed her hand. "The next exhibition game – let's go. You love hockey, let's watch it together."

"Seriously? You hate those games."

Was I inviting Paige to spend time with her, or to watch my man? "Seriously," I smiled, the guilty feeling subsiding. Why couldn't it be both?

"I don't have all day here," the man in the Topsiders

tapped his foot on the wood chips that surrounded the truck.

"I'm coming." I waved to Paige and jogged to the back of the truck.

"Hey Jess," Paige shouted.

I paused with the metal door in my hand. "Yeah?"

"Who are you coaching?"

She had the attention span of a goldfish, but the memory retention of an elephant. "Can you keep a secret?"

Paige turned so quickly I thought that she was going to get whiplash. "Of course."

Kane wanted me to wait until after the last exhibition game, but I couldn't keep it in. I had to tell someone. "It's Kane Fitzgerald. And we're doing more than skating."

25

KANE

TIRED. Happy. Hot. Sweet.

Those were the words I'd use to describe the last couple of weeks with Jessie. I had spent most nights sleeping pressed against the wall in her bedroom, the two of us squeezed together in her single bed.

Watching her skate was my favorite part of the day. We walked into the arena in the darkness, holding hands, and I watched her float over the ice for an hour before we ran drills together. If the dressing room sex was hot, making love to her in her bed was sweet – and I couldn't get enough.

Now, I watched stalker-style from the gas dock as she wiped down the picnic tables at the chip wagon before sneaking up behind her.

"Hi, beautiful," I grabbed her around her waist and whispered into her ear.

"Kane." Her body was tense. "You can't sneak up on me like that."

I kissed her neck, she relaxed but shied away from my lips. "I'm all sweaty."

"I'd call it salty." I kissed her again. I didn't care if she'd just run a marathon and then biked twenty miles, I'd kiss every square inch of her body. "Let's go for a swim."

"Where?" she asked. "Here?"

The water at the marina had a permanent slick from all the boats and the shoreline was littered with cattails and thick mud. "No way, ugh." I grabbed her hand. "Lock up. I'll take you to Pine Hill."

"Pine Hill? What about your dad?"

"He doesn't care if we're there. If anything, *he* should be the one worried about invading *my* space. And don't worry, I think that he went back to the city to spend some time with Tiffany."

Jessie locked up and helped me undo the lines to the Mastercraft. "At the Hilton?"

The damage from the water main break in my dad's city house had been extensive. The mosquitoes had scared Tiffany away from the cottage and she had checked herself into a luxury hotel instead.

"I guess." I shrugged and started the engine. Jessie kicked off her flip flops and stepped into the boat.

"Don't you think that's weird?" she settled into the seat beside me and I navigated out of the marina docks.

"What?"

"That your dad is here alone, and she's choosing to stay there alone?"

"Have you met the woman?" I laughed. I hated Tiffany, but after being alone for so many years, I didn't blame my dad for remarrying. I wished it would've been someone a little more like my mom, although, maybe it was better that she was the total opposite. There's no way that Tiffany could ever take my mom's place in my dad's heart. He'd never say as much, but I knew it.

"She's something." Jessie remained diplomatic.

Even through my Ray-Bans, the late afternoon sun was powerful, and I squinted as I pushed down the throttle on the boat. Jessie held on to the front of her Otters baseball cap.

"Nice hat." I tapped the front of the cap.

She reached up to touch it as if she couldn't remember what was on her head. "It's Dylan's," she said. "He stole my favorite, so I took one of his."

"It looks good on you." She had gotten a little bit of sun and her cheeks were pink, her freckles a bit more intense than they had been on the first day we met.

By the time the boat was docked I was sweating and couldn't wait to get in the water with Jessie. She dipped her toe in. "I don't know Kane, it still feels cold."

"Oh, come on. it's been almost two weeks, it's gotta be almost seventy by now." I bent to pull up the thermometer. "Okay, so it's sixty-five now." I dropped it back into the lake.

"Maybe I'll just wade in up to my knees." She rubbed her arms.

"That's the hard way." I tossed my t-shirt onto an Adirondack chair and hung two towels on the boathouse hooks.

"By now, don't you know that I like to do things the hard way?" she put her hands on her hips and smiled at me.

"And don't you know by now that I like surprising you?"

"Surprising me?" she tilted her head and I charged at her. Her green eyes grew wide. "Don't you dar—," she screamed. "Kane!" She wriggled in my arms as I grabbed her around the waist and launched us into Lake Casper.

When we surfaced, I was ready for flailing hands. "You bastard," she squealed after she gasped for air. "I wasn't ready," she said.

"Sometimes you just have to get thrown in."

"You don't know what you just started Kane Fitzgerald,"

she narrowed her eyes at me, which would have seemed threatening, but they were accompanied with a slight grin which grew into a giggle.

"Bring it, Jessie Moss." I splashed water in her face like a teenager.

"Oh, consider it brought." She lunged at me and grabbed my shoulders, trying to push me under. She was putting everything into her fight. "Your laughing is making you..." I grabbed onto her hip bones and held her away from me. She splashed water directly into my face and I choked, "...weak." I fountained the lake water out of my mouth, directly onto her forehead. "Okay, okay, you win." She swatted at the spray of water. Our laughter trailed off and I could feel Jessie's feet treading water beneath her, her legs occasionally hitting mine as she kept herself afloat.

"You're beautiful." I ran my hand over her wet hair, pulled her close, and kissed her. The warmth from her lips traveled through my body and I wondered if the urge to be inside Jessie would ever subside. I couldn't imagine my world without her.

"Kane, I..." Jessie ran her hand along my jawbone and batted her eyelashes at me. I knew what she was going to say because it was the same thing that I wanted to say. I loved her.

"Kane! Where are you?"

Goddammit. The woman was a bane to my existence, and now she had just interrupted one of the best moments of my life. "It's Tiffany," I whispered to Jessie.

"I know, I can hear her heels from here."

"Kane!" she shouted again.

"Hold that thought, Jess." I squeezed her hand underneath the water and climbed the swim ladder. Jessie followed behind me. I handed her a sun-warmed towel and wrapped the other around my waist.

"What's up?" I asked.

"I have to talk to you about something." Her eyes shot to Jessie. "Important."

"You can say whatever you need to say in front of Jessie." I took a seat on the arm of the chair and Jessie sat in the one beside it.

"Fine." Tiffany rolled her eyes.

My dad stepped onto the dock behind Tiffany. "Hi, Kane. Hi, Jessie." He waved his boat polishing chamois at both of us.

"I thought that you were in the city." I directed my attention away from Tiffany. I wouldn't have brought Jessie here if I knew that my evil stepmother was in the house. Tiffany doesn't believe in interacting with people below her, and in her eyes, Jessie was a Laketownie, the lowest of the low. I wanted to protect her from this bitch.

"I had to pick up Tiffany and get some decorations for her Gala." He opened the door to the boathouse. I have to get the *Power Play* ready, she's a little dusty from all of the pollen.

"I was just about to talk to Kane about the event," Tiffany said, but this time with a weird Cruella Deville smile on her face.

I glanced at Jessie who looked at Tiffany and then back to me.

"I'm not going this year," I shrugged.

"Kent, wait." Tiffany held up her hand to stop my dad from disappearing into the boathouse. My dad shot a look at me and his shoulders slumped. "I don't want to get involved in this."

Tiffany curled her index finger at my dad, and I couldn't believe it when he stepped onto the dock and obeyed.

"What's going on here?" I crossed my arms across my chest.

"So," Tiffany gushed. "Charlene Yates is on the committee for the gala this year." She paused.

"So?" I wasn't impressed by the Yates name.

"It's a big deal, Kane. You know who they are right?" Tiffany said.

"Yes. I know who they are." I inhaled and held back my eye roll. *And who cares?* I added to myself.

"Her granddaughter just flew in from Italy. She's fresh off a breakup." Tiffany clasped her hands and looked like her head was about to explode.

"What does this have to do with me?" I shifted in the chair and crossed my ankle over my knee. I had a sinking suspicion where this was going – and I didn't like it. And neither would Jessie. I glanced over to her and she was following the conversation, her hands holding the towel closed over her wet clothes.

"She needs a date." Tiffany tapped the armrest of my chair with her manicured fingers.

"Good for her. Come on Jessie." I stood up. "I'm not for hire."

"Sit down son." My dad stepped to Tiffany's side and placed his hand on her shoulder. "This would mean a lot to your stepmom."

Tiffany looked at my dad and then back to me. Her smile made my blood boil. "What's the big deal, Kane? You're single, she's single, and she's a model." Tiffany glanced at Jessie as she said 'model.' "And I already told Charlene that you'd do it."

Something in me snapped and I shot up out of the chair. "You did what?"

"Easy, Kane." My dad's voice was calm. "It would be good public relations for Yates Petroleum and Fitzgerald Investments. All you'd have to do is show up to the gala with... what's her name?"

"Bronwyn." Tiffany said. "Bronwyn Yates. The Calvin Klein model."

"And what if I already have a date?" I hadn't planned on going to the damn gala, but it was for the local minor hockey league, a cause near and dear to my heart.

"You just said you weren't going." She was smug.

"Maybe I changed my mind and I've already got a date."

"Who, her?" Tiffany scoffed and gestured to Jessie. "I thought she was just your coach." She crossed her arms over her chest and narrowed her eyes at me.

"She's not just--"

But Jessie didn't let me finish. "I think you should do it." She stepped forward. "It will look good for your family, and I'm busy that night anyway."

"See, she's busy." Tiffany pointed at Jessie.

"No. Nope. You can't make me." What the fuck was Jessie thinking?

My dad sighed. "You're acting like a child. Listen to your friend. Where do you think all of this comes from?" He pointed to the boat and then to Pine Hill. "The taxes on this cottage, they don't pay themselves. Your hockey, your expensive skating coach, Kane. This would help the company, and it's not a big deal."

Jessie stepped beside me. "Kane, I think you should do it." She gave my arm a squeeze.

"Are you sure?" I whispered and looked at her. Her eyes shimmered, but she nodded yes.

"Fine. Fuck. I'll do it."

"That's settled then." Tiffany clapped her hands and made her way back to the cottage and my dad disappeared into the boathouse.

Jessie pulled her jean shorts on over her wet bikini. "Can you take me back to the marina now?"

I didn't want to.

"Sure." I took the towel from her hand and hung it up to dry. "Hey Jess."

"Yeah."

I slipped my finger into the belt loop of her shorts and pulled her to me. "You know I'd rather go with you."

"I know," she whispered.

"What are your big plans that night?" I wondered if she just made up the excuse to placate Dad and Tiffany.

"I'm working."

"Working where?" The chip truck wasn't open at night.

"I'm serving – at the gala."

26

JESSIE

KANE and I had shared an order of chip truck fries while we watched the sun's slow descent. The empty French fry container fluttered in the breeze, weighed down by the pool of ketchup in the corner. Even though I grew up in Laketown, I never got tired of watching the progression in the color of the sky. Kane and I sat at the end of the dock, rising and falling as it bobbed on rolling waves.

"What a beauty."

It was the first thing he'd said in the past half hour. "Is everything okay Kane?"

His spine curved and he stared at his hand in his lap. "There's something that I need to tell you, Jessie."

My heart leapt into my throat. "What?" I croaked.

"You're going to think it's ridiculous." He took off his hat, stared at the Otters' logo, and rubbed the brim with his thumbs.

"You can tell me anything, Kane." I reached my arm around his broad shoulders and squeezed them tightly.

He stared at the water and I waited. After what felt like

an eternity, he continued. "All I've ever wanted is to play professional hockey."

"And you will." I squeezed harder.

"What if it doesn't happen?"

I'd had this exact same question running through my mind for years, although mine was about figure skating. "Where is this coming from, Kane? You're on the scouts' radar and you are an amazing player. I do think this is kind of ridiculous, but I get it. I've had to battle to get those negative thoughts out of my mind. They're toxic, Kane."

"You don't get it."

"Oh, but I do."

"No, Jess. I have this coin."

"Coin?"

"My Uncle Joe, my mom's brother gave it to me. I've kept in in my hockey bag ever since he disappeared."

I dropped my arm from his shoulders so I could move to face him. "What does this coin look like?"

"It's solid gold and has a pirate ship on one side."

"Oh," I said.

His hands were shaking, and I took them in mine. "From the second I got that coin, my luck changed. And I know it sounds stupid, but I always felt like my Uncle Joe was with me, looking over me while I played." He sighed. "That morning, when I saw you at the rink – I was looking for my coin."

"I was wondering why you were there," I smiled, and tucked a strand of his hair behind his ear.

"If I don't have the coin, I don't think I'll make it."

"That's ridiculous, Kane."

"See." He stiffened. "I knew you would think that it was stupid." He put his hat back on his head.

"Listen, I get the superstition thing. You're a hockey

player, it comes with the territory. But a coin doesn't make you skate the way you do. A coin doesn't give you the on-ice intuition you've got. A coin doesn't give you a slapshot faster than any guy in the league." I squeezed his hands again. "Kane, you scored the winning goal in the last game. You didn't have your coin then, did you?"

He shrugged and then nodded. He cupped my cheeks in his hands and kissed me. "And if I hadn't lost the damn thing, I never would've walked in on you changing."

His eyes shimmered and he kissed me again. I held his wrists and let the world disappear around us. After we pulled apart, he rested his forehead on mine.

"Hey, Kane," I pulled back so I could look him in the eyes.

"Yes, baby?"

Baby? I raised my eyebrows. That was a first and I can't say that I didn't love it.

"The Gala."

He groaned. "I know."

"I know that we're taking it slowly, you know, keeping this between us until we figure out what's going on, and that we never talked about whether we were, you know..." As I fought for the right word, Kane held my hand and rubbed my fingers.

"Exclusive?" he suggested.

"That's the word I was looking for." I leaned my forehead against his chest. "We never talked about that."

"Did we have to?"

I looked up at Kane. The golden hour was working its magic and his eyelashes glowed in its light. "Jessie, I haven't been with anyone since I met you. Fuck, I can't even imagine being with anyone else."

I breathed out. "Me neither."

"Why are we taking it slowly again?"

"You aren't allowed to date an Otter's sister."

He snorted. "Fuck Dylan. I bet you he wouldn't even care. And, if we had told him, I wouldn't be stuck being a piece of arm candy this weekend."

There's one thing that Kane isn't lacking, and that's confidence. "In the Calvin Klein model situation, *you're* the arm candy?" I joked, trying to lighten the tone.

The sides of his mouth turned up slightly and then he shrugged. "Are you sure you're okay with it?"

I had thought about it the entire boat ride across the lake. No, I didn't love the idea of Kane going to a black-tie event with a model, but at the time it seemed like the decision was going to make his home life a lot smoother, and I just wanted to keep things simple for him. "Kane, I'm going to be there. It's not like you're going behind my back. I've decided to treat it like a business transaction, and maybe if you do too, it won't bother you so much."

He tilted his head and stared at the horizon. "I hadn't thought of it that way," he said.

"And, I trust you." I couldn't believe those words had just come out of my mouth, and I repeated them, if only for myself to hear. "I trust you, Kane."

Kane draped his leg over the side of the dock and dangled his foot in the water. "Jessie, you are an incredible woman."

"Wait," I said.

He drew his foot out of the lake and looked at me. "I want to amend that statement." I couldn't hide my smile, and the concern lifted from his eyes. "I trust you everywhere except at the end of a dock." I crab walked on my hands and feet away from the edge.

"Come here, Jess."

His voice was serious. He stood and held out his hand, but I hesitated. "I'm not going to throw you in, I promise." I let Kane pull me to my feet.

He stroked my hair. Behind him, the sky looked like strawberry sorbet as he held both of my hands in his. "I love you." The water lapped against the dock as my entire body flushed hot with adrenaline.

Tears brimmed in my eyes and I didn't hold them back. "I love you, too." Tears spilled down my cheeks and Kane brushed them away with his thumbs and then kissed me softly. I whimpered into his mouth and then laced my fingers around his thick neck, kissing my boyfriend hard.

When we finally broke apart, the sun had disappeared, leaving purple streaks across the horizon. It wouldn't be long before the first stars started to appear.

"Do you want to stay at my house tonight?" I asked.

"There's nowhere I'd rather be than your uncomfortable bed, Jess." He slid his fingers between mine and we walked down the dock. As we neared the marina, I pulled my hand from his and pointed to the light that shone out from the garage bay. "Dylan."

"He's still here?" Kane asked.

"He's taken on a second job. That's where he's been every night. We didn't have to worry about him walking in on us at my house after all."

There had been a few nights when I'd shoved my pillow in my mouth to muffle my moans and screams when Kane's face was between my legs.

Kane and I continued walking, but he took a step away from me. "The exhibition series is over on Saturday."

I thought that the player's code was really fucking stupid, but Kane took it seriously – almost as serious as his coin, or not having sex in the dressing room. "Just a few more days, Jess," he whispered. Dylan was suspended for the rest of the season, which included the exhibition games. Until they were over, he was still technically an Otter, and as an Otter's sister, I was technically 'off-limits.'

"He's not going to care," I had argued, but it didn't make a difference. Kane wasn't going to break the code, and I wasn't going to point out the fact that just because no one knew about 'us' didn't mean that he wasn't breaking it.

Once we passed the danger of the marina and were safely seated inside the Volvo, Kane threaded his fingers between mine and I drove to my house with one hand, squinting through the cracked windshield. The radio was playing that Kid Rock/Sheryl Crow *Picture* song and Kane turned it up.

"Really?"

"What? It's a good song," he smiled and squeezed my hand.

From that moment, I knew that hearing *Picture* would bring me back to the time in my life when I'd felt the most complete – and even though I hated the song, I loved it for giving me that memory.

My belly clenched with a combination of excitement and guilt. That coin was in my skate bag. I had completely forgotten about it. I found it the first day I skated at McManus's place and tucked it in my bag, planning to turn it in to the lost and found. I knew he'd be ecstatic when I gave it back to him, but I wanted to wait – he needed to know it wasn't the coin that made him a great player – it was him.

THE BED creaked as I slid under the sheet and I clicked on the fan that sat on my nightstand.

"Did you set your alarm?" Kane asked.

"Three-thirty," I said.

I snuggled into his armpit and he squeezed me tightly, partly to cuddle, but mostly to stop me from falling out of the bed. I ran my fingers through the hair on his chest. He was the first boyfriend I'd ever had with a chest full of hair, and I was surprised to find out that I loved it. Running my fingers through his hair and hearing him murmur in appreciation had awoken a primal side of me I didn't know existed. My lower belly clenched with the urge to feel him inside me. "Kane." My fingertips explored his chest and trailed back and forth between his pecs.

"Mmmmmm?" His eyes were still closed, and I wondered how close he was to falling asleep.

"What do you think people would say if I showed up at the gala with you?"

He opened his eyes and kissed my forehead. "That we look good together?"

"That's not what I meant. I mean, do you think your family will accept the fact that you're with me, and not with someone who has an important last name like Yates?"

Kane propped himself up on his elbows and my fingertips moved their exploratory mission to his now popping six-pack. "Tiffany might, but who gives a shit. My dad won't care, just as long as you're not a Boston fan." His chest shook a little as he chuckled at his bad joke.

"Are you sure?"

"I'm sure, baby. And if for some reason he does, who cares? You're the woman I want, even if your last name is Mold."

I smacked his flexed abs. "Moss is so much better than

Mold." I threw my leg over Kane, straddled his hard body, and kissed him. His cock tented out the sheets and easily bridged the seven-inch gap between our bodies, the tip brushing the crotch of my panties. I pulled the sheet down, revealing his manhood in all its rock-hard glory. "You weren't going to sleep," I said eyeing his cock, my body aching for the moment when its girth pressed into me.

"Guilty." He held up his hands stickup style. "Now get those fucking panties off." In an athletic feat worthy of an Olympic gymnast, he tossed me off his body while somehow rolling me underneath him, so that he was now straddling me. He jammed his hands into the front of my pink lace underwear and ripped them apart.

"Hey, those were new." I couldn't believe that he had just torn them in half.

"I'll buy you a new pair."

His voice was muffled as he kissed the increasingly sensitive space on my belly just below my belly button. My feet involuntarily pressed into the mattress, lifting my hips off the bed. Kane's face was so close, I could feel the warmth from his breath between my legs and my body prickled with goosebumps. "Kane, I don't know how much longer I can take this teasing." I balled my fists up in the sheets as he moved closer, his scruff tickling my sensitive skin as his breathing teased the ache between my legs. He moved to kiss my belly again but returned to tease between my legs once more. I writhed in the sheets.

"I can make you come without touching you."

"Oh god, Kane. Your breath IS touching me," I moaned, and he blew on me like he was blowing out birthday candles. I was convinced he was going to tease me all night long, so when the warmth of his lips finally met my skin, I flinched and then groaned as pleasure rippled through my torso right to my fingertips. I gripped the sheets and it only took about three seconds for the orgasm to crash through my body.

Panting, I laid there, my face flushed with heat as I tried to recover, and I heard the sound of Kane biting open a condom wrapper. He extracted the sheets from my right hand and kissed my palm. "How was that?" He kissed up my arm, his stubble tickling me as he trailed across my collar-bone, holding my hand in his. He kissed my lips and his cock lingered between my legs, waiting. He pressed into me lightly, his hips moving slowly like his lips, teasing me, retreating, then coming back for more. I hooked my leg around his back and pushed on his ass with my heel, urging him to thrust. I needed Kane Fitzgerald to make me feel whole.

"Uh, uh." He resisted the pressure and continued his subtle rocking, his arms trembling at my sides. I grabbed his forearms and nipped at his lip. His eyelashes batted open and he groaned. "I love you, Jessie. And fuck, I love this tight pussy," he growled, and I gasped with the force of him thrusting into me with all his strength. The tender and teasing hockey jock gone, replaced with a wild eyed and growling man. "Oh Jessie," he groaned and gripped my shoulder tight, his cock twitching inside of me before he collapsed on top of me, panting.

Before I could say anything, he propped himself up on his elbows, still hard, still inside of me. "It's so hard for me to control myself when I'm near you, even kissing you, but taking it slowly, that..." He paused to catch his breath. "That was..."

"Incredible," I finished, letting my fingers linger in his hair. He rested his head on my bare chest. "Kane," I whispered. His breath had slowed to the even pace that I recognized. He was sleeping. "Good night."

Letting him go to the Gala with Bronwyn Yates wasn't a mistake. He was mine and no waif-like supermodel could ever replace what we had. I grunted under Kane's weight as I reached for the phone, it was only eleven p.m. He needed some sleep. I needed some rest. For the first time since I'd moved home, I turned off the alarm labeled 'practice.' I wanted to be in Kane's arms more than I wanted to work on that damn lutz. One day off couldn't hurt.

The phone chimed as I held it in my hand. It was a text from my brother.

Dylan: Call me, it's important.

I let my thumb hover over Dylan's number, but didn't want to wake Kane. It could wait until morning. I tossed the phone on my nightstand and nestled into my boyfriend's arms.

27

KANE

SOMETHING WAS WRONG. I felt too rested. Jessie was snuggled into me, holding onto my arm in her sleep. The light on her face was brighter than it should've been.

"Jessie," I whispered.

Her lips parted and she let out a light snore that almost sounded like a purr. "Jess." I nudged her and pulled my arm out from underneath her. "We slept in." She rolled into me and murmured something incomprehensible. "Jess, wake up."

Nothing but a nuzzle and then her light snore-purr, which was cute as hell. I reached over her, and my heart sank when I checked the time on her phone. "Jessie, it's 5:45. We both missed our practice." I shifted her off my body and sat up, trying to figure out what I would tell Covington.

Jessie rubbed her eyes and sat, stretching her arms over her head. "It's okay. I turned off the alarm, I thought we both deserved a little rest." She rested her hand on my morning wood and leaned in to kiss me. As tempting as it was, Kane Fitzgerald didn't blow off practice, and as far I knew, Jessie Moss didn't either.

"Jess, what were you thinking?" I sat on the edge of the bed and patted the sheets looking for my boxers.

She sat beside me and rested her hand on my shoulder. "Come back to bed, Kane."

"No, Jess. I think I'm going to go." I got dressed and slipped my phone into my pocket.

She swung her legs out of the sheets and stood. "Come on, Kane, it was just one practice."

I took a deep breath, holding in my anger. If Dylan was in the house, the last thing he needed to hear was some guy yelling at his sister. "You of all people, you..." I pointed at her and she leaned back, "should know that that's not true. The Jessie I know never misses practice. She knows that she's going to the Olympics and Olympians don't sleep in, they don't miss practice just to what, get a couple of hours of extra sleep and maybe a morning fuck?" I hissed through my teeth.

Shit. Her eyes were filling with tears. "I'm sorry for just wanting a few extra hours in bed with you this morning."

I was an asshole.

"Jess, I—"

She stepped into a pair of jeans and zipped up a green hoodie over her bare breasts.

"What are you doing?"

She turned and her eyes flashed, "You don't have a car here, I have to drive you."

"I'm sorry, Jess. I know how important skating is to you, and you know how important my hockey career is to me."

"It was irresponsible, I get it." Her voice was growing louder in its defensiveness. "It won't happen again." She shoved her feet into her Birks and stomped down the stairs. If Dylan was sleeping, he wasn't anymore. I followed her down the stairs and held my hand on the front door over her head. She pulled hard, but I wouldn't let her open it. She turned, crossed her arms, and leaned against the lace curtain.

"Jessie, come on," I whispered.

"You don't have to whisper." She pointed to the tray of assorted footwear beside the door. "His work boots are gone. Dylan's not here."

I was mad at her, but not enough to turn it into a full-blown argument. I teased her finger, trying to get her to uncross her arms. "Jessie, let's not fight about this."

She opened her mouth to retort, but I didn't give her the chance. "I'm sorry."

She softened and let me hold her hand. Looking down, she said, "You're right, and I don't think that I'm mad at you." She sighed. "I'm mad at myself. We should've gone to practice this morning."

She beat herself up worse than I did. It was something that I saw in other players gunning for the NHL, and I knew firsthand what was running through her mind.

"Hey." I leaned in and kissed her lightly. "Why don't we do something else and call it a cross-training day."

She looked at me and completely softened. "I overreacted. I'm sorry," she said.

"I did too," I whispered into her hair.

"What did you have in mind?" she asked. "For the cross-training."

I scooped her up in my arms and tossed my hat onto the coffee table. "Cardio and core." I kissed her hard and took the stairs two at a time back to her bedroom where we made love, or, fuck that, what we did was hot, sweaty, dirty – and most importantly – pulse racing.

AFTER I DROPPED Kane at his cottage I came home and had a long steamy shower. The sex with Kane had left me exhausted, and true to our cross-training strategy, my entire body was sore - the good kind. I stayed in the shower until the hot water tank gave up its battle and the water ran cold.

As I padded to my bedroom, I heard rustling from downstairs in the kitchen.

"Jessie," Dylan shouted. "Is there any hot water left?"

"Ah, no, sorry."

I heard him groan. "Why didn't you call me last night?" he shouted.

"I was busy," I yelled from behind my closed bedroom door.

"What?" he shouted.

I threw on my chip truck clothes and opened the door, "I'll be down in a sec. Stop yelling."

Dylan was sitting at the kitchen table, waiting for me. "You look like..."

"Shit?" I interrupted. I took an apple from the basket on the counter and crunched a huge bite.

"I was going to say tired," he said. Dylan's work clothes were just as stained as mine, only his were mostly motor oil and probably blood. His eyes were hooded and his skin too sallow for this time of year.

"Ditto, bro. You look like a zombie." He glanced at me, the circles under his eyes matched the dark blue of his work shirt. I poured myself a cup of coffee and joined him at the table. "Dylan, you can't keep going like this." He looked like he was about to fall asleep in the chair.

"We need the money, Jess." He jerked awake and took a sip of his coffee.

He wasn't wrong, and it made my heart ache to see him looking so defeated. A garment bag was draped over the back of one of the kitchen chairs. "What's this?" I started to unzip the cover.

"My suit, for that fundraiser tonight."

"You're going to the Gala?" I raised my eyebrows.

"Yeah. Coach wants the entire team there. All the guys are going."

"Even though you're suspended?"

Dylan laughed. "Yeah, even though I'm probably getting kicked off as soon as the exhibition game is over." He played with the handle of his mug, his lips forming a tight line.

My heart surged and ached at the same time. If Dylan wasn't an Otter, then Kane and I wouldn't be breaking the stupid team code. But that team had kept my brother out of trouble for the past few years. If it weren't for hockey, Dylan would probably be in jail right now, or, I gulped, dead. "You don't know that," I said.

Dylan shrugged, but I knew that he cared.

"Are you taking a date to the Gala?" I thought about Paige and wondered if the two of them were still messing around.

"Nah, just going to show my face and come home." He finished his coffee and then poured himself another. "Is it okay if I take the car tonight?" He sat down at the table. "I completely forgot to check with you."

"That's okay. We haven't seen each other much these past few weeks."

"I guess that's what having two jobs does to a person. Ships in the night or whatever the hell that saying is." Dylan smiled at me.

"Three jobs," I said.

Dylan paused mid-sip. "Three?"

"I'm serving at the Gala tonight, Paige got me the job through Valerock – they're catering it. She's picking me up after my shift at the chip wagon, so you can have the car all night. As long as you promise not to—"

"Drink?" Dylan said. "I actually quit. I haven't had a drink in days."

"Really?" Then why do you look like shit, is what I wanted to say, but didn't. Then I caught a glimpse of myself in the mirror behind Dylan. My eyes looked exactly like his. "Dylan, we can't keep up this pace forever. I want you to stop working nights."

"That's not your decision, Jess."

"You're right." I scratched the back of my head. "But I know why you're doing it, and I'm not going to take the money. I've decided not to go back to the Academy."

A weight lifted off my shoulders as the words tumbled out of my mouth. Words that I hadn't planned, words that had never crossed my mind until that very moment. We were killing ourselves to scrape together money to send me back to the Academy. I couldn't do that to Dylan anymore. My mind immediately rushed to visions of waking up with Kane, of summer nights around campfires, and skinny dipping under the full moon. Of having the kind of summer life that I only dreamed about while I was busy lacing up my skates.

"Oh, shit." Dylan pushed away from the table and almost tipped over backward on his chair. "I can't believe I forgot." He ran to the living room. He returned with a piece of paper in one hand and an Otters' hat in the other.

"Why didn't you call me last night? I said it was important." He returning to the kitchen holding out Kane's hat like an accusation. The number eighty-eight was stitched into the back of it, there was no mistaking its owner.

"I was tired. I fell asleep," I muttered while my brain

raced a million trying to formulate an explanation for why Kane's hat was in our house.

"Jess. Was Fitzy here?"

"He left that," I pointed to the hat, "at the rink after practice. I was going to bring it to our next practice." I didn't look at Dylan while I lied.

Dylan turned the hat in his hands a couple of times and then tossed it to me. "You don't have to give up, Jessie. The insurance money came through." He set the paper on the table in front of me and smoothed it out. The bold 'approved' stood out amongst the paragraphs of jargon. "You can start back at the Academy right away, and with the money we've saved, we should be able to get you one of those costumes designed by that fancy Russian company."

I scanned the letter, it was less money than we had expected, but more than enough to pay the Academy's tuition. I should've been happy, but instead, my stomach clenched into a knot, my visions of campfires and night-swimming disappearing as quickly as they arrived. "Dylan, I'm not going back." The second time the words came out, they came out with conviction. I wasn't going back, I was going to stay right here, with Kane.

Dylan set his coffee cup on the table, much harder than necessary. "What the hell is going on with you? You have to go back."

"Maybe next year," I said. "I'll put my half into a savings account."

Dylan tilted his head and stared at the ceiling, then brought his face between his hands. "This is your chance to get out of here, Jess. And I don't need any of that money. I'm doing just fine. It's all yours – take it and get the hell out of this town."

"I've lost my lutz." It was a partial lie, I was landing it

about fifty percent of the time, but one that he might understand,

Dylan stood and slammed his hand down on the paper. "So, get back to the Academy and find your damn flutz."

Over the years, Dylan had consistently screwed up all of my figure skating jump names on purpose. It must've been such an ingrained habit that he even did it when angry.

"Dylan, it's not your decision." I dumped out the remainder of my coffee, grabbed my backpack, and headed out to the chip truck, my mind racing with the possibility of never having to sweat through another fish frying sauna day again. Maybe it was time to join Paige at Valerock. If I didn't have to get up in the middle of the night to skate, I could get a job that paid good money.

The oxygen pumped through my veins as I pedaled through town. Maybe skating had been a noose around my neck. Was I free? The wind whipped in my hair and flapped my t-shirt against my skin - I certainly felt free.

I didn't have to worry about tuition anymore. The next big thing I had to worry about today was getting through a day of serving French fries, and then seeing my man with another woman on his arm.

NAKED.

That's how I felt in the Valerock uniform. A skin-tight black dress with a scoop neck that plunged to the middle of my breastbone.

"You look fabulous," Paige smiled as I got into the car crammed with four other Valerockers.

"Thanks." I tugged at the neckline for the millionth time. "It's a little big up top here." The dresses were clearly designed for the DD-sized crowd – and glancing at the other servers in the car, they were all members of that club.

"This is Avery," Paige pointed to the driver who waved into the rear-view mirror. "And Maria and Sammi." "Hi," the two pretty blond girls chorused.

"This is Jessie."

"The figure skater," Avery said as she backed the car out of the driveway. "Paige has told us all about you. When are you going to come and work with us?"

"Actually, I was hoping to talk to the manager about that tonight." I was flying by the seat of my pants, but if I stayed in Laketown, raking in tips was a lot better than frying fish for minimum wage. Paige turned and raised her eyebrows at me. "My skating schedule has opened up a little bit." Even though it was kind of true, the reality that I'd just decided to quit, -- no not quit -- pause, my skating career was just starting to sink in.

"I think you'd be the perfect fit." Avery gunned the Volkswagen and we headed through town.

"For sure," Sammi smiled.

"You should probably wait to say that until after tonight." A nervous laugh escaped. "I might spill a tray of drinks on some socialite."

"Honey," Avery shook her head. "Working at Valerock has nothing to do with your ability to carry plates back and forth to a kitchen." Her eyes glanced in the rear-view and then looked me up and down. "You've got what it takes."

It felt dirty and I didn't like it – but I also didn't want to make minimum wage for the foreseeable future. I gulped down the feminist in me and took out my beeswax Chapstick.

"Here." Sammi rested her forearm on mine, stopping me

from applying my lip balm, and handed me a tube of lipstick.

"Thanks." Looking over Avery's shoulder into the review mirror, I applied the matte red color as evenly as I could, pausing until we passed one of the potholes I knew was coming up. So far, the little car's wheels had bumped through every single one of them.

The restaurant's pontoon boat was waiting at the marina with ten other red-lipsticked Valerockers already on board. The boat ride took about twenty minutes and the sun was setting as we arrived at The Island Club. After a quick tour of the kitchen and dining room, we were ordered to light the tea lights on the white linen-covered tables. The volunteer committee members, all in designer couture and updos, flitted around holding clipboards and fussing with the floral arrangements.

"You." I turned in response and pointed at myself. "Yes, you."

It was Tiffany.

I raised my hand in a half-wave like a nervous freshman but stopped when I realized that there was zero recognition in Tiffany's eyes. "Grab that box of auction items and take it out to the patio." Tiffany pointed her tanned arm at a box full of signed hockey jerseys. It was an order.

"Ooookay," I stammered. I wasn't exactly shocked at Tiffany's lack of manners, but I was surprised that she didn't recognize me - unless it was an act - and in that case, Kane's stepmom deserved an Oscar. I picked up the box of jerseys and stepped into the evening air. For the first time that year, a southern breeze brought warmth to the night. A distant campfire flickered on the shoreline and under the strands of white twinkle lights a row of banquet tables featured silent auction items ranging from rounds of golf at the Island Club

Course, to fly fishing trips, to week-long stays at private cottages complete with celebrity chefs, personal trainers, and the hottest DJs - valued at over one hundred thousand dollars.

Another Barbie volunteer barked an order at me. "Fold those nicely and put them in front of the right item number." The Real Housewife of Laketown didn't wait for me to respond and walked away. I closed my eyes and inhaled. *It's only one night* I thought to myself. *You can get through this.*

"Jessica?"

The hair stood up on my arms. I finished folding the last shirt and turned to see Tiffany.

"Hi." I tried to give her a bright smile.

"I didn't recognize you at first." She glanced over my shoulder, studying my folding job. "I didn't think Valerock hired local girls." She stepped beside me and surveyed the table.

What was up with this bitch? My short nails cut into my palms as I squeezed my hands into fists. I wanted to tell her off, but I couldn't lose my job on my first night, and more importantly, the evil woman was Kane's mom, or rather, stepmom. Going for dinner with Tiffany Fitzgerald would be a little awkward in the future if I told her to go fuck herself tonight.

She patted the jersey and leaned into me, her voice barely a whisper, "We've taken an inventory, so we'll know if anything goes missing." Then just to be a total c-word, she picked up the jersey and dropped it onto the table in a heap. "Fold that better."

Frozen with shock, I watched my boyfriend's stepmom walk away after accusing me of being a thief.

"Jess." Paige's voice brought me back to reality, and I

swiped at angry tears.

"Yeah." I wiped my hands on my dress and quickly folded the McManus jersey.

"Team meeting in the kitchen." Paige's smiled faded from her face as she looked at me. "Are you okay?"

I sucked in some air and blinked away the tears. "Yeah, I'm fine. Let's go."

I followed Paige through the glowing dining room, past the flute and guitar duo warming up in the corner and into the kitchen, wondering how I was going to make it through the night without pushing Tiffany into the lake.

Avery gave the team a pep talk and then armed us with trays of champagne flutes filled with Dom Perignon.

"The players are on their way," she smiled and clapped. The servers cheered like they were at a rock concert. I held the tray with two hands, surprised at how heavy and precarious the whole thing felt.

"One hand underneath," Paige whispered through the side of her mouth.

"And ladies," Avery grinned. "Make an impression tonight, but under no circumstances can you go home with the players..." she paused dramatically. "tonight." She winked. "Make an impression and save the fun stuff for later this summer."

There was an excited titter around us, but I was focused on balancing the tray. Paige was right; it was easier with one hand.

"They're here. Let's go, let's go, let's go." Avery led the train of excited women to the dock where the volunteers stood waving sparklers as the first of the line of antique boats approached. My heart hammered in my chest knowing that one of those twinkling lights across the bay belonged to Kane.

28

KANE

THE MASTERCRAFT WAS MY BOAT. And if it was up to me, that's what we would've taken to the gala, but Tiffany had left strict instructions that her family was to arrive in the *Power Play*. My dad didn't trust anyone else to drive his baby, so the two of us stepped into her perfectly detailed interior and headed to the south end of the lake to pick up Bronwyn – my date.

I still couldn't believe that I had agreed to take another woman to the Gala, but Jessie seemed okay with it and it was making my dad happy. At the Yates island compound, Bronwyn stood on the dock, the warm wind billowing out a silky pink dress.

Tiffany had made all of the arrangements and until this moment, Bronwyn and I had never communicated. My first impression? Yes, she was beautiful, in the traditional, I'm-a-model-and-don't-eat-anything kind of way.

My dad idled the boat at the end of the dock, and I hopped out to help my date step into the *Power Play*.

"Hi," I smiled. "I'm Kane."

"I figured," she smiled. "Wouldn't it be quite a coincidence if some other handsome hockey star showed up at my dock at this very moment?"

"Quite," I laughed.

"Bronwyn," she said holding out her hand. I took it and she went in for a two-cheek kiss greeting. Tiffany and her friends always did the same to me, so I was used to it.

"Shall we?" I gestured to the *Power Play*.

"Nice chauffeur," she laughed. "Or is he our chaperone?" she whispered and winked.

I cursed under my breath. She obviously hadn't gotten the message that this was a platonic favor.

"Nice to see you, Bronwyn." She and my dad exchanged the same kiss cheek greeting. She slipped out of her strappy heels and I helped her into the boat. The *Power Play* slipped gracefully across the starry night's reflection in the calm water. Bronwyn edged closer to me and crossed her legs, the high slit in her dress parting to reveal her tanned thin thighs. I pretended not to notice and edged away slightly. As soon as we got to the gala, I would set things straight with her. My blood was boiling that Tiffany had put me in this position and as I kept my gaze on the shore-line, I wondered how well the model was going to take the news.

The clubhouse windows were glowing, and we could hear the music from miles away. By the time we reached the dock, the slips were almost fully occupied with gleaming wooden boats, with a few cigarette boats thrown in for good measure.

The tuxedo-clad attendants caught the *Power Play* and tied her lines, while my dad and I hopped onto the dock. I turned to help Bronwyn out of the boat and let her hold my arm while she balanced, slipping each of her feet into her high heels.

"You go ahead, dad," I said. "I want to have a chat with Miss Yates."

My dad smiled and saluted. I laughed and shook my head. When did he turn into such a dork?

"Bronwyn," I turned to face her. The wind was whipping her hair and she shivered in the breeze. "I think there's been a misunderstanding."

She knitted her brow at me, as far as the Botox would let her. "Miss Yates?" She reached to touch my arm and stepped in close enough that her blond strands tickled my cheek.

"You're a beautiful woman."

Her eyes opened wide and she took a step backward. "You're kidding me?" she muttered.

"Listen, it's just—"

"Unbelievable." She shook her head and crossed her arms. "My fiancé left me less than a month ago, and now you're dumping me before we're even together."

Well, that's presumptuous. I thought to myself.

"I thought you knew that I was doing this as a favor."

She huffed. "So now I'm a charity case? That's rich." Her words were bold, but her voice wavered.

"You are incredibly gorgeous." She smiled and I continued. "I was told that you just wanted to have someone escort you here."

She raised her eyebrows and let out a little laugh. "So, what? You're a gigolo?" Her shoulders softened and she uncrossed her arms.

"I was told that you wanted to be photographed with someone. And have someone to get you drinks, or make sure that your heels don't go through the dock boards. That kind of stuff."

"I wish someone would've told me that," she said.

"Me too," I whispered. "You should also probably know

that I have a girlfriend and she knows that I've offered to be your 'date' tonight."

Her eyes searched mine. "Why? Why would you agree to something like that?"

"We're kind of keeping our relationship a secret for now. And it seemed like the nice thing to do, and my stepmom--" My mouth was running.

She interrupted. "Strong-armed you?" Bronwyn laughed. "She's quite the woman, that Tiffany." The disdain in Bronwyn's voice was apparent. "Kane, I appreciate your candor and it's probably too soon for me to get excited about someone new anyway, although you are a cute one..." She drew her fingertip down the front of my royal blue tie, then snapped it away. Hers was the boldness that came with extreme wealth and good looks.

The weight on my shoulders lifted. "Thank you for understanding."

"But," she held up her finger. "I can't look like a fool here tonight. You said that no one knows about your girlfriend?"

"Not yet."

"Is she here tonight?" Bronwyn pointed to the clubhouse.

"Yeah." I didn't like where she was going with this.

"This just gets better and better." She shook her head. A boat approached the dock and she slipped her hand into the crook of my arm. "Let's walk," she said. We headed towards the sound of music and laughter. "I just went through a breakup that made international headlines. I'm sure that you saw them."

I hadn't, but I kept that to myself and nodded. "Tonight, Fitzgerald, as far anyone here needs to know, you're my date. All I'm asking is to put up appearances."

"Okay. Sure." I thought that was the agreement anyway.

She stopped and gripped my arm tighter than I thought her birdlike fingers were capable, "Don't you dare make a fool out of me."

"Got it."

"I'm serious." Her fingers tightened even more.

"Okay, okay," I laughed and patted her hand. "I got it." How hard could it be?

I knew exactly how hard when I saw Jessie's silhouette amongst the other Valerock girls. As we approached, she glanced up at me and smiled, but it faltered as her gaze flitted to the manicured fingers on my suit. Suddenly, Bronwyn's hand felt like it weighed a thousand pounds and all I wanted to do was rip it from my arm.

"Champagne?" Jessie's lips quivered through her smile.

"Please." Bronwyn accepted a champagne flute.

"Kane?" Jessie held out a glass for me, they were slight, but I saw the tremor rings in the champagne.

"Sure, thanks," I smiled at her and wished that I could tell her that everything was going to be okay. I pursed my lips as Bronwyn slid her hand back into the crook of my arm.

"Shall we, Fitzgerald?" She pointed to the entrance.

"Have a good night," Jessie said.

"You too," I almost reached out to squeeze her hand, but caught myself and shoved my hand in the pocket of my suit jacket. I held the door open for Bronwyn and glanced back, wanting to give Jessie a little wave, something reassuring, but she was too busy handing out champagne to notice.

The club was bustling, and I saw at least three NHL players in the first thirty seconds. Jake McManus was talking to Coach Covington beside the auction table. Even though we were all wearing suits, everyone but me was sporting their team hat, the blue brims scattered throughout the crowd. The band was covering some classic rock songs and I hummed along to *Love the One You're With*. I glanced at the woman on my arm. I can't be with the one that I love tonight, but that didn't mean that I was going to do something stupid. I knew what I had with Jessie was special, the punch-in-the-gut feeling kind of special. Her smile and her touch, both had too much of a hold on me to throw what we had away for an orgasm inside a model's mouth.

"That was your girl, wasn't it?" Bronwyn leaned in and whispered into my ear. "The one with the champagne."

"Jessie," I said. "That's her."

"She is cute." Bronwyn took a sip of her champagne, her blue eyes scanning the action.

Yes, Jessie was cute, but coming from Bronwyn it sounded condescending. Jessie was so much more. "She's a fucking goddess," I growled.

Bronwyn narrowed her eyes and smiled at me at the same time, a disconcerting combination. "Well, she's a lucky goddess to have a man like you." Bronwyn kissed my cheek. "Let's go check out the silent auction and you can introduce me to some players."

"Sure." I drained my champagne and handed it to a passing server. But before we threaded our way through the crowd I turned and saw Jessie at the doorway, her face was white, the forced smile from earlier completely gone.

"Fitzy!" I felt a strong hand on my shoulder and turned to see the huge shit-eating grin on Leo the Lion's face. Mike was just behind him, clutching a beer in each hand.

"Leo." I shook his hand and we did a one-armed hug. "Keeping it classy are you, Mikey?" I pointed to his double drinks.

"It's an open bar," he grinned and then took a swig of beer.

"Leo, Mike." I stepped aside and presented Bronwyn, "This is Bronwyn Yates." The last name went over both of their heads. Neither of them were cottagers. They were from other towns and lived at the Hockey Camp dorms.

"Pleased to meet you." Leo thrust out his hand. Bronwyn accepted and leaned in for her snobby cheek kiss. Leo faltered but quickly figured out what was going on. When they pulled back his face was the color of our practice jerseys – red. Mikey expertly transferred a beer bottle to his left hand. I held my breath, ready for a disastrous interaction and I wasn't disappointed. Mikey went for the opposite cheek that Bronwyn presented, and then when he changed course, his lips brushed hers. I had to hand it to the guy, he wasn't lacking in confidence. Instead of pulling back. he just rolled with it and planted the kiss smack dab on her lips with fervor.

"That's how they do it in Italy," he laughed as a stunned Bronwyn stepped to my side.

"Maybe if you're a mob boss," Leo laughed.

"Sorry, Fitzy, innocent mistake." Mikey stepped backward. If it had been Jessie, I would have been pissed, but he could take Bronwyn out back and have his way with her for all I cared. "Lips off, Mikey," I laughed and punched him in the arm for show. "But the apology should be directed at the lady."

"My sincerest apologies." Mikey took off his Otters' hat and bowed to Bronwyn.

"Apology accepted," she laughed. For an heiress, she had a surprisingly good sense of humor. "That shade looks good on you," she chuckled as she pointed to his coral lipstick stained lips.

I pulled Leo aside while Bronwyn handed Mikey a cocktail napkin. "Can you take her and introduce her to some people?"

Leo raised his eyebrows, "Like who?"

"I don't know. Maybe some of the NHL guys."

"I only know McManus," he whispered.

"Perfect." I clapped him on his back. "Bronwyn, you'll have to excuse me for a moment. Leo, would you take care of my date until I'm back?"

"Gladly," he grinned and crooked his elbow. "M'lady." Leo looked more like a surfer than a hockey player and Bronwyn didn't hesitate to take his arm. Relieved of my date duties I scanned the crowded room for Jessie and spotted her by the entrance to the kitchen. I wove through the crowd, not letting her chestnut ponytail out of my sight.

"Are these smoked salmon?" I whispered into her ear from behind. She turned slowly and presented the tray of appetizers to me. "Line caught from the Pacific," she said.

"They look great," I said loudly. Then quietly, "So do you."

My heart rushed as a blush spread across her jawbone.

"This is harder than I thought it was going to be," she said.

I wanted to reach out to hold her hand but resisted. "You're not talking about the serving, are you?"

"No." Her eyes glanced over to the small crowd surrounding Jake McManus, which now included Leo and Bronwyn.

"Listen." I stepped to her side and ran my thumb along the back of her arm. "I want you to know that you have nothing to worry about. At all." I took a cracker from her tray and popped it into my mouth.

"I know," she smiled. "But thank you."

I brushed my lips with the cocktail napkin. "I told her about you."

"You did?" Her eyes grew wide.

"I wanted her to know that this is just for show." I didn't need to tell her that Bronwyn had different plans at the start of the evening.

"And it looks like she and Leo are hitting it off." I turned to see Bronwyn laugh and then rest her hand on Jake McManus' arm. "Or she and Jake are hitting it off. It's hard to tell from here." She smiled and raised her eyebrows.

"Thank god," I whispered. "May I have another napkin?"

"Sure." She held up the stack. As I took it from her, I linked my pinky finger around hers and gripped it tightly. We locked eyes and squeezed her finger in a swear. She squeezed back.

"Kane," she whispered. "I have something to give to you."

A busty server rushed up to Jessie. "You need to get the sliders out," she barked and then disappeared into the crowd. The band was getting louder and with the free-flowing champagne, so was the crowd.

"Duty calls," she smiled.

"Wait, what do you have to give to me?" She had that twinkle in her eye that made my heart skip a beat.

"You'll have to wait and see," she winked. Before she could walk away, I leaned and whispered into her ear, "I love you." She smiled, winked, and then hurried to get her next tray of appetizers.

The rest of the night was a blur. I think that I held up my end of the deal better than Bronwyn. She spent the night flitting through the crowd, flirting with every single player. I kept my distance from Jessie, letting her do her job, but just because I wasn't beside her didn't mean that I didn't try to catch a glimpse of her any time I could. This woman had done something to me, she had taken a hold of my heart, and for the first time, I was ready to give it away – all of it.

I had a nice buzz from the bubbly, something that I rarely drank, and everything felt right in the world. Then I felt a tap on my shoulder. The unfriendly, I'm about to punch you in the face kind of tap. I turned slowly and a pair of familiar green eyes glared into mine. Dylan's were the same vibrant green as Jessie's, but he managed to make a pretty color look sinister. He shoved something into my hand. It was my Otters hat.

"You forgot this at my house," Dylan said. His eyes were steeled on mine, and I knew he was watching my face for clues.

"Thanks," I said. "I'm not sure how it got there."

Dylan jerked his head toward the door. "I have a fairly good idea. We need to have a chat. Outside."

I wasn't afraid of Dylan, but if I had a sister and one of the Otters had left clothes at my house, I would lose my shit. I wondered how much, if anything, Jessie had told him. I followed Dylan to the balcony that overlooked the docks. The club's flags flapped lightly above our heads and voices floated up from the docks below.

"What's up?" I asked.

Dylan glanced around the empty balcony. "Are you fucking my sister?" he asked, not bothering to whisper.

I recoiled at the language. "Is that the way you talk about your own flesh and blood?" I deflected.

He didn't bite. "Are you?" He stepped a little closer, officially crowding my personal space. I took a step back and crossed my arms. "I saw you talking to her, Fitzy. I know my sister. I know what's going on and it has to stop." He mirrored my crossed arms.

I wasn't going to dignify his aggression with a response, but no one on the face of this Earth was going to keep me away from Jessie. Teammate or not. "I care about her."

Dylan's face fell. "I was afraid of that." The aggression seemed to deflate from his body.

"I know that you're technically still on the team, but..."

"Stop right there." Dylan held up his hand. "I don't give a flying fuck about this whole team rules bullshit." He shook his head. "And I'm probably not going to be an Otter after tomorrow's game anyway."

I relaxed. "Then what's the big deal?" I gestured to the railing overlooking the water. Dylan stepped beside me and together we stood looking at the lake's inky surface.

"Do you want to be the reason she gives up her dream?" Dylan stared out over the water as he spoke.

"What do you mean? Give up her dream?"

"She didn't tell you?" Dylan shook his head, "Of course she didn't..."

"Didn't tell me what Dylan?" I was starting to get angry.

"The reason we were both working two jobs was to pay for her tuition to the skating academy."

"I know. I thought she had enough to go back."

"It was going to be tight." Dylan turned and leaned his hip against the railing. "Did she talk to you about staying here in Laketown?"

I turned and crossed my arms. "What? For the rest of the summer?" I was thoroughly confused.

"No, for good."

"No." I thought back to the past few days. We had talked about plans for a camping trip, that was it. "I thought she was heading back to the Academy after the summer."

Dylan cleared his throat. "I've never seen her like this." His voice softened. "She's in love with you."

"And I'm in love with her." I had said the words to Jessie, but it was the first time I had uttered them to someone else - and it felt good.

"Fitzy. The insurance money came through. She can quit her job at the chip truck. She can stop teaching you how to do crossovers and get back to the city to train – right away. You mean to tell me that she didn't tell you any of this?"

The news hit me like a punch to the gut. Why wouldn't she have told me? "That's great news." The words came out of my mouth before I stopped to think about what it would mean for our relationship.

"Yeah, it is. And she's going to give up on the Academy to stay here."

"No." I slumped. "She can't do that." I had worked my whole life with one moment in mind – hearing my name as a first-round draft pick for the New York Thunder. Jessie was the first woman I'd ever met with the same level of drive, and deep down I thought that was what made us soulmates, we were made of the same stuff. Dylan was silent as I processed the news. I didn't know what to say. Part of me was thrilled at the idea of having Jessie around indefinitely, the other part knew that I would never forgive myself for that selfishness. "She needs to go." I took a deep breath.

Dylan's lips pressed into a closed smile and his eyes were kind. "You really do love her."

"I do." I put on my hat and turned to look at the lake. Dylan squeezed my shoulder. "Then you know what you need to do."

I gulped down the lump in my throat. "I do." As I stared out at the water, the moon disappeared, and I felt the first few drops of rain on my head. "I'll give you a minute." Dylan clapped me on the back and left me on the balcony. I only came in when the rain started soaking through the brim.

29

JESSIE

TIFFANY TOOK the microphone and read the winning bids for the silent auction. I knew that Jake McManus was a big deal, but I couldn't believe that someone had paid five thousand dollars for his jersey.

"Can you believe she paid that much?" Paige leaned into me from our position at the back of the room. Bronwyn Yates was the winning bidder and she smiled coyly as McManus himself presented her with the jersey.

"It must be spun with gold," I muttered.

Bronwyn accepted a kiss on the cheek, and I tried not to stare as she took her place beside Kane.

"It's going to be a late night." Paige surveyed the room and started clearing champagne flutes from the closest table. "We're going to be here at least another three hours." We had tried to keep up, but the copious amounts of alcohol that were consumed had overwhelmed the dishwasher.

"Hey." Kane sidled up beside me.

"Hey," I smiled. "Your date has expensive taste." I elbowed him but he didn't smile back. Bronwyn was smiling and standing awfully close to McManus. "It also looks like

Jake might be stealing your date." We both glanced over just as Bronwyn and Jake broke out in laughter.

"Yeah, so much for putting on an act." He shrugged.

"Does that mean I can kiss you now?" I shuffled the tray into my right hand, trying to figure out how I could meet Kane's lips without smashing an entire tray load of champagne flutes.

"We have to talk, Jess."

He stepped away from me, far enough that I couldn't have reached out to touch him, something that my body had been longing to do all night long. "About what?" My chest constricted. This didn't sound good.

"There you are." Bronwyn interrupted the conversation and looped her arm through Kane's. The woman wasn't a monster, and she shot me a quick wink as she did it. I could read her mind, it was a 'don't worry, I've got a bigger fish on the line wink'. "Jake is having an afterparty. All the New York Lightning are going to be there."

Lightning. What a bimbo. I waited for Kane to roll his eyes and correct her, but he didn't.

"Are you kids having fun?" Tiffany appeared out of nowhere and slung her tanned arms over the shoulders of Kane and Bronwyn, sandwiching herself between the two of them.

"Don't they make a cute couple?" she slurred.

Bronwyn tilted her head and raised her eyebrows at me. She stepped out of Tiffany's embrace, and while rage coursed through my body, I tried to think of a way to extricate myself from the conversation without punching Kane's stepmom in the face.

"We're just friends. Kane was kind enough to be my date for the evening," Bronwyn said, and then to my surprise, draped her long arm over my shoulder. I held onto the tray of empty glasses for dear life. "We were just inviting some of the staff to the after-party."

"Staff?" When Tiffany laughed her face didn't move. "They have way too much work to do here." She set down her glass on the nearby table as if to make an example. "See you two there." Tiffany squeezed Bronwyn's arm and drunk whispered, which was almost a yell, "You're perfect for him." And then cast me an evil smirk as she teetered back into the party.

"Ignore her." Kane shook his head. "She's drunk."

Bronwyn watched Tiffany walk away and then turned to face me. "So, she's not a total bitch when she's sober?" Score another for Bronwyn, who was rising higher in my ranks by the minute.

Kane sighed. "You're right. She's equally bitchy. I just ignore her. I don't know what my dad sees in her."

Bronwyn took Tiffany's glass and set it on my tray. "Jessica, you've got more class in your pinky finger than she's got in her whole body."

"She does," Kane agreed, and then his eyes met mine. "Do you think you're going to make the after-party?" His eyes seemed sad. The shock from his 'we need to talk' bomb was still coursing through my veins, and I studied his body for any hints about what we needed to talk about.

"Paige seems to think we will be here for a few more hours."

"Not on my watch," Paige smiled as she hustled by, her tray of empty glasses jingling. The promise of an after-party complete with the entire Otters' team AND the New York Thunder had injected the Valerock servers with a heightened sense of urgency.

"It will depend on when the work gets done," I said.

Bronwyn glanced between Kane and me and then excused herself from the conversation.

"Sorry about Tiffany," he whispered.

"I'm kind of used to it," I sighed. I reached out to hold Kane's hand, if only for a minute, but he pulled away. The room blurred in front of me. "What do we need to talk about?"

Kane was shifting from foot to foot, and he wouldn't look at me. "It can wait until tomorrow."

I wanted to scream. "You can't do that," I whispered through gritted teeth. "You can't tell me we need to talk and then leave me hanging." Kane's eyes softened and he stepped beside me, sliding his thick fingers through mine behind my back, our hands hidden between my back and the wall. "Are we okay?" My words were shaky.

"Hey, guys." We were interrupted again. This time it was my obnoxious brother and just like that, Kane pulled his fingers free from mine.

"Hey, Dylan," he said. The muscle on Kane's jaw popped at the sight of my brother.

"Fitzy, got room in your boat? I hear you're heading to McManus' after-party."

"Are you?" I asked Kane. We hadn't discussed it, but I had hoped that Kane was going to drop Bronwyn off and then come back and get me.

"Bronwyn wants to hit it on the way home," he said.

"Great." Dylan slung his arm around Kane's shoulder. "Are you okay with a third wheel?"

Kane's lips narrowed to a tight line and Bronwyn returned to the group, her face flushed with excitement. "Are we going?"

"I'll see you there?" Kane asked as he was pulled away by

both Bronwyn and Dylan. I didn't know whether it was a statement or a question.

I gestured around the room. "I'll have to wait and see."

Bronwyn tugged at Kane's arm and he opened his mouth to say something more, but then gave in to her pull. "Hope to see you there." His farewell was generic and cold, and I hated it.

"Bye, Jess." Dylan waved and I turned away, not wanting him to see the redness in my face. I couldn't explain it, but it felt like Dylan had just ruined the rest of my night.

That's when I realized that Kane was wearing his hat.

A chill ran down my spine. What had Dylan done?

30

JESSIE

By the time we polished all the silver and put away the last piece of crystal, it was four o'clock in the morning.

Paige slumped into the chair beside me. I kicked off my shoes and massaged my feet. Waitressing was a lot harder than I thought it would be. "What's up with you?" I looked at my friend who was pouting.

"McManus' cottage is on an island."

I vaguely remembered the timber frame cottage that Kane had pointed out to me on our boat ride. "So?"

"Valerock isn't letting the water taxi drop us off there."

"Shit." As much as I was physically and emotionally exhausted from the evening, all I wanted to do was talk to Kane. The past few hours had been torture, the urge to throw up had waxed and waned as I cleared the tables and replayed my last moments with him.

"I know, right?" Paige wailed. "The best party of the year and we can't get there." She buried her head in her hands. "Unless..." she looked up at me, her eyes hopeful. "Do you think Kane would come and get us?"

If she'd asked me yesterday, I would've said yes, Kane

would show up to get me in a heartbeat. But after tonight, I wasn't so sure. "I'll call him."

His phone went straight to voicemail, so I sent him a text.

By the time the door to the Island Club was locked behind us, I still hadn't heard from him.

"No, go?" Paige sighed.

"No." I slid the phone into my purse. It clanked against the gold coin.

Why hadn't Kane messaged me back? "Maybe his phone is dead?" I shrugged, trying to play it cool in front of Paige and the other Valerock girls.

"Probably a good thing anyway," Avery sighed. I'm exhausted." She nudged Paige's arm with her fist. "Don't worry, Newbie. There will be plenty of NHL parties this summer."

Paige sat up a little straighter, her face brightening. "No biggie." She was trying to play it cool too.

When I got home, I glanced into Dylan's room, he was curled up in the blue and white hockey-themed quilt Mom had made him. While he was sleeping, he looked like the sweet brother I had grown up with. My heart softened as I watched the rise and fall of the quilt as he snored. I shut his door and checked my phone one last time before I fell into a dreamless sleep.

After what felt like hours of tossing and turning, I rolled and squinted at my phone. Still no response from Kane. The last thing my boyfriend had told me was that we needed to talk, and now he was ignoring me. I pulled my quilt over my head and curled up into a ball. It's early, I told myself, he's probably just sleeping. For the next three hours, sleep flirted with me, and my dreams taunted me, varying from visions of a mess of blond hair spread over Kane's chest to Tiffany's blood-red lips telling me she knew Kane would never fall for townie trash. When I bolted upright at nine a.m., I was covered in sweat and the remnants of the dreams made my stomach churn. I ran to the bathroom and dry heaved over the toilet. Something was wrong. I knew it deep down inside.

"You okay, Jess?" Dylan rapped on the door.

"I'm fine," my voice was gravelly.

"I've made breakfast. You could probably use something in your stomach."

I waited for Dylan to walk away and then splashed some water on my face and brushed my teeth. As I entered the kitchen, I was met with the sound of the blender. "What no bacon?" I asked.

"I made your gross smoothie." He held up two glasses filled with a dark green-brown mixture that looked like sludge.

"Thanks." I took the glass from his hand and set it down on the table.

Dylan took a sip of his glass and his eyes shot open wide. "Wow," he said. "This is disgusting."

"That means you made it right." I tried to be funny, but my heart wasn't in it. "How was your night?"

"Meh." He shrugged. "Are you going to try it?" He pointed to my glass with his.

"Give me a minute." I eyed the glass.

"Have you thought more about the Academy?" Dylan sat at the table, drew his lanky leg up, and put his bare foot on the seat.

I hadn't. The only thing that had gone through my mind since the last time we spoke was what the hell Kane wanted to talk to me about. "I didn't know you and Kane were all buddy-buddy," I said.

"We're not." Dylan took another sip of his smoothie and recoiled. "It doesn't get any better." He wiped away his green mustache with the back of his hand. "I just needed a ride to the after-party." Shrugging, he held my gaze, I knew that he knew, and he knew that I knew. There was no point in dancing around the elephant in the room. "Did you talk to Kane about me?"

"You?" he feigned incredulity. "Why the hell would I talk to him about you?"

Dylan wasn't biting. "I thought he might've said something about our lessons."

"Nah," Dylan stood up. "He was too into his date to notice anything I had to say."

"What?" I felt like I had been slapped. "I heard that they weren't even together," I mumbled, trying to recover from my outburst.

"Tell that to the room next to theirs." He finished the rest of his smoothie and then rinsed the glass in the sink. "Apparently, she's a screamer."

"Fuck off, Dylan." I stood and the kitchen chair toppled behind me. I lunged and threw the content of my glass in his face. He sputtered and calmly wiped the green goo from his eyes.

"Why do you care? You're just his coach." Bits of flax seeds stuck to my brother's face as he let the smoothie run down his cheeks and into the neck of his white t-shirt.

I knew that I couldn't defend our relationship. And after last night, maybe there wasn't a relationship to defend. "You're lying," I seethed and ran from the kitchen, my feet pounding up the stairs as I hurled myself back under my quilt.

I collapsed onto the mattress and when I checked my phone for the millionth time, there still wasn't a response from Kane. I knew better, but I couldn't stop myself, and I texted him.

'*We need to talk*.'

I'd backhanded the same gut-clenching words at him.

"WHERE IS SHE?"

I heard Paige's voice from downstairs, followed by her surprisingly heavy footsteps as she stormed up the stairs and into my bedroom.

"Get up," Paige shouted.

"No," I murmured and rolled away from her, tightening in my duvet burrito.

Paige stomped to the bed and yanked the covers so violently I swear I got a little airborne. "Enough of your pity party." I reached for the duvet and she dropped it on the floor. "Dylan said you've been holed up in your room all day listening to Celine Dion and you don't even like her."

"Celine is an amazing vocalist, and Dylan needs to mind his own business." I shivered without the warmth of my cocoon.

"What's going on, Jess?" Paige sat down on the foot of my bed.

"I think that Kane is ghosting me."

Paige crossed her arms. "I could say the same thing about you."

Damn. She was right, there were at least five unopened messages from Paige on my phone. My body crumpled on the bed and I hung my head. "I'm sorry, Paige. I'm such a shitty friend." Paige shifted so that she was sitting beside me and pulled me in close enough that I could smell her grape-fruit shampoo.

"Maybe he's busy. The game this afternoon is a really important one, isn't it?"

How could I have forgotten about the game? "It is. The scouts have been showing up at all the exhibition games, and this is the last one before the summer camps start." I sat up a little taller - maybe Paige was right. Could Kane have just been working on his slapshot all morning? He spent hours doing visualization practices, and pre-game rituals, so it wasn't totally inconceivable.

"And you promised me that you'd go to the game with me, right?"

It was all coming back to me, and yes, I had agreed to go to the game with Paige. "I did."

She must've heard the hesitation. "Did?"

"This whole Kane thing." I shrugged.

"Jessie." Paige shifted away from me so she could grab onto my upper arms.

"Ow," I said, but she didn't let go.

"The guy is busy. It's not the end of the world. You can't just hole up in here because what? He hasn't texted you in the past twelve hours?"

Hearing her say it out loud made it sound completely ridiculous - but she didn't have the whole story. "Last night at the Gala, he said that we needed to talk. Then he left with Bronwyn and hasn't answered any messages since."

"Oh." Paige eased her death grip and dropped her hands.

I rubbed my arms. "And Dylan told me that... that he heard, that um..." I didn't know how to say it.

"What did Dylan hear?" Paige crossed her arms and glanced at the door to my bedroom as if my brother would suddenly appear so she could give him a dirty look.

My throat constricted. "That Kane and Bronwyn got

217

together at the..." I gasped in air, unable to finish the sentence.

"Hold on." She held up her hand. "This is Laketown. I can't try on a pair of jeans without the whole town knowing what brand and size they were. You know that you can't trust anything you hear. Hell, there were rumors that Dylan and I had sex that night at Kane's cottage."

"You didn't?" I couldn't help myself. I smiled wryly as Paige's face registered shock and then a smile when she realized I was joking.

"Come on. Get up. Get dressed. We've got to get to the bottom of this." Paige pulled me to my feet.

"What if he is going to break up with me?" It seemed so surreal to say the words. Perfect isn't a word I use lightly, but dammit, everything had been amazing since Kane Fitzgerald skated into my life.

"Then he's clearly a loser and wouldn't know a good thing if it was taped to a puck and smashed into his loser face."

"Do you want to try to throw loser in one more time?" I asked.

She smiled. "Get dressed. Look fabulous. But..." she paused dramatically. "Be prepared to feel ridiculous when you find out he's lost his phone, has spent the day preparing for the biggest game of his career, and that his girlfriend is listening to the damn Laketown rumor mill."

Maybe he *had* just lost his phone and I was wallowing for no reason at all.

I was going to the game.

31

KANE

THE ATMOSPHERE WAS electric in McManus Arena, but the somber tone inside the Otters' dressing room made it clear that this was more than just an exhibition game. Beside me, Tanner was staring across the room at the wall, his mind clearly somewhere else while his legs jittered beneath his forearms. We knew the scouts were out in full force and that we didn't leave a great impression at our last game.

I emptied the contents of my hockey bag onto the floor, hoping and praying that somehow my coin was going to just magically appear, even though I had searched every last corner and seam of the bag.

Nothing.

It was the first time I had looked for it since I started hanging out with Jessie. I wiggled my toes in my skates, my toe was fully healed; my run of bad luck seemed to end when I met her. I shook my head as if it would get her off my mind. I needed a clear head for the game.

"Still can't find it?" Tanner whispered.

I shook my head and cleaned up the random rolls of hockey tape and single socks.

Dylan entered the dressing room wearing a suit and tie and sat down on the bench beside Mike, and he didn't even look at me.

Coach went over the plays and gave us the same speech he had given for every game I'd ever played. I leaned into Tanner, "You'd think he would've put together something a little more..."

"Inspiring?" Tanner grinned at me. "This isn't the movies. He doesn't want to make this game feel any different from the others."

"Hey, Fitzy." Tanner whispered. "You don't need no damn coin." He shoved his hand into his glove and fist-bumped me. Then he stood up and stretched his arms wide. "Boys. Let's go eat us some Predators for dinner." His commanding voice echoed through the dressing room and the guttural roar that followed practically shook the walls.

THE GAME WAS CLOSE, but the Predators had managed to maintain a one-goal lead on us. I glanced at the scoreboard, something I had avoided doing the whole game, just in case my eyes were drawn to Jessie. She was the only thing that could derail me, and I couldn't think about the hardest conversation I was going to have in my life while I was playing the most important game of my life.

Two minutes remained on the clock and we were tied two to two. Leo had scored right out of the gate and I had gotten the second goal in the third period - short-handed. I was skating circles around guys who were usually hot on my heels; my newfound ability to maintain an insane amount of speed in the corners left gaping holes in the Predators' defensive line.

I hopped off the bench and joined Leo, Tanner, Mike, and Justin on the ice. Almost my dream line, but I hated to admit it, we sure could've used Dylan.

After Tanner won the faceoff, the sound of the crowd morphed into white noise and the movement of the puck went into slow-motion. I felt like I could not only see but sense where all my guys were on the rink at that moment. A Predators player checked Leo into the boards, but not before he backhanded the puck to Tanner. I smacked my stick on the ice and Tanner wound up for the slapshot, but I knew he was going to fake it.

He did and I was ready for it.

I went into autopilot, winding up as the puck lifted slightly off the ice and headed towards me. I was known for my fake shots, but today, I took it. The goalie's water bottle jumped into the air like it had been electrocuted as the puck smashed into the net. The crowd thundered, the goal siren screamed, and as Leo and Tanner surrounded me, yelling and screaming, the bass from the sound system blared, reverberating in my chest. The rest of the team piled onto the ice and surrounded me. We had done it – we had won. I didn't have my gold coin and I had played the best game of my life – and I only had one person to thank.

I finally let myself glance up to the sea of spectators in the arena, and there she was. I knew that she was there. I could feel it in my bones, and I knew exactly where to find those green eyes in the audience. Her hands were clasped in front of her and she and her friend Paige were on their feet. Our eyes met and for the second time that night, the world went silent.

How could it be that the best day of my life was also going to be the worst?

After our celebration, we lined up along the blue line

and Jake McManus presented us with the exhibition series gold medals. It wasn't a cup or a major tournament, but we had played like it was, and I felt just as proud of that medal hanging around my neck as I did when I had skated with the Northern Professional League Cup held above my head.

With the weight of the medal on my jersey, I glanced back to the stands, hoping to catch Jessie's eyes one more time, but my heart sank when I saw that the seats were empty.

With the speeches, showers, and dressing room celebrations behind us, we made our way down the cavernous hallway ready to meet the local press and sign autographs for a bunch of hockey crazy kids.

Someone grabbed my arm. It was Dylan.

"Did you do it yet?" he asked.

"Can't we just do a little celebrating right now?" I shook off his hand.

"She's here. Whatever you're doing isn't good enough." He grabbed my arm again. "I hate it. I know you do too. But you're going to have to hurt her. And hurt her so badly that she never wants to set foot in Laketown ever again."

"You know what Dylan? Maybe we should just trust Jessie to make the right decision for herself."

Dylan stepped in my path and crossed his arms. "You think the right thing is giving up her dreams to live in Laketown to be with you?"

I wished that he weren't right; Jessie wasn't thinking straight. "Over my dead body," I growled. "Jessie Moss is going to make the National Skating Team and go to the 2022 Olympics."

"Good." Dylan stepped aside. "Now make sure that happens."

I felt like I was going to throw up. I couldn't be the

reason that Jessie wasn't on the podium in Beijing. I was scared. I was about to give up the best thing that had ever happened to me and it felt like I was cutting off one of my arms. She had become a part of who I was. She was the last thing I thought about before I fell asleep and the first thing I wanted to do when I woke up in the morning was kiss the freckles on her cheeks. But this morning, my bed was empty. And I was a coward. I told myself that I was focused on the game, but really, I was terrified of losing her. She deserved more than unanswered text messages. She deserved more than what I was about to do to her.

32

JESSIE

"Ow," I grimaced as I was elbowed in the gut by a ten-year-old trying to get a glimpse of the Otters as they left the rink. The crowd cheered as the team, smelling of fresh shampoo, made their way through the lobby.

My heart swelled as I watched Kane. He was a patient man and signed autographs for every single kid that asked him. I knew that he had seen me in the stands, he looked right at me and I wiped my hands against my jeans, waiting for his eyes to meet mine again.

My heart started to jackhammer when we got close enough that I could hear the tenor of his voice and the soft chuckle of his laugh. Finally, his eyes met mine over the top of a gaggle of Otters' hat-wearing ten-year-olds, and my heart melted when he smiled.

Everything was going to be okay.

But as quickly as it came, the smile turned to a grimace - the sparkle gone from his eyes.

"Hi." I stood awkwardly in front of him, not knowing whether I should hug him in front of the team.

"Hey."

Hey? He had never spoken to me so casually. I shoved my hands into my pockets, the fingertips of my right hand rubbing the edge of the gold coin in my pocket.

"Nice skating." My voice wavered.

"Fitzy, come on," Mike yelled as the rest of the team stampeded by, their hockey bags bumping and jostling against the entrance doors.

"I've gotta..." he gestured with his thumb to the door.

"You've gotta go," I whispered.

"See ya."

He didn't even look at me, he just started to walk away.

"You're too good for that, Jess," Paige whispered.

I am too good for that.

I bridged the gap between us. His forearm tensed within my grip and he stopped but didn't turn to face me. "Kane." My voice was stronger than I expected. "What's going on?"

His shoulders slumped and he turned but didn't look me in the eye.

"We can't do this anymore," he whispered.

I knew that the words were coming, but they still got me like a caught toe-pick. "What do you mean, this?"

He gestured to the side of the lobby with his head and I followed him to a quiet corner. "Does this have something to do with Dylan?" I whispered.

"No," he said quickly. Then tried to act casual. "I mean, no. It doesn't have anything to do with Dylan."

"Then, Fitzy..." I reached for his hand. His body softened and he held my fingertips. "What's the problem?"

"It's just...," he stared up at the ceiling. "Fuck, Jess. I mean, I just can't..." he paused as a group of people passed by, "do this. Us."

None of this made sense. "We can make it work. Paige told me I could get a job at Valerock. Fitzy..." I hated the way

I sounded, pleading, but I felt like I was fighting for my life. I was holding onto the thing that meant the most in the world to me by a thread, one that I knew was about to get cut, and there wasn't a thing in the world I could do to stop it.

"No." He pulled his hand from mine. "You can't do that."

"Why?" Now the room was starting to tilt on its axis and the blue painted concrete walls were blurred through my tears. "Don't you get it? I'm not leaving. I want to be with you, Kane. That's all I want."

He brushed a tear from my face. "Please don't cry." I looked into his eyes and he finally met mine. "I'm no good for you."

"But you are, how can you not see that you're the best thing that's ever happened to me?" The tears that rolled down my face were heavy and fat.

"Jessie." The cold voice was back.

I reached for his hands, but he took a step back – just out of my reach. I wiped the tears from my face, worried that we were making a scene. I had lost him. I could feel it in my bones. "Well, if you change your mind, I'll be here. I'm going to take the job at Valerock anyway."

His eyes flashed with an anger I had never seen in him and he stepped close to me. "Jessie. We can't be together. Ever." He paused. He looked at the ground and when he looked at me again, his eyes were dark and cold. "I fucked Bronwyn last night." His tone was sharp, and his words felt like a slap against my cheek.

It was my turn to take a step back. He picked up his hockey bag and then pushed the metal door open so hard it smashed against the side of the building.

The tilting Earth went fully on its side and the last thing remembered before the world went black, were Paige's hands catching me under my arms.

33

KANE

I DON'T CRY.

A week had passed since we won the exhibition game and I lost Jessie. And I had cried, no, sobbed – the kind of sobs that shook my whole body, every single day.

The empty beer bottles rattled in the back of the Land Cruiser – I had forgotten that the bottle return was closed on Sunday, and slightly embarrassed by the number of empty bottles that had accumulated over just one week. Tanner had helped, but the majority of those empty bottles were from dulling the ache in my heart.

Dammit. I cursed under my breath when I saw my dad's car parked in the driveway. I wanted to wallow alone.

"Hey, Dad," I shouted as I bypassed the great room.

"Hi," he said. He was sitting in the porch swing.

I backed up. Something was wrong with the tone of his voice. "Aren't you supposed to be in the city?" He was staring out over the water, rocking in the porch swing. "Is everything okay, Dad?"

His shoulders rose and then he let out a big sigh. "I've decided to leave Tiffany."

Finally.

"Really, why?" I tried to hide the elation from my voice.

"I don't know how she hid it from me all these years."

"What?" I sat down in one of the wicker loveseats so I could see my dad's face.

"Her personality." The side of his mouth turned up and he let out a light chuckle.

Dad and Tiffany had been married for two years, and as far as I could remember, she was a total bitch from day one. "Um…" I rubbed the back of my neck, lost for words.

"I just really miss your mom. Even after all these years. I thought that moving on would help - it didn't."

I rested my elbows on my knees. "I miss her too."

In the distance, a loon called and my dad and I sat in silence. The memories I had of my mom were hazy. She died when I was five and my actual memories were like an old-fashioned slide show: flickery, grainy, and without sound.

The swing creaked as my dad pushed against the painted floorboards with his bare foot. "This divorce is going to be brutal. I'm probably going to shack up here with you for the summer. If it doesn't cramp your style too much.

The Pine Hill keggers had worn thin a long time ago and having my dad home was a great excuse for the guys to find some other party house – probably Tanner's.

"I can move into the bunkie," Dad offered.

"Dad, no. Don't be ridiculous." I shook my head then smiled. "But don't take it personally if I move into the Pinecone Cabin or maybe even the boathouse."

"I won't. Want a beer?" Dad asked.

"Sure, I can get it." I popped into the kitchen, pulled a couple of Heinekens out of the fridge, and returned to the porch. We clinked bottles and drank in silence, the rain dripping off the leaves and onto the roof was the only sound until my phone rang.

"It's Coach." I glanced at the screen as it buzzed on the glass table between us.

"Aren't you going to answer it?" Dad picked it up and clicked the green button.

"I guess I am now." I took the phone.

"Hello?"

My dad stared at me as Coach Covington gave me the best news I'd had in days. I should've been jumping up and down, screaming, and hugging my dad. But instead, I just said, "Thanks, Coach." And hung up the phone.

"What was all that about?"

"The scouts were at the game last week."

"And..." Dad slid to the edge of the swing.

"And they asked me to join the informal training camp." I took a sip of my beer and couldn't believe that I didn't feel anything.

"I thought you were already in the camp."

"Dad." I smiled a little, knowing that the news would make him proud. "Not the Otters' camp – the Thunder."

"Holy shit!" Dad shot to his feet. "Kane!"

"Easy, Dad. It's just their training camp. The informal one. They usually invite one or two guys to practice with them." It doesn't mean anything.

"Don't you dare act like this isn't a big deal." Dad shook his finger at me. "Come on, we have to celebrate." The news had brought my dad back to life. "I'm getting a divorce and my son is going to play with the New York Thunder!" He threw his arms up in the air.

A stray piece of wicker was digging in my back, but I didn't care. I let it poke me. "It's just camp."

Dad lowered his hands from above his head and stared

at me. "Kane. What's up? You've worked your whole life for this, and you look like your dog just died."

I took a sip of my beer. "It's good. I mean. I'm excited."

"You sure don't look excited. What's going on?"

As a retired NHL player himself, my dad knew that this was big news, and it didn't take a genius to read me. I had just been given the best news of my life, but it didn't mean anything if I couldn't pick up the phone and call Jessie. I opened my mouth to try to explain but didn't know where to start.

"Is it drugs?" My dad asked.

"Dad, no."

"Then it's a woman." He sat down. "Out with it. Keeping that stuff inside will kill you."

I knew he wouldn't let this go. "Dad, you remember that girl Jessie Moss?"

"I do. Your skating coach, right?" He tipped his bottle at me. "Those lessons were worth their weight in gold." He smiled and I saw the lightbulb go off over his head. For a shrewd businessman who spent his days reading people, sometimes he could be dense. "There was something more between you two, wasn't there?"

"Yeah." I looked at the ground. "Dad, I did something bad. I mean, it was the right thing to do, but..." I shook my head and a lump formed in my throat, "it feels terrible."

"Dammit, Kane," Dad seethed through his teeth. "I thought you knew better."

He thought I got her pregnant. "No. It's not that, Dad. I do know better."

He exhaled loudly. "Well, then what is it? You just about gave me a heart attack. I'm not ready to be a grandpa."

"I fell in love with her." The past tense sounded wrong. I whispered, "I'm in love with Jessie."

Dad nodded. "I could see that there was something between the two of you. So did Tiffany."

"That's probably why she wanted me to take Bronwyn Yates to the gala so badly, and she was so rude to Jessie every time she saw her."

"Probably," Dad agreed.

"It was terrible. Tiffany was so mean to Jessie. I don't know why she hated her so much."

"I think I do." Dad set his beer on the table. "First of all, Tiffany is a money-hungry, social-climbing snob, and her stepson dating a Yates would have looked good to all of her country club friends."

"Who cares about that stuff?" I asked.

"She does." Dad shrugged. "Maybe it had something to do with the fact that your mom grew up in Laketown."

"My mom grew up here?" I sat up. This was news. "I thought that you two met at the sailing camp."

My dad smiled. "We did. She worked there cleaning the boats." He stared out at the lake. "I'm sorry I brought that woman into your life. If she was rude to your girlfriend, I'll apologize on her behalf."

If only it were that easy. It was time to tell him the whole story.

"Jessie was going to give up her Olympic dreams to be with me. I couldn't let her do it."

"Olympic?" Dad raised his eyebrows. "What do you mean?"

"She was going to quit skating to be with me. She was insistent. Nothing I tried got through to her, so I told her a lie. One awful enough to make her hate me and get her the hell out of Laketown."

"Kane." Dad pursed his lips. "There had to have been a better way."

"I wish there was." My voice cracked.

The loon called again, and this time another called back. Dad stood and collected the empty beer bottles. "Son, if there's one thing I've learned, the kind of love that you two showed for each other doesn't come along every day. She was willing to give up her dreams – for you."

"I—"

"Let me finish." Dad held up his empty hand. "And you. You could've been selfish. You could've let her give up her dreams, but you didn't."

I stood. "Yeah, but I hurt her..." I paused and swallowed the ball in my throat, "and it's eating me up inside."

My dad wasn't an emotional man, and growing up I received plenty of atta-boy slaps on the back, so when he put his arm over my shoulders and squeezed me in tightly, I knew he understood what I was going through. "I miss her so much," I whispered. "And she hates me."

Dad gave my shoulder one more squeeze and then we went back to staring out at the lake in silence, the rain having intensified from a few staccato drops on the roof to a full-on downpour. "Whoa," Dad said as the rain was driven into the porch by the wind. "Come on, let's go inside."

"I think I'll stay out here." I shivered, as the mist clung to the hair on my arms, and sat down.

After Dad left, it could have been three minutes, or three hours, I can't be sure, but I couldn't bring myself to move. Jessie had been part of my life, and with her gone, my body didn't seem to know how to operate.

"Kane." The screen door slid open and my dad poked his head out. "Dinner's ready and a package came for you."

"Thanks, Dad." I didn't look at him and I felt him approach beside me.

"Here." He set a padded shipping envelope on the wicker table. "Come in before your dinner gets cold."

Groaning, I leaned forward and rubbed my lower back. I was too young to feel this sore, but too many body checks will do that to a player.

The package was small, and my name and address were handwritten – it clearly wasn't from a store. I ripped it open and my gold coin slipped out and spun on the glass table. I shook the package and a folded unsigned note slipped out. My hands were shaking as I picked it up and read the note:

You never needed it.

34

JESSIE

Veronica zipped up the black spandex bodice of my long program dress. I shook my hands and then patted at the flyaway strands of hair that had defied my helmet of hairspray. I heard the announcement of Aimee Mathurst's marks and the audience erupted in screams of delight. She was a fellow Skating Academy student, and outside of the rink, a friend – but tonight, she was my foe. The top two skaters from the Regionals would advance, one step closer to Nationals to fight for one of the coveted team spots.

The past two weeks had been hell on my mind and my body. I glanced at my beige tights in the mirror, wincing as I touched my hip. I hoped that the purple bruise on my hip wouldn't show through the fabric.

"Fix your eyes," Veronica ordered and handed me a tube of liquid liner. I pulled my eyelid tight and tried to keep a steady hand, darkening the cat eyes that was part of my *Swan Lake* costume. The girl that looked back at me was someone that I knew well – a skater. I couldn't believe that I had lost sight of her – for a hockey player.

That's what he was. A player – and a skilled one at that.

Just like skating helped me through my parent's accident, it had gotten me back on my feet after Kane's betrayal.

"You have a visitor," Veronica said. I opened my mouth to object, but she had already opened the door – and I saw his goofy grin wide behind a bouquet of roses.

"Hi, Dyl." I hadn't seen him since I high tailed it out of Laketown, but we had talked every day.

"Wow. You look scary." He kissed me on the cheek and handed me the flowers.

"Thanks." I was about to lob the insult right back at him but couldn't. Dylan's eyes sparkled; his skin was golden – he looked the healthiest I had seen him in years. "But you're supposed to give me these after the performance."

"You know I don't follow the rules."

That's when I noticed that he was wearing his Otters' jacket. I pointed to the logo on his chest, "I thought you were going to get kicked off the team."

"Me too," He said. "It turns out that Coach gives second, even third chances."

"Good. It will keep you out of trouble," I smiled.

"Never," he laughed.

"Jessica. It's time." Veronica gently squeezed my forearm.

"I'm out of here. Good luck, kid. Nail the fuck out of that flutz," he yelled and strode out of the dressing room.

"Quite the character." Veronica fluffed the feather skirt of my costume. "Aimee skated well, but she doesn't have the axel." My coach transformed back to business and squeezed both of my wrists; her brown eyes locked on mine. "Breathe. Be Consistent. Just like practice."

I nodded, pulled my shoulders back, and flicked the switch. All the sounds from the arena dulled to a buzz around me. The audience turned into a sea of color; the announcers voice garbled in the background. A man in a headset opened the door to the ice surface and the second my blade hit the ice; I knew I was going to nail it.

After my name and skating club were announced, and I took my place at center ice, the arena went silent. The violin's opening notes sent my body into autopilot, and I opened with a triple toe, triple toe combo – and stuck the landing. The rest of the program was the most flawless skate of my life, but the lutz was still coming up.

I gathered speed and set up for the jump, my foot poised beside the gliding skate, and I don't know why, but before I reached out to stab my pick into the ice and launch me into three full rotations, I looked to the audience. Dylan was on his feet, his arms up in the air, and beside him – Kane.

Already in motion, I couldn't stop the momentum, and I pulled my arms in tight, praying while the arena spun around me once, twice, three times.

It was too much – I was too far back on the landing. The heel of my free skate dug into the ice and I knew I was going down. I slid about twenty feet, leaving a cleared swath on the ice.

Dammit.

The audience gasped collectively. I squeezed my eyes together tightly, and as I had done so many times before, sprang up from the ice and launched into my finishing spin – a flying camel.

The audience clapped and cheered, and I brushed the snow off my bruised hip as I skated off the ice. Even though I hung my head in failure, cellophane-wrapped roses littered the ice – obviously, the fans didn't agree with me.

Veronica was waiting for me in the 'kiss and cry' section. The qualifiers were televised, and I tried to look away as the camera zoomed in tight to my face. Viewers would've seen tears, but they wouldn't have known that they were tears of anger. How dare he show his face here? Tonight. At the most important competition of my life.

But, why did I look?

"You broke focus," Veronica whispered as we waited for the marks.

"I know."

She patted my hands. "It was a good skate, Jessica." Up until the lutz, she was right. "You're going to get a deduction for the fall, but I think that the axel will make up for it."

I nodded and trained my gaze on the scoreboard. The audience cheered as the numbers came up. "It's a good score." Veronica seemed to relax beside me, but I wondered if it was good enough.

Then the standings were posted.

First Place: Aimee Mathurst, Second Place: Jessica Moss, Third Place: Katherine Travis.

"You did it." Veronica squeezed my hand.

I should've been ecstatic. I squeezed back, handed the flowers to Veronica, and walked past the TV cameras into the quiet of the warm-up area. Yes, I had made it one step closer to my Olympic dream, so why didn't I feel anything but sadness?

The medal ceremony was scheduled for later that evening and I sat to undo my skates.

"This is for you." Veronica held out a small envelope – the kind that comes with flowers.

"What's this?" I asked.

"I told your brother it was better if you got this after your skate. Not before."

She pressed the tiny envelope into my hand. It was heavier than I expected. As I ripped it open, I knew exactly what was in it. The flowers weren't from Dylan, I should've known he wouldn't have bought long stem red roses, they were from Kane. I pulled out the card and left the heavy gold coin in the envelope. I had never seen Kane's writing before, and it was exactly what I expected – barely legible.

Beijing 2022. Take this with you.

I turned the card over. He hadn't signed it, but who else could have written it? Was it an apology? Why the hell would I want his damn coin? To remind me of my first real heartbreak every time I looked at it? I shook my head and shoved the card back into the envelope and zipped it into the pocket of my warm-up jacket.

"Meet you back here at nine for the medal presentation." Veronica disappeared behind the curtain. I shoved my skates into the bag and carefully got out of my dress and into my warm-up suit.

"Good luck," I smiled at the pairs couple who were scheduled to take over my dressing room. "It's all yours." I pulled the curtain back and gestured to the cordoned off room.

"Thanks," the duo, who I recognized from the Academy, chorused.

I wheeled my skating bag behind me and draped my garment bag over my shoulder. My phone chimed three times in succession and I ignored it. Making my way through the crowd, I heard it sound again and again. I joined the other members of the Academy who were seated behind the judges stand, opposite the arena from where I'd spotted Dylan and the asshole.

"Great performance, Jess." Jack, one of the male skaters stood up to let me pass by. I took a seat next to him and watched the couples warming up for the pairs event. My phone chimed again. And again.

"Are you going to get that?" Jack raised his eyebrows at me.

"Oh, sorry. I guess it is annoying." I pulled the phone out of my pocket and clicked it to silent.

"You think?" Jack smirked and then reverted his gaze to the ice surface. I studied that ice surface and every skater as if I was going to be given a test. There was no way I was going to look up at the stands or try to find my brother. My blood was boiling. Dylan knew what Kane had done and he brought that cheating asshole onto my turf.

The first flight of skaters finished, and the Zamboni took to the ice. The driver was sporting a tuxedo complete with tails and a bow tie. There was no way Andy would've ever been seen in an outfit like that. I sighed. One of my biggest regrets was leaving Laketown without saying goodbye or thanking Andy. Without him, I wouldn't have been able to keep up my skills. Without him, I wouldn't be stepping onto the podium here today.

"Excuse me, pardon me. Yes, you, get out of my way." Veronica's British accent, posh yet rude at the same time caught my attention. My coach was making her way towards me. She was pretty much a celebrity in the skating world, and everyone moved out of the way to let her through, like the seas parting. She dropped into the seat beside me. "You didn't answer my calls."

Shit. I had assumed that it had been Dylan blowing up my phone.

"Oh shoot. The ringer must be off." I pulled out my phone and made a show of turning up the volume. Jack rolled his eyes. "What's going on?" I asked. I had missed five calls from her.

"There's something we need to talk about." Her voice was stern.

"Okay..."

"Not here." She grabbed my hand and pulled me from my seat.

The second flight of skaters had started, and I could hear Vivaldi's *Four Seasons* from speakers above the ice surface. "What's going on?" I was totally confused but let her pull me up the arena's stairs and into the lobby.

"I'm fine, Coach," I said. "I'm good now."

"Now?" she raised her eyebrows. She led me to the wooden benches underneath the viewing windows and we sat.

I huffed out all the air in my lungs. I didn't want to have this conversation with Veronica. "You're my coach, not my therapist."

"Same thing. Your performance was impacted tonight, and we need to figure why and how to stop that from ever happening again."

"There was this guy, back in Laketown..."

"You lost your focus because of a man." She pursed her lips.

I thought that she was going to lose her mind, but she didn't seem upset or even surprised. "They can do that to you." She smiled to herself as if remembering someone, or something.

"Anyway, I thought I was over it and then he showed up here tonight."

"I know," Veronica said. "I told him to stay away until after your skate."

"That's why you took the envelope."

"Yes." She pursed her lips and nodded.

The envelope sat heavily in my pocket, weighed down by its contents.

"We were going to wait until after the medal ceremony, but I think it's important that we break this news to you now." In an uncommon show of affection, Veronica took my hand in hers.

"Boys," she said loudly. Dylan and Kane appeared from around the corner. I tried to pull my hand from Veronica's, but she held on with a death grip. "Just listen," she said and then patted my hand. I gripped the edge of the bench and gritted my teeth.

"Jess. I'm so proud of you," Dylan smiled and opened his arms out for a hug.

I remained seated.

"What are you doing here?" The question was directed at Kane, but Dylan answered.

"Watching you skate?"

"Not you." I narrowed my eyes at Kane.

"You."

35

KANE

IF SOMEONE HAD TOLD me that Dylan Moss was going to become one of my closest friends, I never would've believed them, but over the past few weeks, that's exactly what happened. I had convinced Coach that the Otters' offensive line would have a gaping hole in it if Dylan got kicked off the team. And if it wasn't for him, I'd still be drinking away my sorrows. Was I trying to keep Jessie close by spending time with Dylan? Maybe, but I never asked him how she was doing. He dropped those morsels of information on his own.

Dylan, of all people, stopped me from drinking myself into oblivion every night, and it was Dylan and my father who came up with the plan that would bring Jessie back to Laketown. I just needed to talk to her, to get close enough to make it happen.

But she wouldn't take my calls and that's when Dylan offered to take me to the competition.

Her *Swan Lake* program was the longest I've ever gone without breathing. I don't know the names of all of her jumps, but I do know the lutz – and when I saw her leading into it every muscle in my body was tense. She had hit every jump in her program, and I had never seen her look so radiant, so in her element. Tears welled up in my eyes as I watched the woman I loved, doing what she loved, and fucking killing it.

When she skated, she went into what we both called 'the zone'. I winced as she looked into my eyes right before she jabbed her toepick into the ice; I knew that she'd lost her concentration.

"Dammit," I whispered as she slid across the ice.

"Shit," Dylan said beside me.

She got up just as fast as she'd fallen and finished off her program with that fancy leg out spin that I really liked.

Her face filled up the video screen and the intensity in her eyes as she watched the scores made my heart feel like it was ripping in half. Could I have ruined everything for her? First, I hurt her; I sent her away, and now, I distracted her when she needed all of her focus.

The announcer read the marks and then the standings were posted. Dylan started screaming and jumping up and down beside me. "She did it," he yelled.

I looked at the rankings. "She got second," I said.

"It's the top two who go," Dylan hooted and clapped his hands as the names were read over the loudspeaker.

"Come on." He slapped my leg. "Let's go find her."

"Maybe you should be the one to tell her." I didn't stand.

"Get up." He smacked me again. "Put on your big boy pants."

We searched that damn arena for at least an hour. Dylan called and texted, but Jessie wasn't answering her phone.

"Dylan." The voice that shouted his name was loud. We turned and saw Jessica's coach, Veronica walking towards us like an enraged momma bear. "You were supposed to wait until after she skated." She pointed her blood-red fingernail at me. "That could've cost her everything."

"I'm sorry. I just really wanted to see her skate. I shouldn't have come," I said.

"What's done is done. I think that she will be open to the plan, but I'm not going to be the one to break it to her. That's up to you Mr. Fitzgerald."

Now, here Dylan and I were, hiding behind the snack bar, waiting for Veronica to lure Jessie out into the open where we could talk to her. We all knew, including Veronica, that Jessie would never agree to speak to me. It seemed tawdry, but we had to trick her – and the coach was in on it.

"What are you doing here?" she repeated. "Dylan, why did you bring him here?" Her voice shook.

"Jess." Dylan sat down beside his sister. "Please just listen to him."

Her eyes softened at her brother, but when she turned to me, they narrowed. "What do you want?"

"Jess. You didn't return my calls."

"So?"

"I'm sorry."

"Sorry isn't going to cut it, Kane Fitzgerald. You slept with someone else."

"No, he didn't," Dylan interrupted. "I told him to say that. If you want to get mad and throw someone out of your life it should be me, not Fitzy."

"Is that true?" Her eyes were wide. "Why would you do that?" She looked back and forth between Dylan and me.

I sat down beside her and tried to take her hand, but she pulled it away and held it herself. "We wanted to make sure you went back to the Academy. We didn't want you to ruin your life, to stay in Laketown, when you truly belong on the ice." A lump was forming in my throat. "Jessie, you were beautiful out there." I tried to take her hand and again, she ripped it from me.

"You two decided what was best for me." Her voice was guttural.

"It was the hardest thing I've ever had to do, Jess." My voice wavered and I tried to hold it together.

She stood up. "It was shitty." She pointed to Dylan and then to me. "Both of you."

"We just wanted what was best for you Jess." Dylan scuffed at the rubber floor with his Vans.

"I decide what is best for me. Not you. And definitely not you." She pointed at me but shoved Dylan. She started to walk away. I didn't dare grab her arm, but Dylan did.

"I'm sorry," he said. "I made Kane do it. He didn't want to."

She looked at me. As much as I didn't want to throw Dylan under the bus, it was time that everyone started telling the truth. I nodded.

"Then you're no longer my brother." Jessie shook her arm out of Dylan's hand. "You didn't sleep with Bronwyn." She looked to me for confirmation as if she needed to hear it from my mouth.

"No," I said. "I love you."

"But the rumors..." her voice trailed off. "It doesn't matter. This is my life now. You two made that decision for me."

"You might change your mind when you see this." I set my backpack on the bench and pulled out a manila envelope.

"What is this?" she asked.

"Open it."

She pulled out the dog-eared proposal, the same one that we had given to Veronica. "What is this?" she repeated, and smacked it against her hand.

"Read it," I urged, and pushed the thick paperwork towards her.

"It's a proposal." Her eyes scanned the first page and then she flipped quickly to the second and third. "For another ice surface in Laketown?" She flipped the document closed. "What does this have to do with me?"

"The Laketown figure skating arena's roof leaks and the building is about to fall. Fitzgerald Enterprises is investing in the new ice surface." I couldn't hide the excitement in my voice.

"Your dad is building a figure skating arena?" She slid the papers back into the envelope.

"Not exactly." I rubbed my neck. "There isn't enough ice time for all of the hockey teams; the players need a secondary surface – and they'd be willing to share."

"I still don't understand. What does this have to do with me?"

The classical music that had been playing in the background stopped and we were interrupted by the cheer of the audience. We had to speed this up because, in just a few minutes, the lobby was going to be bustling. "Well, the skating club needs a new elite coach. And we just hired Veronica."

As if on cue, the raven-haired woman walked into the lobby, followed by throngs of figure skating fans.

"Veronica, is this true? Are you moving to Laketown to coach?"

Veronica smiled. "Only if my top skater comes with me. The decision is yours, Jessica."

Dylan had been hanging back but stepped to his sister's side. "You can have it all now. You don't have to choose between skating and the life you want."

By that, he meant me. I was jostled by some fans and the space between us was quickly filled with people waiting around for the medal ceremony.

"Jessie. Come home," I pleaded.

36

JESSIE

KANE'S EYES searched mine and I wanted to launch myself into his arms, but something held me back. The two men in my life, my brother and my boyfriend had conspired against me.

"I need some air." The smell of popcorn, one of my favorite snacks, had become overwhelming. "I need to get out of here."

Before anyone could stop me, I wove through the crowd, bursting from the arena into the humid June air. The door opened behind me a few seconds later and Kane appeared. "Please, Kane. I need to be alone."

"Can we talk? There's a place near here that I think you'll like."

"I don't think that I want to go anywhere with you."

He tilted his head and his lips drew into a line. "And I get that," he said. "Let me show you this place, and then I'll leave you alone."

"If I say no, will you leave me alone anyway?"

"Not a chance," Kane said. The sides of his lips turned into a smile and I turned away because I could feel mine doing the same. I had to stay resolute. I wanted to be mad at him.

He kept his distance as we walked side by side down the busy sidewalk. "I went to a skills camp at that rink and on days when I couldn't take the city, I would come here." The path he led me down was so overgrown, I never would've known it was there. Kane held the branches of the trees back, so they didn't whip me in the face as we bushwhacked down his secret trail.

"I have to be back for the medal ceremony," I said. "We can't get lost."

"We're almost there." He held a branch and gestured for me to walk ahead of him. I stepped into a clearing and my breath caught in my throat. "It's beautiful," I said. Not everyone would think a swampy lagoon was pretty, but as we took a seat on a rickety bench, a blue heron took flight, its wings leaving rings on the surface of the pond.

"I thought you could use a good place to think. Nature helps."

"It does," I whispered. The sun glowed on fuzzy cattails, giving them the same glowy halo that shone on Kane's hair.

Kane turned to walk away. "Where are you going?" I asked.

"To leave you alone."

"Oh." My heart sank.

"Jess, I want to stay here with you. I want to wake up in your crappy bed in Laketown with you snoring against my chest. I want you to go to the Olympics. But those are all things that I want. I need to start listening to what you want. And right now, you want to be alone."

It wasn't a bluff. He turned and walked away, and within seconds the royal blue of his t-shirt had been swallowed up by the overgrown trail.

"Dammit," I whispered to myself. I didn't want to be alone. At all. I charged into the trees. "Kane," I shouted. It was quiet in the trees and I scanned both left and right, but there was no sign of Kane or the trail. I took a deep breath. He couldn't have gone far. "Kane," I shouted. "Come back."

Thump. Thump. The only sound I could hear was my heartbeat whooshing in my ears. My eyes tracked for any sign of movement amongst the trees, and then it came. Sticks cracked and it sounded like a bear was rumbling towards me – if bears wore blue Otters' t-shirts. Kane swiped branches away as he charged at me, wrapping his arms around me, and burying his face in my neck. Squeezed in Kane's arms I felt like I was home. I inhaled his soapy musky scent and all the emotions I'd held in for the past weeks escaped. Hot tears streamed down my face and Kane held me even tighter, his big hand cupped around the back of my neck, underneath my ballerina bun.

When I looked up at him, I saw something I'd never seen before – tears in his eyes. They didn't fall, but the shimmer made his ice blue eyes even more intense.

"I love you, Jessie," he said. "I'll spend the rest of my life supporting you, but ultimately your life is up to you." He cupped my face in his hands. "I just hope that you decide to come home and make it with me." He smiled and one tear escaped from his eyes. I reached up and swiped it away with my thumb.

"Kane." My voice was shaking. "It doesn't matter where I am. If I'm with you, I'm home."

A slow smile spread across his face. He wrapped his arms around my back and kissed me tenderly, starting with my lips and then he kissed the salty tears from my cheeks. "Does that mean...?" His eyes searched mine.

"Yes, Kane. I'm coming back to Laketown."

EPILOGUE - KANE

THE WARM AIR from the lobby mixed with the arctic air in the arena as I sneaked in to watch Jessie's practice. I shivered and rubbed my bare arms. Unlike McManus's place, with its suspended heaters and comfy seating, the community rink was old school – and that meant cold. I cursed myself for not bringing a sweatshirt and sneaked into the bleachers as quietly as I could, hoping to go unnoticed.

Veronica had banned me from Jessie's practices, but I missed watching her skate.

Veronica was wearing an ankle-length fur coat and shouting as Jessie glided across the ice. I held my breath – I knew the lutz was coming.

She stuck it.

It took all that I had not to scream out loud. My hands were balled in fists and my chest puffed out with pride as she did it again. Jessie was ready for Nationals.

I stealthily made it back to the warmth of the lobby and pretended to have just walked in as Jessie and Veronica made their way to the entrance.

"Hi," I smiled and waved.

"Hi." Jessie slid underneath my arm and hugged my waist.

I glanced at Veronica and she shook her fist at me, but with a smile. Of course, she had seen me.

"Bye, Coach," Jessie shouted over the rumble of her wheeled skate bag.

"See you tomorrow," Veronica shouted and made her way to her Mini Cooper.

"You hungry?" I asked.

"Famished." She leaned into me. "I've got my lutz back."

"That's amazing, babe." I kissed her temple and then opened the passenger door of the Land Cruiser. I took her extremely heavy skate bag and tossed it into the back. "There's a party at Tanner's." I put the car in gear. "He told me he's ordered forty pizzas."

"I feel like I could eat sixty," she smiled.

Since she'd been home, we'd fallen into a comfortable routine together – something I never thought I'd want – let alone savor. My dad had moved to the sanctity of Pine Hill to wait out his divorce and I had moved into the Pinecone cottage, one of the bigger guest bunkies, to give him space. Jessie didn't technically live there, but she might as well – we spent every night together.

A routine isn't a bad thing – especially when it consists of waking up with the woman that you love – and lots of skinny dipping.

Tanner's cottage is on the other side of the lake, so it was faster for us to hop in the boat and drive across Lake Casper than it was to drive around it. Jessie had permanently stolen my Otters' hat and she put it on backward as I pushed down on the throttle and we headed into the setting sun over to Tanner's place.

Leo was sitting on the dock when we arrived and stood

to catch the boat as we reached the slip. "Hey, Fitzy. Hi Jess." He smiled his million-megawatt grin as he helped to tie up the boat.

The guys had given me a tough time about Jessie, but with Dylan's blessing, they seemed willing to overlook the whole teammate's sister thing. They were also distracted with the hazing plans for the new rookies.

I slung my arm over Jessie's shoulder. "Pizza or a swim?"

"Pizza then a swim," she smiled, and I slipped my arm down so we could walk hand in hand to the timber frame cottage. Three naked guys that looked like zombies ran at us and our hands ripped apart as we jumped out of their path. They were covered in what I could only assume was baby powder or flour, and it provided very little modesty. They were pushing and shoving each other, and we turned to watch as they raced down the dock and flew into the air spectacularly. Flour man one did a cannonball, number two a front flip, and number three went with a swan dive.

"What was that all about?" Jessie asked.

The surface of the water was coated in white, and when the trio hoisted themselves onto the dock they were covered in a gloopy mess. "Oh no," Jessie turned away – with most of the flour gone, their nakedness was clearly apparent.

"Hazing," I laughed. "Come on, let's go."

Since she'd been home, Jessie had an extra glow to her face. Her friend Paige was at the party and I watched as the two of them talked animatedly in the corner while Jessie wolfed down a slice of pepperoni pizza.

"Hey man." Dylan slung his arm around my shoulder. "Did you see the rookies?" he laughed.

"My vote is for the cannonball guy. A naked c-ball? That takes some guts."

Dylan laughed. "No kidding."

He followed my gaze over to his sister and Paige and then waved. There were rumors about Dylan and Paige, but both of them denied that anything had ever happened between them.

Jessie pointed to the slice of pizza and then at me. I nodded.

"See you around." Dylan smacked me on the back and then disappeared into the crowd.

Jessie found her way to my side and presented me with a paper plate loaded with three pizza slices. "Thanks, babe," I smiled, and then took a giant bite. I nodded to Dylan and Paige, who were lined up at the keg. "Is something going on with them?" I asked.

"I thought you didn't care about stuff like that," she laughed.

"I don't."

She leaned in close. "I think that they're officially in the friend zone."

"Really? They seem to get along so well."

Jessie looked around the room and when she seemed sure no one was listening in on our conversation, pulled me close and whispered, "Paige has been partying with some guy from the Thunder – she won't tell me who though."

"You'll have to wait another month to get the inside scoop," I whispered back. It was going to be a busy summer; I was going to attend both the Otters' and the Thunder's training camps. Jessie had been so excited for me when I told her about my walk-on spot. I tried to brush it off like it was no big deal, but she saw right through it.

"And Dylan," she whispered. "The other night, a text message showed up on his phone – a girl had sent him a topless photo."

I didn't want to tell her that as a player, that happened

all the time. Or, it used to happen all the time. Her eyes sparkled. "It was Bronwyn Yates."

I almost choked on my pizza. Of all the guys in Laketown, Bronwyn Yates was messaging Dylan? I was secretly impressed. The guy deserved a break.

Someone turned the music up, and the front veranda turned into a dance floor. The rookies, now thankfully covered up in floral bedsheets tied toga style, were surrounded by puck bunnies in bikini tops. "Those guys have no idea what's coming," I said to Jessie and laughed.

"I think I know that guy." She pointed to the tallest of the three rookies.

"That's Brodie, he's a..." I almost said Laketownie, but Jessie and I had agreed to strike that word from our vocabulary. "He's from here."

"Dyl," she shouted and gestured at her brother to come over.

"What's up?" he asked.

"That guy, the rookie." She pointed to the guy doing a keg stand. "Do you recognize him?"

"Yeah, that's Brodie Bishop."

"I thought so," I yelled to Kane. "He was a couple years younger than us at Laketown High."

Brodie Bishop was the local triple-a hotshot. He was cocky, arrogant, and I hated to admit it, good.

"Looks like he's come into his own." Jessie rolled her eyes as he lowered himself down from his keg stand and draped his arms over two of the closest blonds, kissing them each on the cheek. Then some old school hip-hop blared out of the speakers and he launched into the air in a swan dive and then proceeded to breakdance, doing 'the worm' across the balcony.

"You ready to go for a swim?" I asked. The room was getting rowdy.

She looped her arms around my waist and pressed her hips against mine. "I am." She shot me her 'I'm horny' smile. She squeezed my ass and my cock twitched in response. She leaned in so close I could feel her breath on my earlobe. The twitch turned to a throb. "But I want to do it without this." She tugged on the bikini string at her neck.

"Say no more." I grabbed her hand and the two of us left the debauchery of the first Otters' kegger behind. "Let me take you home."

If you loved *Not a Player*, be sure to check out *Hating the Rookie*!

HATING THE ROOKIE

The hot new hockey player is a lot of things...

Number one: he's a talented player.
Number two: he's cocky as hell.
Number three: he used to be my best friend.

Get ready for more skinny dipping, campfires, and a little enemies-to-lovers action in "Hating the Rookie".

Hating the Rookie
Laketown Otters, Book 2
Now Available

SNEAK PEEK: HATING THE ROOKIE

Even though it was hot in the train car, I shivered and looked away from the town's welcome sign. It was an illustration of a busty woman in a red, old-fashioned bathing suit, waving as she waterskied behind a wooden boat. The bright town sign didn't make me smile or feel warm inside. No. That fire engine red lipstick wearing woman brought back every single feeling I had before I left my hometown for college.

Shame. Betrayal. Rage.

At the bottom of the retro sign hung a blue sign that I had never seen before. I lifted my sunglasses and squinted to read the addition: 'Home of the Otters.' I dropped my Ray-Bans back onto my nose and groaned.

I hated my hometown.

Even though the train had slowed, my heart raced. I wiped my palms on my jeans and paused the lecture series podcast on my phone. I caught a glimpse of my reflection in the blackened screen and attempted to tame the flyaway hairs that were sticking straight up from the top of my head. When they didn't comply, I tossed my hair into a messy bun.

As the train jerked to a halt, I scanned the platform for any sign of my parents. It didn't take long to pick out my dad. His hair, which was longer than mine, but totally gray, hung down his back, in a ponytail, from underneath a worn Panama hat. I took out my earbuds and hopped off the train.

"Dad," I shouted. He was walking in the wrong direction. I shouted again, but when he didn't stop walking, I had to break into a light jog. I caught up with him and he jumped when I tapped him on his shoulder. "Dad," I repeated.

He turned. "Bree." He opened his arms and I let my dad hug me tightly. He smelled just as I remembered, like sawdust and marijuana – and I loved it.

"How was your trip?" he asked.

I shrugged. "It was okay. The train left on time. Nobody sat beside me."

"Ha." My dad laughed and squeezed my shoulders. "Glad to see college hasn't changed my salty daughter."

But I had changed. A lot. Leaving Laketown and all the drama that had swallowed me up here, was the best thing I'd ever done. The Bree that grew up on Portage Street was long gone, replaced with someone who didn't worry about running into the mean girls at the corner store.

With the bags loaded in the back of the faded red Toyota Tercel, my dad pumped the gas a couple of times before turning the key, and the tiny engine whirred to life. The radio crackled, tuned to the local radio station, and then some twangy country song came blaring through the speakers. I unrolled the window and listened to the louder-than-it-should-be muffler as my dad navigated the car through Laketown.

The streets were lined in red tulips, and my stomach growled as the smell of waffle cones filled the car. It was barely noon and the lineup for the ice cream shop was already out the door. Nothing had changed.

"I brought you some booch." My dad pointed to the mason jar of orange liquid in the cupholder.

"Thanks, dad." I unscrewed the lid and took a sip of my mom's homemade kombucha. As a kid, I had been embarrassed by my hippie parents. I wanted a green lawn and swing sets in the backyard, but every square inch of our yard had been covered in tomato plants or chickens – my mom was an urban homesteader before it was cool.

"Are you hungry? We could stop for something." My dad slowed as we reached the one traffic light in town.

I was starving, but the last thing I wanted to do was run into anyone from my past. I also knew that eating out was an extravagance that my parents couldn't really afford. "I'm fine dad. I just want to get home and have some of mom's sourdough."

My dad's eyes crinkled as he smiled. "There's a fresh loaf with your name on it." He pulled off his hat and tossed it into the back seat. Clouds had crept onto the horizon of the bright blue sky. "Feels like rain." He murmured. "We need it."

As we continued creeping along at old-man-in-a-parade driving speed, I checked out the new stores along Oak Avenue. Over the years the main street's stores had gentrified from bargain shops and convenience stores to expensive boutiques, art galleries, and gluten-free bakeries, all catering to the summer crowd.

Shit.

I hadn't expected to see anyone I knew five minutes into my summer. I averted my gaze from the two blond girls who had just walked out of the smoothie shop. Slinking down into the passenger seat, I perched my elbow on the window ledge and tried to hide my face with my hand. I stole a sideways glance through my fingers, relieved to see that the smoothie sucking duo was oblivious to me. My heart thumped in my chest and I took a deep breath before taking a sip of the spicy kombucha. In the side mirror, I watched the two girls strolling down the sidewalk like they didn't have a care in the world, enjoying their ten-dollar smoothies, probably talking about their great sororities, or their summer jobs at Valerock. I knew that it was petty, but I hated them. They didn't have to wonder if their high school nickname, B.J. Anna, an immature combination of blow job and Brianna, was going to get shouted across the street. They didn't have to worry if someone was going to take those smoothies from their hands and pour them over their heads.

"Are you okay Bree?"

I hadn't realized that the jar in my hand had been slowly pouring kombucha on the floor mat. I jerked the jar upright. "Yeah, dad. Just lost in thought there."

"Equations on your mind?" My dad had a little smile on his face.

I had been known to wander the streets of our subdivision, pondering calculus equations for hours. "You know it," I lied.

"Want to drive by the old house?" he asked. But before I could answer he had already turned onto Portage Street.

The last thing I wanted was to drive by our old house. That meant driving by *his* house.

"I don't need to see the house dad. It's been over two years since you moved."

"No. You need to see the terrible color the new owners painted it." I tried not to look at number sixteen, Brodie's house. Instead, I fixed my gaze on my childhood home, number eighteen. Growing up, the house had been painted pumpkin orange with blue trim. Now, it was a tasteful dark gray with cream-colored trim.

"Isn't it hideous?" Dad shook his head.

"Terrible," I smiled. It looked like any other house on the block now. And it was an improvement.

"They even ripped out your mom's gardens and planted grass seed. Can you imagine?"

"Of all the nerve." I drained the last of the homemade drink, avoiding the slimy scoby at the bottom of the glass. I let myself take a glance at number sixteen. The white porch swing sat empty.

As kids, Brodie and I had fantasized about swinging the wooden seat from its metal fastenings. That swing had seen a lot of action, from forts to hide and seek as kids, to my first kiss as a teenager – with Brodie. I tried to stifle a sigh of nostalgia as I remembered the feel of his lips on mine. But sentimentality was replaced with anger as I remembered the snarl on his lips the last time we spoke.

"How did you know they ripped out Mom's gardens?" I craned my neck as we drove away, trying to get a glimpse of the back yard.

"Brodie told me."

"Brodie?" It felt weird to say his name. "Do you still talk to him?"

"What?" Dad shouted.

It hit me then, my dad was losing his hearing. I turned down the staticky Johnny Cash and stared at my dad. "Do you still talk to Brodie Bishop?" I spoke slowly and enunciated each word.

He tilted his head to the side and then nodded. "Of course." The car shook as we sped up on the highway and headed out of town towards Casper Cove Road. "We needed some extra help with the grounds this spring. That Brodie's been a lifesaver."

The world started to blur. "Brodie is working at the cabins? Your cabins."

"Our cabins," my dad emphasized. "They're going to be yours someday, you know."

The gravel crunched under the tires as we turned onto Casper Cove Road and dad started swerving like a maniac to avoid millions of potholes. The canopy of maple trees shaded out most of the light and my world got a little darker. I had agreed to come home for the summer to help my parents with the cabins – without knowing a vital piece of information - that they had hired the only person in the world that I truly hated. If they knew what he had done to me, they never would have hired Brodie Bishop. Not in a million years.

And now I'm going to have to see that asshole, every day, for the entire effing summer.

Get 'Hating the Rookie' Now

CONNECT WITH A.J.

www.ajwynter.com

www.facebook.com/author.a.j.wynter
www.instagram.com/author_aj_wynter

Printed in Great Britain
by Amazon

26603797R00155